"Elaine Isaak's *A Wreck of Dragons* is a rocket punch to the mecha v. kaiju genre. Energetic and thought-provoking, the adventure thrills while posing questions about sentience, purpose, and finding common ground in a vast universe."

R.W.W. Greene, author of *Mercury Rising*

"When world-building rises to an art and alien biology takes your breath away, you're reading a stellar work of science fiction. Add a battle of conscience as large as a planet and memorable characters — plus an ending I will not spoil for you, but still makes me tear up — and you've *A Wreck of Dragons* by Elaine Isaak, your new favorite. Bravo! Very highly recommended."

Julie E. Czerneda, author of *To Each This World*

A WRECK OF DRAGONS

ELAINE ISAAK

For Gabriel

1

B EYOND THE TWIN SUNS of a system in Capricorn, five Colossus robots reached toward each other like survivors of a shipwreck in the vastness of space. They revolved slowly, coming into alignment and matching speed, their feet pointed toward the failure far below. The planet Johari had rejected hung there like a moldy meatball, clouds of gray striated with bands of white and glimpses of the dreary green sludge beneath its tainted atmosphere. The bots, and their human companions, came here in search of a home, and they had not found it.

Turning away from that uninspiring sight, Johari focused instead on the complicated dance of the robots reaching toward their union. He floated, weightless, in the chest compartment of Colossus Norgay, drawing ever closer to the others with brief bursts of maneuvering thrusters. To their right, Colossus Earhart slid a vast arm over Norgay's shoulders, and Earhart's partner, Maya, gave a brief cheer that echoed through the communication channel. Johari smiled. Only three years younger than him, why did she strike him as such a child?

To his left, Colossus Zheng He entered the group, its pale green tone made mirror-bright without an atmosphere to disperse the light of the nearest sun. Each bot stood about forty meters tall, though their humanoid forms took different proportions to suggest their individual capabilities. Where their bodies met, they inflated a thickly insulated bubble of atmosphere, uniting all five and cutting off the view of the planet below.

"Johari," Norgay said, a deep baritone that echoed inside Johari's skull and through his bones. "I suggest you hold on in case of any difficulties with the union."

"There've never been any before," Johari pointed out, but he looped his arm through a strap that floated in the canopy nearby.

"Thank you. It does ease my mind."

Johari snorted. "Oh, please."

Norgay rumbled with quiet laughter, then the canopy separating Johari from the outside world peeled back. In spite of his bravado, tension knotted Johari's shoulders. That canopy, nearly a foot thick, protected him from everything from micrometeors to hostile atmospheres to the simple and sinister vacuum of space itself. To achieve union and gather the team in one place, the canopy shifted away, giving him freedom, and leaving him vulnerable.

The white insulated chamber bridged the space between them, smart plastic couplings sealed with a soft zip. The bots arched overhead like the guardian statues of some weird church dome built by the ancients, as if their young human partners were somehow holy.

Into that space, each bot deployed an array of communication tools, spinning out tablets that drifted, awaiting their users. Finally, the bots merged their communication systems to project whatever the team required into that central space. The bots reminded Johari of a vid he'd seen — a scene repeated hundreds of times in thousands of hours of captured sportscasts from the time before the Ruin. They resembled giant football players leaning in, eager to hear the team strategy. Made more sense than the church image he conjured earlier. If football were the metaphor, then Johari was the coach, hoping to lead the Saturn Five to victory. All he had to do was come up with a game plan. His own bot, the colossus Norgay, formed his metallic face into a smile. "We stand ready."

Johari launched from his command chair in Norgay's chest cavity and soared into the temporary habitat with a hoot of joy, his dark hair waving back from his face. Tolui, pushing off from Colossus Armstrong, met Johari half-way and caught his wrist, spinning them both. They brought their feet together and pushed off from each other, arching into moves impossible in real gravity, or in the confines of their separate robots.

"Hey!" From Earhart, Maya tried to emulate Johari's launch, but ended up in a tumble, colliding with one of the drifting tablets, giggling all the while. Her bot's face, high above, flared the blue sensors that served as her eyes and a rumble of bot laughter moved through the space.

Emerging from the shelter of their bot, Zheng He, Emm hooked a foot around one of the inner struts and stretched out gracefully, capturing Maya's hand and bringing her to rest nearby.

"You good?" Johari righted himself in relation to his friends. Maya gave him a thumbs up, and Emm released her to float more carefully just off the wall.

The final member of the team, Shawntelle, reclined in the air on one elbow, her blue-tipped dreadlocks hovering around her face as if her whole head were electrified. "We gonna get down to business here or what?"

Tolui and Johari shared a look, then Johari paddled himself toward the floor, caught a strap and settled onto the "ground," with a sigh, reluctant to give up the freedom of such a large space after months confined to Norgay's cramped interior. Emm joined him, their Egyptian-turquoise eyes framed by pale hair cut short in a style that made Johari a little self-conscious about his own, less practical choices. Tolui settled next to them, strapping down for business. "What are the prospects?"

Maya flailed in their direction, then caught a strap and pulled herself down to join the circle. Shawntelle settled opposite Johari. She popped open her hand to reveal a small projection of the planet they were currently orbiting. "One stinking, methane-flooded mess of a swamp. Nice pick, Johari," she said, then flicked the virtual planet toward him like a pool ball. "What's next — something snowbound maybe? How about an eternal lightning storm?"

Johari snatched the planet's image and slam-dunked it into a tiny basketball hoop provided by Norgay's projector system, after which both planet and hoop vanished to Tolui's light applause. Johari said, "All we can do is go by the data and make a judgment call — blame the long-range scans."

"In a couple million years those methane-producing bacteria could be trees or animals, who knows?" Tolui said.

"And in a couple hundred years, or less, humanity's gonna be remembered only by the broken hulks of Fleet ships aimlessly drifting through space. Eriksson's been having a bunch of little material faults." She pointed up toward her bot, with his eternally grim expression. "I have to keep doing external inspections, trying to keep on top of decay. The bots just weren't meant to last this long."

"This is true," Eriksson rumbled, "though all of the flaws have, so far, been easy to overcome." He sounded annoyed, as if Shawntelle's remarks embarrassed him. Could the bots even get embarrassed?

"Your geological studies are pretty rough on your systems, though," Maya said. "I've been adding all the maintenance reports to a data cloud."

"That's a good point about the specializations," Johari said. "Should we be talking about duty rotations? Norgay's been on Civilization for decades, and so far, he hasn't had much degradation."

"That's because he's got nothing to do," Shawntelle broke in. "There's no civilization out here but us — such as we are."

Through the implant at the back of Johari's skull, Norgay's voice spoke, taking advantage of the private channel. "*There have been some concerns about my joint membranes, you may recall, but I would not wish to be partnered with anyone but you.*"

"*You just don't want to get stuck with Shawntelle,*" Johari subvocalized, and Norgay answered with a quiet warmth of his assent.

Emm said, "Scout duty rotation has been found to increase a sense of isolation from the Fleet and from the mission."

"Spoken like a counselor," Shawntelle said. "How about Delta Force? What've they got?"

Emm's raised eyebrows were the only sign of exasperation.

Maya took up the question. "They targeted a system with two planets in the goldilocks zone. Do you want me to review their reports?" She brought up a window display showing the send-off from the other scout mission, five bots and their companions launching into hyperspace, a publicity vid replete with Fleet insignia, pre-recorded cheering, and the words, "Delta Force: Find us a home!" The coordinates of Delta Force's prospect planets showed beneath. Each time a scout mission launched toward a new system, Fleet circulated a vid like that through all channels across the ninety-eight ships that made up the Fleet. When Johari was just a kid, there were four teams. Now they were down to two. Scouts died of filtering malfunctions on distant worlds, or in the flare of a coronal mass ejection from an alien sun. Dead scouts became shooting stars for the worlds they sought to explore.

When humanity got lucky, it was just the kids who died, and the bots could rendezvous with the Fleet for new partners then head out again on their mission. The geniuses who created the Colossus units hadn't survived the Ruin of Earth, leaving the remnant population with dozens of bots, technological wonders they had no hope of repairing. The records they left behind about their work showed signs of heavy tampering — probably to foil any competitors who wanted to reproduce the robots. Over the nearly two hundred years since the Ruin, only ten fully functioning bots remained, plus a few too damaged for interstellar capability. Those had to stay with the Fleet, limping along like broken-down horses put out to pasture. Definitely he'd watched too many Westerns during their last hyperspace flight.

Johari brought himself back to task. "Thanks, Maya, but if Delta Force finds the new Earth, we'll hear about it."

"Big time," said Shawntelle. "They'll be the heroes of the Fleet for generations."

"Still hoping that'll be us," Tolui said. "I've got a few more months"

Johari gave him a thumbs up. "I'm doing my best. I've identified three prospects, two at Capricorn twenty-seven —" at his gesture, three-dimensional representations of the planets blossomed in the space between them, casting a blueish light on their faces and obscuring Shawntelle completely. He tapped two planets in turn, letting them grow. They revolved slowly, accompanied by scrolling lists of statistics. "No detectable signs of civilization at any of them — no radio signals or orbital structures, so that's a plus." Not that they'd ever found any signs, not since humanity first started looking. "What do you have on the solar monitors, Maya?"

Maya splayed her fingers to trigger her own data. "Their star's a bit iffy. It's like, almost changing color in the spectral analysis."

Her bot, Earhart, explained, "It's been showing increased activity while we were investigating here. Capricorn 27 is already on the older side of the spectrum."

Johari winced at the numbers. "I'd hate to give the all-clear to colonize a planet about to get eaten by a supernova. The third prospect is a little further, but —"

A sharp tone sounded through the habitat and through his implant. "Incoming public message from Fleet Comm, priority one," Norgay announced.

Priority one? Oh, frack. Not many things earned that designation. Maya gave a little gasp. The team settled back, and Johari disappeared his virtual planets. "Ready."

In the projection space, a flickery image of Fleet Commander Roxanne Shen materialized. Over her prim uniform, she wore a flowered collar to indicate a celebration, and Johari relaxed a little. "Greetings, citizens of the Fleet, and thank you for your attention."

He subvocalized, *"How long ago was this sent?"*

Through the implant, Norgay replied, *"Approximately twenty-one days. I transmitted a tight-beam with the results of our most recent exploration, but this message appears to have already been in transit."*

"At one pm, Fleet standard time, I will be pleased to virtually host an allocation ceremony. Prior to that time, all current lottery submissions will be reviewed for medical and societal eligibility. Those of you in the lottery will be informed of your eligibility status prior to the allocation. We have four resource allocations available, and we anticipate that excitement will be intense." She said it all through a bright smile. "Good luck to everyone in the lottery — we look forward to welcoming four new citizens in about nine months!"

She spread her hands, taking a pause for the cheering and applause that would have greeted the live broadcast. "At this time, and especially for the benefit of our brave scouts, I'd also like to announce that Tolui, Colossus Armstrong, is nearing his eighteenth birthday! At the end of his current rotation, Tolui will return to Fleet to take up full citizenship and enjoy the benefits of a Fleet posting. Congratulations, Tolui!"

Johari led the cheering and clapped Tolui on the back, reveling in the flesh time contact they got so little of. Maya flung herself over to give Tolui a quick embrace, then drew back immediately, as if she'd gone too far. A grin flashed across his deep-brown features, but he glanced up toward Armstrong — the bot towering far above.

"Tolui and his team, the Saturn Five, are currently on deployment to Capricorn where maybe — just maybe — they'll find us a brand new home!" Shen clapped a little herself. After a moment, she continued, "In honor of Tolui's eight years of scout service, Fleet Command is reserving one allocation for Tolui, on his return — assuming he meets the eligibility criteria. Congratulations, Tolui! Only four months until we welcome you home. Or maybe —" Shen leaned in, her tone rising, "You'll be the one to welcome us! Keep up the great work, Saturn Five. Remember, it only takes one!"

Over her palm hovered an image of the Earth, as it had been back in the twentieth century, before mining and construction projects cluttered near-Earth orbit, before the Climate Wars that left it uninhabitable. Before the conflagration of natural and man-made disasters they referred to simply as "the Ruin." The clouds glowed white and the oceans blue, the idol of all their hopes. In spite of the beautiful orb she held like a queen with a scepter, Shen's expression was fixed like a holomask. She must have delivered that reminder a hundred times, just like her predecessors. One planet, one place for mankind to settle, but they still hadn't found one. Commander Shen's image blinked out.

"They're saving an allocation for you? Wow, Tolui, that's great!" Maya clapped her hands, and a fountain of sparkles scattered through the projection space like tiny fireworks.

Tolui's eyes glittered and he blinked fiercely. Johari reached over and punched his shoulder. On the subvoc, he opened a private channel. *"Way to go, man. You've earned it."*

"Given they ate my fracking parents, I thought I'd fail the lottery on genetics alone." Tolui grinned. Aloud, he said, "I'm in fracking Capricorn, how'm I supposed to find a partner?"

"I wouldn't worry about finding a volunteer. Empirically speaking, of course." Emm spread her hands, opening up a world of possibilities. "Or… you could request a posting at the Office of Compatibility, and find your own partner. Your temperament and your biological training make you a good fit."

"I'll be your partner!" Maya shouted. She jumped free of her restraint and turned a somersault in the air. "Come on!"

With a whoop, Tolui sprang after her. He caught both her hands, giving her a twirl that sent her spiraling across the space, and him flying backwards. Earhart generated another stream of fireworks that spun about them as they danced. Even as the sparkles fell, Johari's smile fled. Absently, he rubbed his fingers over the Fleet insignia printed on his tunic, the designation of "Scout" imprinted underneath.

An allocation as a reward for service. That was huge, no doubt, especially for the son of outlaws, and Shen always phrased the allocation lottery as some big party. It was a big deal, allocating the resources to have a child. Given the tight restrictions on oxygen, water, and food in the Fleet, they practiced a strict replacement doctrine. In order for five babies to be authorized, it meant five people had died. Johari's throat felt dry. "Oh, frack. She didn't mention promotions."

Across the circle, Shawntelle, normally quick with the sarcasm, sat silent, and her near-black gaze met Johari's.

Five allocations, no promotions for the lower-ranking citizens who would have been training for those jobs. Five people died so young they weren't employed — or when they died, their jobs died with them.

Emm's eyes softly closed. "Oh," they whispered, but the sound traveled. The party atmosphere inside their little habitat dissolved in an instant. Tolui's expression matured in moments, well beyond his seventeen years. He guided Maya back to the circle. As she tucked herself under the restraint, Maya's glance skipped from one to another of the older kids. The sparkles evaporated. "Why do you guys look so weird all of a sudden?"

"It was Delta Force, has to be," Shawntelle said.

"We don't know that." Johari put up his hands to forestall the tension. "There might have been an accident at the school or something, an external work detail that screwed up. There's no need to jump to —"

The chime sounded again. Johari raised his eyes toward the bots' faces looming above. Norgay, too, had lost his smile. "Incoming tight beam on private channel, scouts only," Norgay reported, modulating his tone to a soothing low. Who was he kidding?

"It was them, wasn't it? Delta Force went down." Johari's chest tightened and Tolui set a hand on his shoulder. Emm's fingers knotted through his on the other side, and even Shawntelle allowed Maya to draw her into the circle as they edged closer together. For a moment, only the humming of equipment and the whisper of clothing filled the chamber.

Norgay expelled a soft sound, like a sigh. "I regret to inform you that Delta Force has been lost. The scouts and their colossi. Their final transmission indicates they entered hyperspace in a united formation. There is no indication that they ever exited. Their emergency beacons triggered in cascade and fell silent in almost the same instant."

"All five?" Maya shivered, and Emm wrapped an arm around her.

"Hardware failure?" Emm inquired.

Norgay replied, "Most likely."

"Whatever happened, the failure occurred in united mode," Johari said. And the same could happen to them at any moment.

"I can do some trouble-shooting with the data cloud." Maya's fingers flew over her tablet as she called up her data. "Maybe I can figure out what kinds of problems uniting would —"

A low mechanical creaking spanned the silence between them, and Maya's fingers froze, poised over the screen as her eyes flared wide.

If Johari's team were becoming stars, he'd rather it be in the metaphorical sense — after they found humanity's new home. He pulled free of the strap that helped him stay put. "Scramble — come on!" He grabbed Maya's hand and flung her toward Earhart's compartment, the motion propelling him back toward Norgay as the other three dove toward their own bots. "Prep for separation!"

"Aye, sir!" Tolui replied. In the shared space, the projection equipment spooled backward, each bot reeling in their components.

"It's that smart plastic — all those couplings! They weren't meant to last for hundreds of years," Shawntelle called as she vaulted into Eriksson's chest habitat, already strapping down and helping to guide the equipment back into place.

"I've been organizing the work of el Mohtar and Kwame," Maya said through their implants. *"There's gotta be clues about their formula."*

"Yeah, cadet, but you haven't found it — after two hundred fracking years of everybody looking, nobody has." Shawntelle's hand hovered near the trigger for her canopy. "Johari — where to?"

Where indeed? Each of them would hurtle through hyperspace alone within their colossus, hoping the next planet he chose would be the One. Two planets at risk of supernova, and the last one ... "Planet number three! Norgay —"

"Sending coordinates," the bot replied. "Seventeen days in hyperspace. I hope your entertainment options are fully uploaded." He extruded Johari's command seat and the straps that embraced him. Johari caught a floating tablet and locked it down, then his hand, too, rose to the trigger. Each member of the Saturn Five leaned back into their bots, hands at the ready, and Johari's wasn't the only one trembling. The last explorers for mankind.

"We've got this. We've all been doing our inspections. There's no reason to think anything will go wrong." Johari met eyes with each of them in turn: Maya, frightened, Tolui, grim; Emm, focused; Shawntelle flashed him a cocky salute.

"See you on the outside," she called across the space to him. "And remember, it only takes one!"

Let it be this one. Johari tapped the trigger.

2

RIDING SAFE IN THE HEART of Colossus Norgay, Johari emerged from the nauseating stretch of hyperspace into the presence of a whole new world. Norgay's automatic systems adjusted rotational momentum, halting at a safe distance. Just at arm's reach, the shield wall in front of Johari curved away in a matte metallic darkness that reflected the tall and narrow range of his existence. The first few hours of the transit, he twitched at the slightest change in Norgay's status alerts, but when his bold words proved true, and nothing went wrong, he let himself relax into the long journey, reviewing monographs of the latest atomic paintings, and listening to some improvisational stomp tunes produced by a band in one of the mining vessels. Maybe not worthy of Fleet's definition of Civilization, the ideal they hoped to resume, but not half bad. Again, as they approached their emergence moment, Johari tensed, listening for any sign of plastics gone bad. When it didn't come, he eased into his seat and reached for the new world.

Where his finger touched, the window began scrolling a series of figures: measurements of the planet's size and calculations of its orbit, length of days and years, likelihood of rapid decline, the composition and age of its star. Spectrometer readings marched down the far left. Carbon, oxygen, methane. The holy trinity. And the holy grail: water vapor. The truth rushed over Johari, his mouth going dry. His team had gathered data from afar, analyzing so many possible worlds, and he chose this one. He had interpreted the data correctly: this could be the place, for real: the One.

"Systems up, Norgay," he commanded, peeling back the smart cloth hammock and kicking his feet free.

"Colossus Norgay unable to respond at this time," replied the calm voice of the giant robot. "With deepest apologies, Master Johari, please stand by."

"Now, Norgay! Come on — we're there."

"Colossus Norgay unable —"

"Cut it out — are you doing Fleet coms? Or watching some season finale?"

The unmistakable whine of the shower hose stretching out. "Hey!" Johari pushed up on the restraint which snapped away, and turned about in the low-g. The round metal head of the shower hose hovered over him like a curious snake. "You've had seventeen days in hyperspace to binge-watch. That's how they structure the shows, they want to make you keep watching. Besides, haven't you watched every video that survived the Ruin?"

The hum of Norgay's basic functions penetrated deeper into his consciousness. Norgay was messing with the controls again, reducing his noise-damping function just to annoy his partner. Johari imagined Norgay from the outside, his enormous humanoid form folding his arms, or maybe covering the sides of his head with his hands like a toddler that didn't want to listen to its parents.

"I know that's you, Norgay. None of this stuff has to make any noise at all unless you want it to." Johari waved his hand at the wall behind him. Personal care cubbies and hidden compartments spread vertically from his hammock tethers, above to the Command and Study unit, below to Recreation and Habitation. Big titles for regions separated only by the workout center, the hammock, and the chair that stuck out within Norgay's chest canopy. As if at his command, a series of white doors popped open and shut, and drawers slid free with a little crescendo of music, their movements orchestrated to a familiar symphony.

"Bach, ah, 'Goldberg Variations'?" Johari suggested. The doors that held his field kit clapped open and shut.

"Old fracking news — what are you doing still in bed?" Shawntelle's voice over the com, loud and clear, as abrasive and insightful as ever. Sometimes he caught glimpses in her of something deeper, maybe darker, something she was working very hard to conceal. But most of the time, she drove him up the wall. Right now, he was just relieved they'd both survived hyperspace.

Johari glared at the nearest visual sensor. "You're letting her see me? Jeez, Norgay, I thought you were on my side."

"I am on the side of humanity, Fleet, and you," Norgay's baritone rumbled through him as much as around him. "In approximately that order at this time."

"At this time?" Johari pushed the hair out of his face. What was that supposed to mean? "Glad you decided to join me."

"At your service, Master Johari," the bot managed to sound droll and still a little irked at being taken away from his other pursuits. "As it happens, I was in communication with Earhart."

"Hey, let's focus! Johari's the guy who steered us here, and you're still messing around," Shawntelle's voice said with a tinny echo. Norgay manipulated the sound of Shawntelle's voice as well. Uncharitable, given how useful she was to the team, but a nice apology for his failure to turn off the cameras. Johari patted the metal strut supporting his hammock, the touch relayed through Norgay's systems to whatever passed for his heart.

"Johari, have you looked outside yet?" she demanded.

Norgay replied, "I have not yet cleared the window, Miss Shawntelle. Master Johari often requires the judicious application of caffeine to achieve an optimal state, and I believe he may require additional preparation for the moment at hand."

Already, the smell of hot chocolate warmed the chamber, topped with just the right splash of coffee. Oh, yeah, Norgay was on his side alright, and he felt at least the slightest bit guilty for dodging orders.

"Just clear the window — we don't have time for that," she insisted.

"I believe that Master Johari —"

"Hey, you need to stop it with the 'Master', and maybe stop it with the worm shows — that Peace Masters crap is just irritating, okay?"

"*Masterpiece Theater,*" Norgay said, sounding quietly aggrieved.

The nearest wall panel slid open and a steaming mug extended beside Johari. He wrapped his hand around it. Most of the time, beyond that window, he had seen nothing but blackness and the distant prick of stars. Once in a while, they paused for materials at some undistinguished planetoid or grabbed hydrogen from a comet streaking around a distant sun, but those were just way-stations, bits of solid ground that relieved the endless openness of space. Then, a handful of days like today, when they confronted a prospect world, ready for exploration. And every time so far, the search proved futile.

In the back of his mind, he recited the odds against his being the one to find a new Earth, the odds against it even happening in his lifetime. For almost two hundred years, what little remained of humanity had been living in a hodgepodge of spaceships: mining and freight vessels, opulent pleasure ships re-purposed for long-term habitation, plus a few asteroid repulsion vehicles and exploration craft surrounding the Ring, the circular orbital station that had been the largest thing near Earth at the time of the Ruin.

Fleet, such as it was, limped through interstellar space conserving resources and cobbling together repairs as best they could, employing the bots — the greatest technology humanity ever produced — as their scouts in the desperate hope of finding a place to someday settle down again. The loss of Delta Force still echoed in the back of his mind. He tried to ignore the fact that the future of all humanity could rest upon his team. He tried … and failed.

Taking a swallow of his mocha, Johari braced for another disappointment. "I'm as ready as I'm gonna be. Clear the window, Norgay, or she'll just keep at it."

"Indeed." The window swept clear, the metallic sheen going translucent, then transparent. All the calculations, speculations, and scrolling data streams in the universe could not prepare him for the reality of what he saw. Round and green and white and blue, the planet filled his vision, shining against his skin.

The mug slipped from his grasp. The chamber went suddenly weightless as his mocha cascaded silently past his feet and Norgay manipulated gravity to contain the liquid before it got any place they'd hate to clean. Johari lifted from his hammock, his hair rising from his shoulders, his hands reaching out. The planet glowed faintly beyond his reach — but not by much. "It's blue."

"And white!" Shawntelle shouted. "White! That means atmosphere. Eriksson's initial measurements suggest breathable."

"It's not all white." Johari tapped the window in the upper left quadrant of the world that hung before him. A series of orange pock-marks pierced the planet's swirling cloud cover. Colossus Eriksson hovered to the far right, a vast humanoid form, the shape of Shawntelle barely visible his chest canopy as she, too, leaned in toward the planet.

"Some kind of gas vents, around the equator, but the poles should have plenty of arable land. Zoom in, check out those rivers!"

Johari hovered before the world. "Jeez, Norgay, I can't believe you almost slept through this."

A jet of cold water slapped the back of his head and dispersed into tiny, floating spheres around him, each one reflecting his astonished face, and the world — the glorious world that floated with him.

Johari tore his gaze from the view and dove toward his drifting breakfast drink, slurping up a few globules, hot, sweet, then bitter. His wet hair tangled into the air around him. "Come on, Norgay — where's the rest of the Saturn Five? Did you ping —"

"Already on it, Master Johari. Zheng He and Armstrong are incoming in seventeen point three minutes. Earhart is experiencing drive difficulties and is undergoing a maintenance power down cycle."

"No, no, no! This could be the one!" Johari smacked his palm against the window which shimmered with a simulated shattering. Norgay's idea of a joke. If this were the one, the Saturn Five would go down in history as the saviors of humanity. But Earhart, and Maya with her: the knowledge of what happened to Delta Force gnawed at him. "Ping Earhart. Is there any risk to life support or critical systems?"

A pause, then Norgay replied, "Negative. Shall I prep for flyover?" His voice held a hint of excitement, the sort that Johari could never tell if it was genuine or an AI artifact intended to build friendship between them. As if it needed to.

"Absolutely!" Turning about, Johari launched himself upward along the habitat and caught the locker door as it swung open. He pulled out a tunic and loose trousers, diving and leaping into his clothes.

"Flyover in ten… "

"I'm not ready!"

"Nine…"

Johari scrambled up the holds to the top of the habitat and pulled into his seat as it extruded from the wall. Up here, his head rested inches from the rounded top and front of the window. He tugged the straps over his arms and locked himself in.

"Eight …"

"Flyover?" Shawntelle chirped from the comm. "Are we doing this?"

"Affirmative," Johari replied. "Ready."

"Excellent." The series of whirrs this time around were the real thing as Norgay shifted from their transit mode. On the window before him flashed a series of procedures: the rounded, torpedo shape of transit flattening out, solar sails sucked inside, then wings spreading, and the suggestion of Norgay's true form revealed. To the right, he caught a glimpse of Shawntelle's partner, Eriksson, performing the transformation: a sleek, silver shape converting smoothly, Eriksson's enormous head aiming forward and down, the structure of a jaw smiling at this brave new world.

Then he thought of Earhart, stuck a few days back, working on propulsion, and he frowned. "Toggle Earhart, would you?" A moment later, an image swelled into the upper left corner, Maya's face streaked with tears.

She tried to wipe them away, her gaze focused somewhere else, as if avoiding him would help her get under control. "Is it true you've got a planet? A good one?"

Johari winced. She looked awful. At thirteen, Maya was the youngest member of the Saturn Five. When she was brought to the creche as an unlicensed infant, it was three-year-old Johari who named her, seeing in her round face some resemblance to the sculptures of the ancient Maya people they were studying at the time.

They'd been close ever since, and nothing thrilled him more than when she, too, had been chosen as a scout. Now she'd been left behind to deal with mechanical failures while the rest of them explored a new world, maybe the one they'd been searching for all this time. Maybe the one humanity had been searching for for centuries.

"Yes, Maya." He sighed. "Really good."

She bobbed her head, compressing her lips, and saying nothing.

"Do you have a status update?" Norgay had already asked Earhart, but sometimes it helped to feel at least a little in charge.

"Uh, the left-hand power coupling failed during our last transit? We think it had to do with polymer fatigue." She sniffed, then straightened and flicked her fingers over her command screen. "We're building a new one, but it has to go in layers and have time to cool between layers, so… at least another seventy-two hours." Plus the time they would need to catch up with the team, assuming there were no other repairs.

By which time, they'd be deciding about planetfall. Beyond her tearful face hovered the magnificent orb of green and blue and white, so close Johari could reach it. So close, he could be down there in a matter of moments with the right combination of jets. A planet where maybe the atmosphere would allow them to remove their helmets for the first time, breathing in unfiltered air, the natural scents and breezes of a living world, to feel the spring of grass beneath their feet and stand with their toes in the tide of a new home. A new home that meant nothing without people to share it.

Johari took a deep breath. "Maya, I'm coming to get you. Norgay can sustain both of us for a few days, until Earhart is ready to catch up."

"You would do that, for me?" Maya's eyes widened. "Delay the whole thing?"

"Master Johari," A low warning tone, half pleading. Norgay wanted this, too, the fulfillment of their joint mission, one Norgay had been pursuing for over a hundred years with nine previous partners. A long time to be searching without success.

Johari stroked the nearest pliable surface, and felt an answering warmth, the same warmth he'd been enveloped by since Norgay adopted him after his parents died in the last colonization attempt. "This is what we're here for — not for exploration, not really —

but for each other, right? To remind the bots that humanity is the important thing."

"Oh, frackin' dark matter, you are not serious!" Shawntelle shouted over the open link, and Maya's gratitude transformed into something like terror. "We are not going to hang around in orbit while you go baby-sit!"

"Hey — we're supposed to be a team, remember? We should've taken a pause when we jumped out of transit to make sure all the bots were ready to go."

"Yeah, maybe, if we hadn't seen the planet!" Still, Shawntelle's voice softened with that mixture of excitement and regret he knew they were all feeling. "It's not a critical failure, right? She's not going all Delta Force on us."

Johari stiffened at that.

"She's right," Maya sniffed. "She's right, you should go on without me." She shrank into her seat.

Johari threw up his hands. "It doesn't have to be all or nothing. The failures aren't critical yet, but I'd rather have Maya close in case they reach that point. Besides, taking Maya with us gives Earhart more latitude for repairs — she can shut down life support entirely and not be concerned about minor material flaws. She'll probably catch up faster on her own. In the meantime, Eriksson, Armstrong, and Zheng He can take the lead. They'll tight-beam their data to Earhart while I'm in transit. Short jump, right? I can be there in a few hours, and back here by the end of a day."

"You're the civ guy, Johari, we need you. I can't imagine doing this without you."

"Are you volunteering to go for Maya?"

Shawntelle fell silent.

"Right." She had a point though: what were they going to do without him? They'd have noticed any obvious signs of civilization by now: satellites, transmissions, air and water pollution — those brown divots in the cloud cover could be showing them something, but something small and localized — the bots could do recon from orbit, and get close in reflective mode before they were noticed. He took a deep breath, and said something he'd never imagined he would, not to Shawntelle of all people. "Use your best judgment."

"Yes, sir," she said, her voice ringing with delight. "See ya later!" Beyond the window, Eriksson accelerated from a silver presence to a golden gleam across the face of the world.

"Thanks, Johari," said Maya. "This means a lot."

"Don't mention it," he said, his throat tightening. "Norgay?"

"Already on it, Master Johari. And may I say what a pleasure it is to serve with such a fine example of humanity."

"I hate it when I can't tell if you're being sarcastic."

"Then you shall simply have to take me at my word. Engaging transit, short jump."

"Wait a minute — if Earhart gives you the specs of what she needs next, can we be manufacturing a few layers for the coupling on the way? It'll shave a few hours off the wait time, right?"

"An excellent suggestion, sir. Now, if you will hold on…"

Johari's seat absorbed his weight as Norgay plunged into darkness.

3

"ARE YOU READY FOR THIS?" Johari gestured toward the broad sweep of his view window, opaqued for the moment, with the churning display of tight beam data flowing like a cascade down the far left.

"Oh my god, am I ever." Maya wriggled in her seat, extruded a little lower than his own. He watched her as he gestured for the window to clear.

As the glowing green filled her face, her lips parted. She drew in a breath and looked weightless, with that naked delight he remembered from the first time she'd seen the bots. Any time a bot considered adding a child — their external hands in a more agile form, and their internal conscience, the living reminder of their mission — they had to test the kid's receptiveness. Maya had run up to Earhart's foot, patting and banging on it until the bot relented and extruded a set of rungs for her to climb up. Even now, the graphic at the lower left that indicated Earhart's progress on the repair showed an image of Maya, climbing.

Yes, okay, the delay had been worth it for that expression on her face, and so far, the team hadn't reported any hint of civs, so it's not like they had needed him. The only things in the atmosphere down there were some kind of flying reptiles, some with feathers, and the only unusual markings on the ground lacked the patterns of organized activity, but he'd have to get closer for a better look.

"Let's go in reflective."

"Are you certain it's necessary, Master Johari? All signs indicate an unoccupied planet."

"You want to just go down there and fly around naked? Who are you trying to impress?"

"He calls you 'master'?" Maya interjected. "That's weird."

"It's a new thing. He got interested in this vid series from Old England. I tried to get him hooked on *Fleet Fighters*," but he didn't go for it."

The comm pinged. "Armstrong to Norgay, ears up?"

"Ears up, Tolui," Johari confirmed. "What have you got?"

"I have all the scans I can do from this altitude. We're negative on signs of intelligent life. I want to land and take samples."

"It's about time!" said Shawntelle.

Maya groaned.

Reaching out to the screen, Johari spanned an image of the world with his hand and gave it a slow twirl, finding Armstrong's beacon near the southern ocean, not far from the brown-patched skies. Eriksson performed a flyover of the largest mountain range on the other side of the world while Zheng He moved in a slow pattern over a dense area of forest. As they worked, the image of the world became more detailed. "We're pretty dispersed. We should come back together before anybody goes for planetfall, in case anything goes wrong."

Shawntelle's face, lean and dark-skinned, framed by a nimbus of coiled blue-streaked hair, appeared in the corner. "I can understand you worrying, after what happened to Delta Force, but may I remind you, they were close together when it happened. You told us to use our judgment — we each found the spot with the greatest level of data for our specialty. Which one of us should give up the job because you're afraid of phantoms?"

Tension crept along Johari's spine. "Phantoms killed my parents."

Maya's teeth snapped together — she had never known her parents. Fleet chose orphans for their scouts because, with a tweak in the fertility treatments for approved parents, babies were easy enough to get. Fleet already had too many mouths to feed: that's what made the resource allotments such a big deal. It wasn't that Fleetcom were heartless, just that would-be parents who'd already shown their value to humanity represented a stronger investment than kids who got left behind when bad things happened.

The lighting shifted a little dimmer and a little warmer as Norgay responded to the changes in Johari's biorhythms. Maya reached for the window and started scrolling through images and data packets, flicking them this way and that to sort the files.

"I don't know if that's exactly true," Shawntelle replied, but in a subdued voice, her glance aimed a little off from his.

"Close enough. And they died on an approved planet, more than five years into colonization, never mind a complete unknown like this one. I don't want something like that to happen here. Besides, we're the last scouts — we can't risk the bots."

"I'm the one who wants down," Tolui inserted. "Come be my back-up. You and Maya both."

"Maya hardly counts without Earhart," Shawntelle pointed out, then an instant later. "Yes, totally, if you're worried, that's what you should do. Just in case Armstrong can't handle whatever's out there."

"Those flying reptiles seem pretty fierce." Johari captured one of the files Maya was generating and expanded it to examine one of the creatures. Scrolling measurements detailed a wingspan as broad as Norgay was tall, a short tail between muscular legs. The creature's long neck swung back and forth as it flew, its arms clutched tight against its leathery chest. The skin was mottled green on top and pale underneath. Something like gills opened and closed along the neck, revealing glimpses of feathery membrane, and in the broad, flat head: a series of round divots marking at least three pairs of eyes, slit nostrils, and a mouthful of teeth. Fierce, yes, but strange and beautiful, like the creatures drawn in the margins of ancient European manuscripts, or the ones who guarded wisdom in old China. Beguiling.

"Armstrong can take them one handed," Tolui replied. "Like that King Kong guy you like so much. Are you coming? Come on, Johari — you've got to see this place!"

Shawntelle added, "It's not like there's much for you to do, anyway."

"Except maybe name the place." Emm's voice, chiming in from where they methodically examined the forest below.

"How come he gets to name it?" Shawntelle protested.

"His role is civilization. In the absence of such, it is also his part to be the ambassador of ours. But if you prefer, we can use the celestial designation —" Emm read off a string of digits.

Maya giggled. "No way! Johari names it. After we get to see the surface? Please?" She looked up at him, and their eyes met, just like the little sister he'd never had. According to his research, little sisters were considered highly exasperating, but everybody seemed to love them in the end.

"Hold position, Armstrong, we're on the way."

Norgay soared over a deep blue-green sea, following the coastline. In deference to Johari's concern about being spotted, he flew reflective — his surface material optimized to make light bend around him. Johari and Maya's seats swiveled forward, the ocean rippling beneath them with the swirling fins of strange fish.

Cliffs of yellow and blue banded stone crumbled into that pounding sea, and huge broad-leaved trees bent down at their tops as if searching for someone who'd fallen below. On a grouping of off-shore rocks rested thick-bodied birds of some kind — that was Tolui's department — birds with skin flaps they stretched as they lounged, liquid pulsing through the veins that showed in the translucent skin. Their flaps sealed as Norgay soared directly over them. He might be invisible to the eye, but not to every other sense. Interesting. "Norgay, those things — they notice us."

"Then we shall hope they do not have a taste for robot."

"Or people," Maya added. "Preliminary analysis shows a high level of biodiversity, concentrated around the coastline and the dense forest. Zheng He is capturing a variety of audible tones, but it'll take a little while to figure out who makes what sounds, or even how many creatures are making them."

"What do we know about those?" Johari pointed toward their horizon, coming up fast on a rock formation that seemed to blend seamlessly into the brown murk of the sky. As they approached, the formation resolved into a series of stone towers channeling thick smoke from thermal vents. Like the formation of volcanoes, the heated liquid lay down mineral layers over eons to create huge stone chimneys.

"It resembles a tornado, but not moving," Maya said. "Powerful chemical mix, according to some samples that Eriksson snagged on the way by. Heavy sky. That's so weird."

The surface of the sky indeed swirled slowly, striated like milk being stirred into hot chocolate. On the near side of the smoking chimneys a small group of creatures soared, drawing together enough to overlap wings, then spreading apart again. Smaller than the one Maya had already begun to diagram, they were clearly the same species, their side-pointing eyes open, their heads comparatively large. One of the group swung sharply downward and steered them all closer to shore.

"Stay straight! See if we can weave, or duck beneath them."

"If we pass too close to the water, we'll create ripples that will alert them to our presence," Norgay observed.

"Up, then! Up, up!" Johari cried as eight winged creatures slid through the air around them.

One flew directly in front of them, huge wings outspread, twisting just a little to tilt the creature to the side. Dark gray on top, with scintillating streaks of greenish light, and pale blue-green below, the wings cast a long, sweeping shadow over the sea and over its companions.

One of those below dodged aside and slipped downward in a dizzying arc. Johari wished they could follow, wheeling down after the creatures. He wanted to spread his arms and soar along with them. Flying with Norgay gave him his greatest joy — how much more incredible if he could soar into the wind, hovering on a breeze, feeling the tingle of ocean spray against his skin and breathe in the world. So many living things, an entire landscape of them, but with the window separating him from all of that, it could be nothing more than a clever vid or a VR game, a projection, just like all the images he'd ever seen of trees or cliffs or oceans.

The altered course gave them a broad view across the coastal ledges and out to sea where a series of low islands broke off from the land. Low islands topped by round knobs. Johari caught his breath, then magnified, leaning forward into the window. That portion of his view zoomed in. Strangely symmetrical islands protruded from the sea not far from a southern spit of land, and each one carried a series of shapes that resembled leather stretched over a frame of branches. "Norgay, seven degrees east. Are those huts?"

"Huts?" Maya stared with him. She prodded her files around again, frowning. "The atmosphere is inconsistent with large-scale agriculture, but it doesn't rule out smaller, more primitive farming."

"Hold position, Armstrong — we've gotta check this out." Huts! For a moment elation rushed through him. Civilization at last! But civilization meant the planet was a no-go. They'd have to abort their exploration and find a new target. Every man, woman, and child in the Fleet depended on finding a planet where they could finally settle down and have a home.

The weight of their hopes and expectations dampened his enthusiasm. Was it worth displacing or destroying some native civilization in order for humanity to survive? When nuclear and volcanic destruction swept over the surface of the Earth, those off-planet looked on in horror. Those scientists, miners, and laborers, along with the crews and occupants of a handful of pleasure ships, became the seed of the Fleet, a working-class remnant population mostly black and brown, and determined to rise from the ashes to create a better humanity.

Fleet's founders, acknowledging the thousands of exoplanets found by decades of astronomers and buoyed by the spirit of union after humanity's wars were finally over, vowed not to ruin someone else's world as they had their own. They vowed not to inflict the same horrors that had once been imposed on their own ancestors by groups of warlike or even well-meaning colonists.

Half of Johari's lessons as he prepared to take on the role of civilization envoy for the Saturn Five focused on understanding everything humans had done to each other in their quest to better their own lives at the expense of others. Trouble was, those vows were made a long time ago, and nobody still alive in Fleet had signed that contract.

"Hurry it up, would you?" Tolui replied over the comm. "Or better yet, save the location and get back to it later."

"Taking a closer sweep, Master Johari," said Norgay. "We should still arrive only shortly off schedule." He pronounced it "shed-jewel". Thank the long-dead British Broadcasting Corporation for that one. He soared a little higher and nearer to the curious mounds. No sign of life, no smoke of fires or anything moving among the structures. Closer-to, they looked more like dead leaves of giant plants than any kind of construction project. Some were little more than empty vanes, whatever had covered them disintegrated with time or weather.

"Are those some kind of dead cabbages?" Maya wrinkled her nose.

"Tolui — what do you think?" Johari swiped a few still shots and slid them across the screen to send to Armstrong.

"Got it." Silence for a long moment, then Tolui's voice again. "Weird but not unnatural. Cabbages is a good analogy." Maya beamed at this acknowledgment. "No sign of tools or tool use. If I had to guess, I'd say some kind of sea-vegetation that probably revives when the water gets high enough."

"You guys want to see something unnatural," Shawntelle chimed in, "Check this out. From my southwest quadrant." An image popped onto the view screen showing a cluster of holes in the water. It lapped over the edges and trickled inside. "Mineral in origin. Lava tubes, maybe, but super smooth. Can't get a good view of them."

"Wow — that is so cool! Maybe I can rappel down one of them." Maya expanded the image and drank it in.

Johari tapped the image of the "huts" and regretfully filed it away. Nothing. They'd investigate later, of course, and find out what kind of plant or animal or plant/animal hybrid might have lived or died there. Tolui had a complete ecosystem, replete with potentially useful organisms, and Johari had only a handful of dead cabbages.

"Come on, Jo-jo! Don't keep me waiting."

"On our way," Johari replied as Norgay performed an elegant sweep and turned back for the shore. His disappointment vanished in moments. The sea and the sky rippled with secrets, and the lack of civs meant they had all the time they needed to explore. They only needed one — and this planet looked, every moment, like it might be that one.

4

ARMSTRONG'S BEACON ALERTED to their proximity, and Norgay veered inland, sliding carefully out of the flocks of creatures into a cove where the vegetation parted in a series of large, round bowls. Maybe where trees had fallen?

His window overlaid the image of Armstrong, outlined in blue to indicate that he still moved in reflective mode. Even as they slowed their approach, Armstrong rotated in the air and his stabilizers drew back in as his arms separated. The smooth shell of his flying exterior crinkled and folded to reveal joints: waist, hips, knees separating from the whole, huge silvery feet hovering as gently as butterflies.

Armstrong's hands flexed through a series of movements. Fingers longer than Johari extruded a variety of tools ranging from chisels and bolt drivers to guns, nets and suction tubes. The opaqued window at his chest concealed Tolui's chamber, the habitat, office and control room, as if Tolui were Armstrong's living heart.

"Awesome. Let's go!" Armstrong's careful jets and repulsors leveled his feet to the ground over a patch of stone and he set down with a little puff of dust. Maya cheered and clapped. Their previous planetfall, that methane swamp inhabited by water striders as big as toddlers, hadn't been nearly as pleasant. Johari grinned. What would he name the world? They had a list of themes proposed by Fleet Command, and suggestions from the col itself — probably millions of them by now — but in the end, it would be up to him, regardless of whether they stayed.

The thought gave him a little chill. Stay. On a planet, bound by gravity you couldn't turn off, surrounded by people you didn't even know. The list of names from Fleet included words like "Freedom," "Liberty," "Unity," "Prosperity". The suggestions from regular citizens were stuff like, "New Earth," "Happiness," and simply "Home".

Johari settled back into his seat and Norgay swelled a little around him, cradling him, as he always had. The only definition of home Johari had ever known.

"Wow!" Maya leaned forward and Norgay obligingly stretched out the chair so she could press her palms to the view. Her breath made little clouds against the window. Beyond, Armstrong's various tools collected bits of foliage, soil samples, a cloud of some tiny creatures. Insects, or what passed for insects around here. Over the rounded pits hung immense blossoms in dripping rings of yellow and red, with lolling fronds around their stems. Armstrong's cameras beamed close-up images of the fronds where streams of liquid pumped along, and little things swam inside. As Johari watched, a larger, worm-like entity detached from the inner wall and slurped a mouthful of the smaller creatures then glided downstream and burrowed against the wall again. A whole ecosystem in a single plant. Freaky. Emm would want to know about that for their botanical studies.

Armstrong moved carefully forward, a serene statue in a garden of wonders. He leaned down and reached into the nearest round pit, then adjusted his position, and leaned further, almost precarious now, sending one of his suction tools toward a pile of stones.

"What does he want with that?" Maya said aloud.

"Bacteria, probably, or lichen. Or maybe Shawntelle asked him to bring her one for chemical analysis."

The suction tool rose slowly, the barely-captured thing wobbling on its end. A second suction tool tried to assist, but overcompensated. With a tearing sound, the thing broke open and the unmistakable goop of an egg spilled out onto the ground.

"Gross." Maya flinched back from the window.

"Tolui. What are you doing?" Johari tapped and magnified. A thicker blob lay amid the murky pool. The egg had been fertilized. Gross indeed. The crazy flowers swayed and arched backward in slow-motion. Sensitive plants. Cool.

"We need to gather one. I suspected they were eggs. If the proteins check out, the eggs could be used to recharge our kitchen pods. From the air, the pattern of these bowls reminded me of fish nests, but above ground."

"Yeah — dragon's nests." Maya nibbled on a fingernail.

"Dragons?" Johari protested.

"Giant flying reptiles? What would you call them?"

"We think they may be amphibious, actually," Tolui offered. "I'm going to try again."

"Negative. Check your position! Armstrong's gonna fall in there and get egg all over. One or two samples for testing is fine, but we didn't come here to wreck the place."

Armstrong straightened and turned from the waist, scanning the pits all around them. Most were empty. In those that contained eggs, the eggs clustered close in the middle. Johari pictured the bating wings of one of those — okay, fine, dragons — as it tended its nest. They would need that kind of span between the egg caches.

"You got a point," said Tolui. "I'm going EVA."

"No way! We're not close to ready for that. We need more samples, a broader range. Comparative analysis, you can't just —"

Tolui's face appeared in the center of Norgay's view window, his expression direct, his bronze-tone features almost too handsome, to judge by Maya's sudden reddening as she studied her files. Johari suspected she had a crush on Tolui — at seventeen, their oldest member, and the guy who should have been Civs, if he wanted it. He didn't.

During the flight from their last planetfall, Tolui had shaved his black hair into a familiar shape: the back and sides of Armstrong's head. That was new. Of course, his short, sharp beard undercut the effect — unless Armstrong planned to extrude one so they could still be twins. "We don't have time for that," Tolui said. "The atmosphere tests fine. This won't take long. One egg and

I'm back." He flashed a grin, then vanished. Armstrong squatted near the pit and extended one arm, swiveled at the shoulder to reveal a staircase.

"The atmosphere is one thing, we don't even know if the suit's filters can handle the local pollen and spores! Tolui!" No answer. Johari sagged in his chair.

"We want to hurry, right?" Maya asked. "I mean, if stuff is starting to break down."

"That doesn't mean we want to rush and screw this up. The only other time scouts okay'd a planet for colonization, they overlooked a few tests, and the colony got destroyed." His parents had been there; Johari barely escaped with his life — the only survivor.

In the view before him, a hatch opened where Armstrong's ear would be and Tolui stepped through, wearing a slick EVA suit. At least he was wearing a helmet in spite of the encouraging atmospheric testing. Tolui descended the stairs from Armstrong's shoulder and made his way down the slope into the broad, round pit. The pile of eggs stood as high as his waist, the eggs themselves double the size of his head. At the perimeter, the flowers stretched upward.

Johari sat up straighter. "Something's happening. Tolui — come back. Those flowers —"

One of the nearest gave a sudden burst, spewing greenish liquid across the pit. It spattered Tolui, knocking him sideways. He flailed his arms, righted himself, and the sound of laughter came through the comm. "And you thought the egg was gross! You had no idea." He reached a hand up and swiped gunk away from his faceplate, then he gave a shudder. The liquid still contained the organisms Johari had noticed earlier. Now the small ones crept over the surface of Tolui's suit. And the larger ones, the predators, wriggled toward his joints. Shit. "Armstrong! Norgay — we've gotta get that stuff off of him."

Tolui spun about, stumbling back toward the slope, his movements jerky as he kept pausing to slap away the creatures. Armstrong's left arm pivoted and bent at the elbow. A barrel emerged and he blasted Tolui's suit with a fine etching powder designed to remove any foreign matter before re-entry. Norgay zoomed closer, shooting out a cable that latched to Tolui's suit and drew him up the slope.

A shadow swept over the stone, and the flowers recoiled as huge wings rushed downward.

5

"INCOMING!" JOHARI SHOUTED.

The dragon reared upward, its hind claws snatching toward Tolui's wriggling form. Norgay launched between them, releasing the cable, which Armstrong snatched up to reel his partner out of the pit. Huge and pale blue, the dragon's wings beat at Norgay as the bot barreled into it, forcing it back.

Maya shrieked and grabbed the arms of her seat while Johari braced instinctively, then dropped a hand to grab one of hers as the dragon loomed against their window in startling close-up.

The gills flared around its head in brilliant scarlet and its mouth opened, a gulping maw lined with razor-teeth pointing backwards, meant to grab something and never let go. It flailed, scraping across the exterior window and battering some of the cameras and sensors. The forelegs flexed, revealing one especially long, sharp claw on each as if it could spike them straight through the bot's canopy, then Norgay triggered repulsors.

The dragon swung its head to and fro wildly as the bot's repulsors drove it from its nest, and Johari realized they were still in reflective mode. The dragon literally couldn't see what hit it. The writhing leather form slashed through the sky, rebounding and clearing his view. Maya relaxed a little as the dragon retreated, and Johari drew back his hand, gliding through a series of diagnostic controls. Framed in the broad view, the dragon soared up and dove toward them again.

Maya's seat retracted as far as it could go and she pulled up her legs as if to stay out of reach. "Johari! What do we do?"

The sound of her terror gave Johari an eerie calm. Testing and simulations were no match for the real thing, and this would be a hell of a time to find out Maya couldn't handle it — one of them had to. Johari zipped up his own fear and stuffed it away.

"Stay calm — Norgay's got us. Maya: manage the data stream, make sure we can get this footage to the others. Norgay will keep us safe." Great — but where was Tolui? Johari slapped the lower viewscreen and brought up the other cameras. Tolui lay at the top of the slope, twitching. Armstrong's torso opened at the bottom, creating an airlock to get Tolui back inside. The outside of the suit undulated in a weird way, and Johari couldn't tell if the creatures had gotten inside. Oh, god, what if he was infested? Johari's stomach churned. Could one of those things have gotten through the suit's defenses?

Johari slapped open the comm channel. "Armstrong, don't! Don't take him inside!" His eyes burned as he said it. Was he condemning Tolui to some hideous death? But the team was expendable, he knew that — they all knew that. The bots weren't.

"How can I not?" Armstrong roared, and his eyes blazed over Tolui's fallen form.

"Make him an evac sled."

"I cannot secure an evac sled and defend it at the same time, Johari, and I will not lose him." Armstrong's voice resonated through Johari's bones.

"We can't afford to lose you!" Johari slapped the release button and leapt from his seat. "Humanity needs you — all of you."

Maya twisted around. "What are you doing?"

"The dragon returns," Norgay's voice, calm and clear. "I must take flight to perform counter measures if Tolui is to escape."

Johari plunged downward, sliding his hands along the rails like a fireman with a five-alarm blaze. "I know, I know! Twenty-six seconds, right? Use the repulsor again." Twenty-six seconds; his personal record for donning an EVA suit. "Don't hurt it if you don't have to."

Slapping her own buckle, Maya said, "I'll help."

He glanced up. For an instant their eyes met and he gave a sharp nod as they dropped to the bottom of the hab. He slid his legs into the suit. The assist mechanisms wrapped the suit to his form, presenting the sleeves for him to slide his arms inside. Maya toggled the helmet free. He shook back his hair, tipping up his chin so she could place the helmet. "You stay here. Norgay will keep you for now. This is not how the Saturn Five go down."

She gave a hesitant smile then backed away as he toed the release lever, dropping into the lower airlock, then outside the instant the upper hatch sealed. He hit the ground, crouching as Norgay thundered upward, the barest ripple revealing where he'd been.

Head up, Johari ran. Armstrong knelt over Tolui, protecting him with his own bulk. A keening wail filled the air around them, and the flowers curled into themselves as if bracing for impact. Armstrong bristled with gear, sprouting guns and clear shielding. He had planted one huge fist between Tolui and the dragon's nest. The evac sled separated from his forearm and whirred into place as Johari ducked the bot's arm and dropped next to Tolui.

"Tolui, can you hear me?" Between the dragon's screeching and the rumbling air of Norgay's attack, Johari could barely hear himself.

Tolui's thrashing diminished, and he got a hand under him, shoving himself back. Johari pulled away, hating it, but knowing if he touched his friend, they could both be down. The whites of Tolui's eyes flashed in stark contrast to his skin, but even his skin looked weirdly pale.

Johari switched to his implant. *"We're taking care of you, Tolui. It's okay."*

"Don't touch me!" An anguished yelp, his voice shaking.

"I know." Johari reached for the sled and helped its guidance system draw it alongside.

"And don't let Armstrong take me in." Tolui's voice broke, and Johari had never wanted to hug someone so bad in his life.

"I won't. We've got a sled here. Armstrong and me, we'll get you to safety." The ground shook beneath them as something heavy struck nearby. Johari froze, his breath catching. *"Norgay?"*

"*I am unharmed,*" Norgay's voice a soft buzz at the back of his head.

A wing scraped the ground near Armstrong's fist. The robot swung its fist out to the side and bullets streamed from two of the swivel-mounted guns. The dragon's scream shot pain through Johari's head. He grabbed at his neck as if he could make the pain stop. The creature tumbled against the surrounding growth, then sucked upward, flailing. The blur that was Norgay came about. He must have deployed the tractor function meant to guide him into a docking station and used it to pull away the dragon. With the dragon tethered, still screaming, Norgay took off, full power into the air, dragging the monster with him.

"Okay, okay, let's do this," Johari muttered.

He worked the controls, syncing the sled to his own codes and the sled rolled sideways, unfurling a series of feelers. They crept beneath Tolui and steadied, stiffening, then lifting him upward as the sled rotated into place underneath.

Johari made a gesture, turning and releasing his fingers, and the feelers released Tolui into the cushioning below. It molded to him, and Johari triggered the settings for maximum containment. The sled, designed for evacuating injured colonists or soldiers, included provisions to contain contamination from viruses and invasive nanotech. Hopefully, some of those provisions could help Tolui.

A clear cover slid into place over Tolui as the feelers became straps that secured him in place. He stared at Johari through the double layer of his helmet and now the sled. Johari placed his palm on the cover, and managed a smile. "We've got you, Tolui. Armstrong is right here with you — stupid. He's probably talking to you now, am I right?"

"Johari, we must run," Armstrong rumbled. "More dragons are coming. If we stay reflective, there is a chance they will not notice us."

Run? "Tolui is secure — what should I do?"

Armstrong replied, "Hold on."

Thick cables fixed the sled to Armstrong's waist, and he was already pivoting and rising to his full height, towering over Johari. Johari leapt onto the sled, grabbing the external handles and locking his gloves to them.

The sled zoomed into motion, thirty feet off the ground and a few feet away from Armstrong's back. Armstrong ran using his repulsors, bounding over the growth between the nests, aiming his feet toward the empty ones and pushing off again. The bot could move at least five times faster, but any faster would cause too much disruption and make their path obvious. Even the curled-up plants couldn't avoid being rocked by a wind like that.

In the sled beneath him, sensors scanned Tolui, linked in with the suit's own devices, and readouts continually updated his vital signs and streams of data. Tolui's eyes closed and his face relaxed as the sled anesthetized him. Together, they plunged through an alien landscape with a furious robot as their only hope.

6

J OHARI BARELY REGISTERED the bizarre landscape they pounded through: towers of stone where the lichens snapped shut as they approached, and a waterfall where creatures with gossamer wings hovered, snatching food from the thundering spray.

They avoided the thicker jungle, and emerged with a sudden halt on the edge of a cliff. Armstrong reared back, dropping one hand to catch the sled as it nearly shot past him. His huge metallic fingers clasped the nose of the sled with infinite tenderness and pushed it carefully behind him. The sensors would relay Tolui's vital signs, and cameras in the bot's arm and hand would show him Tolui's sleeping face, but he still turned and glanced down.

The bot's face resembled humanity only in its proportions with features functional rather than beautiful. Vast blue eyes contained high definition cameras that sensed all wavelengths of light and a bunch of other things as well. The mouth served as a docking port when they took on a transit form, but closed into something like a smile the rest of the time. Functional and inhuman, and yet … reactive metal framed the features and formed the nose, the bots' main outlet for creativity. Emm's bot, Zheng He, kept their nose simple, patterned after a robot from an old film. Norgay preferred a more human appearance, a roman nose and sculpted eyebrows that could form a variety of expressions. Armstrong's face, as he regarded his partner, shifted subtly, his forehead and nose more broad, his cheeks a little more full. Did he intend to resemble Tolui?

Armstrong's gaze focused to meet Johari's. "Are you injured?" His tone sounded a little more calm — thank the stars!

"I'm okay. We need to find a secure location, someplace far away from the dragons, and circle up."

Armstrong gave a rumble and Johari wasn't sure if he implied consent or frustration. The bot straightened and turned to survey their surroundings.

Johari released one hand and sat up on the sled, scooting to a more comfortable position where he got a better view. His other glove remained locked to the handle. If Armstrong decided to take off again, Johari meant to go with him.

The cliff before them broke down in a series of chunks the size of shuttlecraft and freighters, a jumble of bluish stone leading down to the sea, and no sign of dragons. The fall had been recent enough that no vegetation had re-grown yet. "What about down there? That flat, level stone: I think there's room to inflate a hab."

Armstrong brought his attention to the slab and did not answer.

"I don't want to go much further without having a chance to check over Tolui. I think he's stable, but —"

Armstrong sprang forward, leaping down a series of stones to the enormous slab, the sled hovering along with him and Johari's arm yanked straight out so that he banged against both sled and stone until he got hold of a second handle on the same side.

Not far from Johari's face, Tolui's gloved hand rested inside the sled and something gelatinous crept over the silvery material. He needed to get baked, ASAP. The sled settled a good distance from all the edges of the slab. Armstrong detached the cables, using one as an anchor. Johari let go and slid his feet to the ground, feeling a twinge of pain from a bruised knee. "Do you have a backup tent? We'll need two."

Armstrong's fingers moved through that pattern again, each bending in turn, hints of the tools and weapons they concealed ruffling the surface metal. "Because he cannot be with you."

Johari walked slowly toward Armstrong's foot, thinking about how he could fold his arms over Norgay's toe and rest his chin there. With Armstrong, he dare not take any liberties. Given the bot's current mood, if Johari tried it, he figured Armstrong would kick him half-way around the world.

Instead, he held his hands out low. "I'm not going to leave him, Armstrong. You know that. You also know we have to be cautious. We don't know what those things are, and we can't afford to have them spread any further."

Johari's subvocalizer gave a brief pulse. "I have called the others," Armstrong informed Johari. "When they arrive, I will initiate a program of extermination toward the dragons." He turned away, scanning the ground with those vast, empty eyes.

"What? No, you won't."

"They represent a significant threat. The colony cannot arrive under such a threat." As he spoke, Armstrong released a packet that struck the ground and immediately began to deploy into a tent of strong, silvery material. Like the bots, it could be charged with reflectivity, to make the light bend around it and become almost invisible.

"No, no, no."

Armstrong was already on the move, and Johari scrambled after him, tugging free the anchor tubes and setting them to the surface where they sucked the tent snug against the stone. "Armstrong, listen to me. We just got here. It doesn't matter how perfect the place looks, it's clearly not. If we're not staying, we're not slaying. We're not going to upset the ecosystem any more than we already have."

The bot deployed the second, smaller tent not far from the sled, then returned to the first one, extruding a nozzle for the rapid inflation sequence.

Johari ran the perimeter, securing the rest of the anchors. "Would you slow down? I take eight steps for every one of yours — if you inflate before I anchor, we'll lose the tent, then what's Tolui supposed to do?"

Armstrong's head swiveled, and his eyes appeared to blink, then turn down. The pressure of air entering the billowing tent slowed while Johari caught up and finished the anchors. Together, they moved on to the second, smaller tent. The tent hatches could be joined together to form a larger space with multiple chambers, but Johari anchored the smaller tent at least a botstride away. No chances. Not even for Tolui. Not if they were going to get off this planet alive.

After securing Tolui's sled in the smaller tent and checking the perimeter, making sure the reflective function of the tents — and of Armstrong — was fully engaged, Johari stepped up to the larger tent, turning his back to it and triggering the seal. It latched onto his suit, which opened at the back into the atmosphere he knew and loved.

Johari wriggled out of the suit and flopped onto the inflated flooring. It didn't coddle him as his own bed in Norgay's habitat would, but still, it was good to feel safe for a little while. His stomach growled violently, reminding him that he hadn't eaten for a few hours.

He found his way to the survival cases automatically deployed along with the tent and dug out a few tubes of food: A green one, an orange one, and something with the pinkish gray of "meat." Norgay insisted on balanced meals. Where was his partner now? He felt a twinge of envy knowing that Maya sat in Norgay's canopy, flying where he should be.

Squeezing the first tube into his mouth, Johari wondered about the egg. Three years ago, when Maya had joined the Saturn Five, Fleet com served a meal of eggs and greens from the farm that occupied part of the colony's central ring. Humanity needed to maintain the skills of farming, but of course they couldn't raise enough to feed everyone fresh food all the time. For special occasions, the command staff brought out the best. Eggs — chicken eggs — fit in a palm, and it took two or three to feel full. That dragon egg could feed eight or ten people, easy. Even if they had to convert the proteins, they could still get a huge nutritional load from a rank of nests like that. Of course, it depended on two things: not killing all the dragons, and the dragons not killing them. Yeah, right.

Refreshed, Johari lay back again on the springy material and cast himself into the Realm.

His avatar stood on a grassy slope in front of an oversized Colonial-style house, made of wood with a shingled roof and windows of old-fashioned glass that remained clear all the time. A virtual dog bounded out of the door, wagging its tail and slurping his virtual hands.

When he was a kid, entering the Realm for the first time, everything he saw had a label on it, a floating glossary to tell him what all this stuff was and what it meant. Pets. Houses made of wood. Glass that kept the weather out, and let the view in. All the comforts of "home."

He walked up the slope and rang the doorbell — alerting the rest of his crew that he had entered virtual reality — then let himself inside. The Realm gave them a place to gather when they couldn't meet up in person, critical now that their capability to unite was faulty. VR also facilitated face-to-face communication with Fleet, not to mention being a nice respite from the unbroken spaces between the stars. Ordinarily, the bots protected their partners' inert forms during VR interaction, but while they were planet-side, it might not be safe to stay in the Realm for very long.

In the entry hall, a half-round table carried a bunch of letters, ranging from ordinary white envelopes to the annual fancy scroll for the Founders' Day celebration. He didn't bother interacting with the icons. Instead, he called up the list of messages, letting them scroll down the wall.

Routine stuff, back and forth with Fleet, a few alerts or congrats for the previous planetfall on Capricorn 27b, things that weren't important enough for a tight-beam. Still, the more recent ones pulsed in a variety of increasingly urgent colors. He should have been in contact with Fleet directly already, and entering the Realm would alert them as well. What was he supposed to say? Found a planet, attacked by dragons, Tolui did something reckless and got felled by a plant?

For a moment, he imagined the version of the Realm occupied by Delta Force, possibly even a twin of this same suburban house, with a twin of this very table, covered by blinking, urgent messages that would never be read.

Johari wet his lips, and began. "Message to Fleet Com. Saturn Five has made planetfall at new target. Exploration continues. Some difficulties encountered. More time needed to determine suitability. Johari, Colossus Norgay out." His words shimmered on the wall, then flicked away. Terse. Probably suspiciously so. "Recall that," Johari said. He paced the short hallway and the dog, a tri-colored creature with long fur, plopped down to watch him, wagging its tail when he looked its way. Somebody at Fleet had way too much time on their hands if they spent it programming the reactions of virtual pets. Johari relented and stroked the animal's head. Finally, he straightened.

"Message to Fleet Com. Earhart remains damaged, and we are hopeful she will join us in another forty-eight hours. I elected to pick up Maya using Norgay to bring her to the site while Emm, Shawntelle and Tolui commenced the atmospheric testing. The Saturn Five team has now entered the atmosphere and dispersed to determine planetary suitability. Some of the biology appears hostile, but the atmospheric gas blend appears conducive to human life. Water testing will commence shortly. Johari, Colossus Norgay, out. Send."

The new message shimmered, and blipped as it transmitted to command. Good. Done.

The door opened, and a compact girl with a ponytail of blue-tipped dreadlocks stepped inside. Shawntelle. She flashed a brilliant smile, then ruined the effect with an exaggerated glare, as if she deliberately sabotaged her beauty. "Does Armstrong really want us all to just give up what we're doing and go to ground? That's crazy. There's gonna be wildlife — deal with it."

"He wants to deal with it by killing it all."

"Fine by me. Makes it easier to see the rocks." She kept walking as if to step right through the dog, but it dodged out of the way at the last moment, preserving the illusion of the virtual realm. It managed an aggrieved expression, and Johari smothered his grin. For a pet that didn't exist, the dog still made him feel better. Presumably, that meant it was fulfilling its programming.

A bright red envelope appeared on the table just as the wall above it began to flash with the Fleet symbol. They wanted into the Realm.

"Fleet's knocking, you gonna let them in?" Shawntelle nodded toward the screen.

"Tolui got himself shot with alien life forms and I can't be sure they haven't gotten past the suit. If I have to reveal any of that, his chances for keeping that allocation are nil. No, I am not going to let them in, not until I have something more conclusive to say."

She chewed on her lip. "Dunno, Jo, they seem pretty insistent."

He faced the wall. "Message to Fleet Com. Appreciate the contact. We will initiate when ready. Johari, Colossus Norgay, out. Send."

The tall, willowy shape of Emm stepped through the door, walked up to Johari, and wrapped him in their strong, wiry arms. "How's Tolui? How are you?"

Johari returned the embrace, his implant supplying the sensation of warmth and the pressure of Emm's grip. Each of them had two roles on the team, one for crew, and one for planetary action. As the team's counselor, Emm's compassion should feel like a mere job requirement; instead, it touched him, every time. "I'm okay. Tolui ... he's in iso, in an evac sled. His vital signs look okay, if a bit rattled. The sled is running diagnostics to see if any of the critters got through."

Emm backed off a little, but didn't release his shoulders. Their keen blue eyes searched his face. "You didn't touch him?"

"He's smarter than that, by a long shot," Shawntelle called from the other room. "So's Tolui, for that matter. What was he thinking? I mean, I'm as eager as anybody to claim this thing, but you can't just rush in, right?"

"I've been analyzing the sound profiles picked up by Armstrong's sensors. That pulse hit frequencies similar to our own subvocalizers, I think —" Emm broke off as Johari gave a little start.

"Yes. It was like something stabbed me in the back of the head." His hand rose to the spot involuntarily. Beneath his hair, he traced the faint pattern of the scar that marked his implant.

"The pulse also seems to have triggered the plant's reaction. Some kind of sound dampening field might prevent future exposures."

"That's perfect."

From the doorway beyond, Shawntelle called out, "Come on, guys, don't just hang out in the hall."

Emm offered a shrug and glided past in that direction, only to stop short at the doorway. Come to think of it, Johari didn't remember any doors on that side the last time he entered the Realm.

Johari came up alongside Emm and found himself staring into a cavern gleaming with crystalline colors, a slowly shifting range of amethyst, quartz, and smooth sheets of chalcedony creeping from rumpled layers of agate lit from within. Jagged forms emerged and sank back again, sometimes fusing into larger geometric shapes that latticed before him. In the middle of this remarkable geode, Shawntelle lounged on a smooth granite shape, like a boulder rounded off by an ancient river.

"I don't believe I've seen this simulation before," Emm remarked.

Johari said, "What the hell is this?" He leaned in, sensing a warm breeze that stirred the shapes around him. Bulbous mounds of malachite, striped in several shades of green intruded from the near side.

Shawntelle reclined into a cushion of thread-like white crystals. Gypsum? "I made it. You spend all your time in transit studying up on Civ crap — watching worm shows and listening to their music, I've been doing this." She waved an idle hand as if infiltrating the Realm and programming her own VR were just a way to pass the time. Impressive.

Some of the shapes seemed eerily familiar and Johari sprang into the space, letting himself drift as he pursued one vein of lapis, the dark blue sparked with flecks of gold.

"That's Armstrong," Shawntelle explained. "Fleet's got this subroutine that tracks our vitals, and the bots —"

"And updates our avatars when we log in, sure, but it doesn't interpret the data in visual form. At least, not like that." He turned, scanning. Another pattern, changing and echoing in the layers of malachite caught his eye, and he followed it with his hand, conducting. Bach. "Me?"

"You're getting it." She finally grinned. "Why should the Realm — our Realm — look like worm crap? Even when they do get a planet to settle on, it's not gonna look like that." She waved her hand dismissively toward the door and the house beyond.

"I'd've thought biofeedback analysis would be part of my role." Emm stepped away from the door, a perfectly ordinary wood-panel door now hanging in the crazy space of Shawntelle's geode.

Shawntelle tipped her head. "I just needed an algorithm I could graft with my simulated mineral growth patterns. This made the most interesting designs."

Emm swam to the boulder and sank down cross-legged. A perfectly formed wand of aquamarine took their weight, its cool depths reflecting Emm's own. "This is extraordinary. I didn't know you could do that."

Shawntelle tapped the crystal and it gave a soft chime of resonance. "Didn't know it could be done, or didn't know that I could do it?"

"At all. The Realm is Fleet-space. We can control invitations, open or close the door, as it were, but we don't control what happens inside, any more than we control what happens inside the bots."

The breeze felt suddenly warmer and Johari regarded Shawntelle in this new light. She testified to his own intelligence, while letting herself be underestimated. What else might she be capable of?

"What'd you want us all here for anyway?" she asked. "Oh, wait, is it the Founders' Day celebration? I got the vid." A flick of her hand triggered a display that hovered in the space between them. It showed a few thousand people gathered in the colony ring, dancing and cheering. In the center, holograms of the Founders appeared, towering over the descendants of people they united.

The vid camera soared closer, circling them slowly for the benefit of broadcast to the other ships of the Fleet. Their names hovered before their images: Dr. Nguyen, of NASA; Foreman Superior Reyes of the United Asteroid Miners; Commander Pei of the Chinese National Space Agency; President Andra, of Lunasity's Helium 3 operation; Understeward Traore of the Spaceliner Galactica; and Allesia Shapiro, the Artist-in-Residence from the short-lived Martian space complex. Every year, these same six faces with their expressions of determination. Every year, the chanting, the cheering ... the easing restrictions on the consumption of alcohol. How much of the Founders' Day party was the spirited renewal of their common purpose, and how much was simply spirits?

The holograms turned in unison, placed their hands together. "For the good of all mankind, we hereby renounce all ties of nation, class, rank, and discipline —" as the Founders' words echoed through the broadcast, Johari found himself chanting along. Okay, in spite of the perspective gained by distance and a few years, the words still moved him. Emm followed along as well. Shawntelle made a puppet of her hand, flapping its "mouth" along with the familiar words.

"From tragedy shall a new humanity be reborn. From the ashes of ruin, we shall rise into a space-faring future. In the face of nightmare, we embody the dreams —"

"Oh, for frack's sake, you guys really believe this stuff?" Shawntelle broke in, then she carved her hand through the air, sweeping the image away into shards like the faceted crystals that grew around them. "I haven't bought into that crap since I was — " she paused. "Maybe ever. It's a lot of pretty words that didn't mean anything. It's not like it lasted. They renounced all those things, only to adopt an austerity code the next year and start doling out the ranks again, military ones, this time —"

"It has lasted. Two hundred years," Johari pointed out. "You think all those different kinds of people could have formed the Fleet and kept it running for so long without some form of discipline?"

From the hallway outside, a gong sounded, deep and resonant; it swelled through the door, and no doubt echoed through the rest of the house, the one place where their subvocalizers powered down unless called for. Armstrong's alarm.

Stopping himself in mid-air, Johari executed the escape function, powering up his implant. Nothing happened. "What the Hell? Shawntelle, what —"

The others, too, sat alert. Shawntelle's eyes flaring, then narrowing. "I didn't intentionally shut down the 'plants, if that's what you're thinking."

He dove for the door, Emm bursting past him. "We're on the way! Maybe an hour," they shouted as they flew through the door and tumbled to the floor beyond. Emm vanished from the Realm. Outside the geode, the normalcy of the Realm reasserted itself and Johari hit the flooring at a crouch, then triggered Escape again. An instant later, he blinked up from the cushioning of the tent. "Armstrong, do you copy?" He leapt to his feet and ran for the suitlock.

"A dragon on the horizon over the ocean. I would have already shot it down, save that I do not wish to signal Tolui's location."

In the limited tech of the temporary shelter, Johari spent precious seconds longer checking his own seals, sliding the helmet shut, missing the speedy assistive servos of Norgay's compartment. Reflectivity was already triggered, thanks to the tent controls, as he stepped away from the tent and ran across the plateau. As he ran past Armstrong's location, his helmet display showed the blue outline of the giant bot in a posture of vigilance, scanning the ocean. Both arms revealed heavy weapons, but the bot remained reflective.

"Don't shoot, Armstrong, please. The others are coming." Except that he hadn't heard anything from Maya and Norgay, who should have been closest of all.

Johari's heart pounded double-time. He summoned up helmet magnification and scanned the horizon. There! The broad wings of a dragon cut the sky far out at sea. Instinctively, he dropped low behind a bit of rubble, watching. The dragon did not turn toward them, nor did it fly with any great urgency. Rather, it circled the same area, then took a position nearly vertical, beating those huge wings slowly as its neck waved, its gaze aimed at the water below.

With a sudden swerve, it pulled out and down, wings tucked, neck outstretched. It struck the water with a geyser of spray, then turned again, sliding along the surface. Its head reared up, a struggling creature clasped in those jaws. The dragon soared skyward, carrying its prey. Those curved front legs snatched forward and it brought its head down to meet them. The two big claws came together, carving into the thick hide while the smaller claws kept hold of the separated skin. Starting at the head, those jaws chomped and chomped, swallowing the wriggling thing even as the forelegs skinned it. The dragon dropped the empty pelt and it tumbled away below. With a final great gulp of its jaws, the dragon finished its meal. Its flight path smoothed out again and it started another search pattern, a little bit nearer.

Armstrong emitted a tone that Johari's implant echoed. Proximity alarm. Norgay must be here at last! He turned from the ocean as a shadow cut off the sun. A second dragon swooped overhead, neck extended, head swaying. Searching.

7

'NORGAY, WHERE ARE YOU?" Johari subvocalized.

Armstrong bent his knees as the dragon soared over the encampment, passing through the space where Armstrong's head had been a moment earlier. Johari pressed his back against the rubble as the shadow passed over. The dragon's gill-like structures flared and rippled in the sky, beautiful and terrifying. What if they weren't gills at all? What if they were some completely different organ, some kind of sensor or even a weapon — more akin to jellyfish tentacles than breathing apparatus? Johari's throat felt parched. This was only the third planet they had found with any life forms at all, and the first one had just been at the cellular level. Why hadn't they just stayed there, with the bacteria, and found a way to make it work? Fleet needed complex proteins for their recombinatory food production system. They wanted trees. They wanted grass, and dogs, and all the things they couldn't have, which — they should fracking well face it — they had never seen except in VR. Shawntelle was right: worm crap. Meaningless memories of a lost world.

Johari's head swam and he let out the breath he had been holding. Whatever the dragons sensed, his breath would be the least of it.

Across the way, Armstrong remained in a crouch, the two tents silhouetted behind him, and all outlined in the blue indicating their reflective status. The bot raised his weapons, tracking something. Johari toggled an external cam on his wrist and extended his arm past the stone, trying to replicate what Armstrong could see. The dragon wheeled slowly, turning around a wing point.

The sun shone through the membranes, revealing a complex network of veins and vessels framed by the dark strokes of bone. One wing showed speckles of light and a ragged edge that oozed liquid. Armstrong's bullets had made an impact back at the nest site. This visit wasn't the random intrusion of a coastal creature.

Its head swayed, exactly as the other's had while it was hunting. Two eyes faced out to the sides, two others faced forward, along that wicked snout. Where was their zoologist when they needed him? Struck down by a botanical attack. Two sets of eyes, facing in different directions. A lower pair of bulges, covered by a leathery skin, suggested a third set of eyes currently closed. Those wild gills made him think of the pulsing veins of color in Shawntelle's VR chamber.

It beat slowly, hovering, then returned, its shadow sweeping the camp again. Johari froze, his arm still sticking out, in case moving too quickly caused a blink in the reflectivity. His wrist cam remained pointed out to sea, where the first dragon abandoned its hunt and turned ninety degrees, soaring along the coastline, head waving.

"I am close, Johari. I'm almost there." Norgay's voice resonated through Johari's head.

The dragon overhead let out a painful screech and Johari flinched. Wind rushed down at him, making the suit sensors flare. He spun about to find the dragon lunging toward camp, hind legs extended and wings tipped back. It screeched again, overwhelming his auditory interface. Armstrong fired a barrage of bullets, both guns, battering the dragon back toward the sky. Wailing, it twisted in the air. One wing slapped the ground near where Johari sheltered as it struggled to flee. The wail pierced the back of Johari's neck, where his implant hid, and he, too, screamed. Last time, that sound seemed to trigger the plant's attack. Thank God they had chosen a site without vegetation. As he jerked his arm back, instinctively getting smaller, he caught a glimpse of a second soaring form wheeling back in their direction.

Stone scraped and the plateau's edge crumbled as the dragon righted itself. It launched over the ocean, tail lashing. A spatter of blood fell in its wake. Armstrong took three steps that thundered the rocks and launched after it. "No — don't leave!" Johari screamed. What was he supposed to do? Tolui lay in his healing sled, oblivious, and the other bots were still many klicks away.

As long as the reflectivity network remained intact, the dragons couldn't see them. He calmed himself with this thought as he scanned the plateau, tracing the bluish outlines of the tents in his display. And there, in the middle of the larger tent, a rippling area of darker space. The torn outer layer vented air and nanofibers worked to bring the edges back together. In less than five minutes, they would have an intact shelter again. In less than five seconds, they could be dragon food.

Overhead, another round of gunfire, something heavier this time. As the second dragon closed in, Johari ran to the smaller tent. He punched the emergency protocols — they could always re-inflate with more atmosphere, but if the thing ripped through and found Tolui — expendable be damned!

Johari put on a burst of speed, diving through the airlock into the tent. The sled rose off the ground, its power cells humming. He grabbed the handle on one end and hauled it after him, back outside toward the gap where this plateau broke off from the main cliff. The second dragon gave a screech of its own and bore down on the plateau.

Johari yanked the sled to one side and let its momentum carry him into the gap. The hover function could only operate with a solid surface below, and the motors whined as it exerted greater and greater force, just enough to keep them from crashing as they came to rest in a heap of broken stone. The crevasse above him went dark as the dragon swung overhead. Gunfire sounded in the distance.

He couldn't just cower in a ditch and hope for the best. Johari scanned the area, and pulled the sled over some rough stones to a hollow in the cliffside. Tolui lay peacefully inside, sleeping through the battle. Just so long as he didn't wake up to find himself alone on an alien world.

A ping vibrated the back of his neck. Norgay. But why wasn't he talking? Johari used the suit's microflares to assist as he scrambled back up the plateau and peered over the top.

For a moment, he saw no dragons, just the outlines of the shelters, then a shadow from above, growing larger. The second dragon must have spotted the tear in the shelter. It dove straight down, about to rip their temporary home to shreds. To the right, over the sea, the dragon with the pierced wing flashed its frills in a dazzling display. The second dragon broke away immediately and swung out to sea.

Not far off, Armstrong hovered, guns drawn, fully visible. Seventy feet tall, a silver humanoid robot with heavily armored limbs, Armstrong confronted his enemy, reflecting the span of those bold, green wings.

No wonder the dragon stopped attacking the tent — there was the real threat. Armstrong's rockets flared and he soared out to sea, two dragons streaking with him, drawn away from the vulnerable humans. Johari didn't know if he should cheer or weep. Vulnerable humans: two on the surface, and seventy-eight thousand marooned in space, depending on these bots to find them a home. This was no time for Armstrong to be a hero.

Pebbles and sand bounced on the plateau's surface and Norgay, outlined in blue, landed a few feet away. Johari ran for him, flinging himself onto the robot's foot. In this world's lower gravity, he could leap as high as the bot's ankle, then slide down to the top of his foot. The metal hummed and produced a familiar warmth that made Johari want to curl up and rest. But if he did that, Armstrong might never return. *"We've gotta go after him."*

Norgay extruded a set of rungs and Johari scrambled up to the airlock, slapping the seals and peeling off his gloves as the lower door sealed. "Maya! Suit up — Tolui's down in that crevasse, and I don't want to leave him alone."

"Are you okay?" She dropped through the upper hatch and fumbled the helmet he tossed to her. She managed to keep hold of it, her hands visibly shaking. He needed to take over for more reasons than one.

Johari nodded. "You?"

"We tried to lead the dragon away. More of them came, so we had to move carefully. It was so freaky, being surrounded by those things. I guess Armstrong gave up on staying invisible?"

"He'd do anything for Tolui. That's why we have to go after him. Maybe Norgay can reason with him and get him to stand down. Once the tent is healed, you guys can move back in."

She stuffed the helmet over her curls and climbed into the suit, giving a little wave as she dropped away to the plateau surface. Johari finished his climb and the hatch closed behind him, then gravity suddenly shifted and he flew upward. He put his arms out like a superhero, giving a whoop of joy. This had been one of his favorite games as a child, slingshotting around the habitat's interior as Norgay played with gravity, bouncing, tossing and catching him as if he were a gymnast. As he soared nearly to the top, Johari turned a somersault. He set his feet gently against the upper canopy, doing a hand-stand to catch his seat. He dropped into it as Norgay returned the hab to normal. Johari snapped his belt, nestled once again where he belonged. Breathless, he started to grin, then said, "Why didn't you answer me earlier?"

"I am glad to see you as well. And I am fine. Thank you for asking." Norgay took three long strides across the plateau and leapt into the air. "I believe the dragons can sense our transmissions."

"They can hear us talking?"

"Not precisely, but they are aware when we do. It triggers a response."

No wonder the dragons knew where they were. Armstrong's summons to the other bots had called to them as well. If the dragons' emissions bothered them, it made perfect sense that the feeling was mutual. "Oh, frack."

"Indeed. We'll need to run some tests to determine their accuracy and frequency range. It may be possible to switch to an alternate system."

"I'm glad you're safe."

The seat cradled him with comfort. The ocean below gave no sign of their passage. Sea stacks — towers of that same blue and yellow stone rose up around them. Flocks of enormous, flightless bird-seal hybrids lounged at their base, sheltering where it would be hard for dragons to scoop them up. Johari thought of the one he'd watched being skinned and he shuddered. Norgay made an inquisitive noise.

"The dragons. They hunt those things. They use the big claws on their front — wait a minute. Two dragons. One of them was out hunting over the ocean, turning circles. Armstrong and I were keeping an eye on it, to see if it turned hostile, and that's when the second one came up behind us. I mean, we got sensors on it, right, but it couldn't know that."

"You think the hunting dragon served as a distraction."

"A deliberate lure so we were looking the wrong direction. That's teamwork. It suggests a high level of cooperation among individuals." As he spoke he started tapping notes on a pop-up screen. "Coordinated attack, and likely communication. The decoy had to be pre-planned. Maybe they don't have civilization, but that behavior puts them past the level of pack-hunters like wolves, probably closer to dolphins or chimps on the evolutionary scale."

"We have not yet noted any tool use."

"Would we even recognize their tools? What kind of tools would they use?" Johari's finger hesitated over the screen. "What if those plants around the nests are deliberate? An early alert and defense system? They could be evidence of agriculture."

"We would need to establish that they are cultivated for a purpose."

"Right — what's the barrier for pre-civ intelligence factors prior to colonization?"

"Confirming … "

A distant sound of screeching drew Johari's attention. A cluster of darkness in the sky, jagged and swirling like a flock of birds, only the nearer they got, the bigger the birds, and the broader their leathery wings. In their midst, he glimpsed silver. Dragons mobbing something just like seagulls in the old vids. Johari tapped a few video links, tracking and seeing if they had a model for the behavior. Facts flashed by. Crows mobbing eagles. Seagulls came in colonies on land or flotillas on the sea. When they washed up dead on a beach, scientists called them a wreck. As he watched a dragon, wings tattered, plunged toward the sea. A wreck of dragons.

8

"MAYBE IT'S TIME to de-cloak and draw them off — at least swoop in a little faster, even if they can feel us coming." Johari set his fingers lightly on the window before him, and the scene zoomed closer through Norgay's enhanced vision. Seven, eight, nine dragons darted and wove around Armstrong. Most of them showed streaks of blood and wounds where his bullets had struck.

"Fearsome as they may appear, I don't believe they have any defenses capable of truly damaging one of us." Still, Norgay increased speed.

"Then he's got to stop — they're intelligent, at least. We've got to stop this thing before it escalates too far!"

The fallen dragon flapped against the surface, its neck arching back. A surge of water rose to the left, waves rising, edged with some kind of glowing bacteria.

Something approached beneath the water, something so large and powerful that its body thrust the ocean aside into mad eddies that gleamed like swirling nebulae. Green spirals expanded as the wave grew and the dragon thrashed all the more, but one of its wings and the entire back half of its body did not respond. All three sets of eyes flared open, rolling wildly as if searching for aid.

Johari's hand rose as if he could reach out to it and pluck it from the sea. The gills along its neck sparkled, reminding him of neural activity. The dragon glittered with frantic energy, gorgeous and horrifying. It squealed as a series of spines broke the surface of the water, then the wave plunged downward, sucking the dragon below with it. Its tail slapped against the surface, raising an arrowhead pattern in the gleaming sea.

A flicker of spikes and the water settled again, though the arrowhead lingered, the ghost of the dragon remaining on the surface, a warning. The other dragons hesitated, swooping apart and rising higher off the water. For a moment, Armstrong hovered among them, his feet and legs now clear of dragons.

"Down! If he goes to the water, they won't follow," Johari shouted.

Armstrong turned in the air, glancing down, then shifted his rockets and dove. The dragon with the torn wing — the same one that attacked the plateau, Johari was sure of it — swung about in the air, flapped hard, then tucked its wings and dove with him.

In order to make the plunge, Armstrong powered down the central booster at his spine. He pulled back his arms, making a sleek shape to penetrate the water's surface. The dragon grabbed at him with its powerful hind legs, claws scraping along the surface as he pulled in every extrusion possible. But the central booster was non-negotiable.

The dragon's claws caught and Armstrong jerked to a halt. He fired his thruster, shooting across the surface of the ocean, his wake streaming to either side as the dragon's wings strained and cut into the water, carving deep grooves splashed with blood.

In the sky above, the other dragons swirled and followed in a disorganized mass. They screeched the danger call Johari was coming to recognize.

A ripple of spines cut across Armstrong's wake.

Norgay was catching up, pacing them now, close enough that Johari no longer needed magnification. Those spines stood at least as tall as he was, and the creature that bore them was gaining.

Johari opened comms. "Armstrong, pull up! There's a sea monster!"

On the bot's back, the dragon flexed its wounded body and brought those short forelegs down, with its two huge claws. They dug in around the powerpack between Armstrong's shoulders and metal ground.

"Can we send a pulse through the water and stun the monster?"

"Indeed." Norgay dropped lower and shifted power. Johari felt a lurch as the thrusters turned, then a deep, powerful boom echoed through his body.

The spines sank away, and the dragon thrashed free of Armstrong's back, something metallic glinting in its claws. It pumped its wings fiercely and started to gain altitude. Armstrong slowed and rolled, raising an arm. Aiming.

"No — it's got to stop! Norgay, full shields."

"You wish me to dive between Armstrong and an alien lifeform."

"Yes! Absolutely!"

They changed course and shot forward, water rushing up to either side then crashing back again behind them in a sparkle of fluorescence. Norgay rammed between the dragon and the bot, rolling to place Johari's habitat on the safer side of that confrontation.

"Colossus Armstrong, stand down, by order of Fleet representative Johari Norgay."

Even as he said the words, Armstrong's lights flickered, then the bot was dropping. As he fell, his extremities smoothed out, any exterior vents sealing up, and he dropped into the sea.

"Armstrong!"

Johari's implant buzzed with a brief pulse of bot-to-bot communication, then Armstrong's signal vanished into the deep of an alien sea.

The dragon screamed and plunged downward, smacking hard into the habitat. Johari flinched as its sharp breast smeared blood across his window. The hind claws scraped, scrabbling for purchase. Its front claws still clutched something, the metal torn from Armstrong's back. His nuclear generator: a small unit, enough to power the bot for a long time when he couldn't deploy solar sails or other energy sources, the nuke had to be outside, accessible to engineers, and able to be readily jettisoned if a malfunction might cause an explosion.

Tearwing launched itself upward, beating hard and hauling its prize. Was the unit already damaged and leaking? If so, what might a radioactive exposure do to these creatures? Worse yet, what would its loss mean for Armstrong, sinking to the bottom of the sea? He might have enough power reserves to maintain his own systems, but not enough to escape the depths.

The other dragons swarmed Norgay, just as they had been doing to Armstrong moments before. Norgay spun about and streaked upward, using his jets. One of the dragons flung out its wings, trying to brake in mid-air, but Norgay's trajectory blew straight into it.

The dragon's shriek became a wail of pain, its leg and wing smearing across the window then it fell aside. Johari saw the ripples of rising green and forming vortices of the sea monster's approach and the dragon was gone. Still reflective, Norgay continued on course, acceleration pushing Johari back into his seat as they left the dragons behind. He turned and dodged the brown pillar of the chemical storm and gained altitude for a few long, silent moments. Johari watched the scanners intently, but no more dragons edged the radar, either in front or behind their position.

Norgay slowed a little and curved in toward the landmass, drawing a long arc around the campsite. The tents, fully repaired, resumed their invisibility, while the blue outline of a bot stood on the cliff beyond, the bulky presence of Eriksson. As they curved back toward the water, Johari caught a glimpse of a second cloaked bot, Zheng He, in position between the plateau and the cliffside, hidden in the deep fissure, facing out to sea.

Norgay decreased both speed and breadth and cycled down to a landing near the larger tent, taking one knee, one of his hands resting knuckles against the ground, the other pressed against his chest, the vast fingers splayed over Johari's habitat, Norgay's palm held as if against his heart. The bot bowed his head.

Johari unbuckled and pressed himself against the inside of the window, his body splayed to meet Norgay's hand. "We'll get him back — he's not gone."

The habitat felt strangely silent, as if they both held their breath.

"Johari. You are safe." Norgay's voice a whisper through him.

"Yes."

They stayed that way a long moment, Norgay holding his internal gravity just so, enabling Johari to ... hug him. What other word could there be?

"Will you please come out? I need you."

Outside? Weird, especially at a time like this. The flow of diagnostics down the side of Johari's vision suggested only superficial damage — nothing that a quick hose-down wouldn't take care of. "I need you, too, buddy. I'm on my way."

With a sigh of reluctance, Johari peeled himself off the window and drifted downward to the suit bay. Maya had his primary suit, but he had a back-up as well: Fleet was very big on redundant systems. As he suited up, Johari asked, "What's the matter?"

"I am unable to deploy my nozzle system. I believe there is a mechanical failing."

"Right." Johari pulled on the helmet. The first twist failed to latch it. He groaned, and tugged again, this time hearing the hiss as the suit's internal systems booted up life support and the pressure pads conformed to his body. He slipped from the hatch and clambered onto Norgay's bent knee. Norgay lifted his fist from the ground and propped his huge elbow on his knee, offering his hand.

"The problem is here." Norgay spread his fingers, or tried to. Something protruded from the slight gap between the first and second knuckles.

Johari stepped onto Norgay's arm and walked along his wrist to the back of his hand. He knelt down near the trouble spot. The broken tip of a dragon's wing stuck out, torn membrane flapping and pale bone slicked with blood jutting toward the sky.

Johari edged a little closer and dug in his gloved hands at the base of Norgay's metal frame, trying to get a grip on the fragment. He wrapped both hands around the bone and wiggled it back and forth, tugging upward. It finally came free and he tumbled back, landing on Norgay's hand with the flap of wing and broken bone across his lap, a hideous blanket.

Johari's throat stung as if he might vomit, but he swallowed hard and pushed the thing aside. Until today, he had seen the insides of living things only in videos depicting hunting or battle scenes recorded hundreds of years ago. Now, he was living inside those movies, his friends breaking down or incapacitated, his own long-time companion, Norgay, involved in the killing. His life translated from VR and deep space into vivid reality, the torn wing of a dragon oozing in real time. How did that ancient quote go? *"Months of boredom, punctuated by moments of extreme terror."*

He could not afford to give in. The Saturn Five were depending on him, and Fleet was depending on them. After a few deep breaths, he picked up the wingtip. Tolui would want to examine this, when he and Armstrong came back together. Shit.

Down by two bots, and one team-member. Would Tolui and Armstrong ever come together again? Only if the one could be rescued from the bottom of the sea, and the other released from isolation. Johari clung to the bone, his fingers barely wrapping halfway around, and this must be the very tip of the dragon's wing. A slender claw sprouted there.

"I did not mean for it to die, Johari," Norgay said within him.

"You were trying to get both of us away, before any more damage could be done. I know. I wish —" Johari broke off. He wished Armstrong hadn't taken off like that? Then he and Tolui would probably be dead. He wished Armstrong had found a less impulsive response? Definitely. That was exactly why they had teammates. The bots tended toward binary responses: Leave the planet alone, or destroy everything that might be hazardous. Still, he hadn't expected Norgay to be so affected by the fight. Was it losing Armstrong, one of his peers, or killing the dragon, a member of an alien race they had barely begun to know?

"We should leave," Norgay said.

That brought Johari's head up. Norgay's enormous face barely changed and yet embodied a heart-sore sadness. The blue bowls of his sensor arrays stood in for eyes, gazing down dimly. Part of Johari's job meant reading the expressions on that mechanical plane. *"This is humanity's best hope in a long time, isn't it? This planet? We have a duty to stay and learn everything we can, to be sure."* A lump formed in his throat. *"Humanity is counting on us, Norgay. We can't allow a couple of setbacks let us forget that."*

Norgay remained silent a long time, then said, *"You are correct, Johari. It has been a long time."* Another pause. *"It has been twenty-two years since we had such a strong prospect, Johari. That was Eden. Where your parents died."*

9

"H EY, JOHARI, are you ever coming inside?" Shawntelle's voice cut in over the low frequency radio they used for local communication. "We got Tolui's sled back in, and the cycle is ramping down, so any external parasites will be fried at this point."

"Great, good." Johari lingered a moment, his hand atop Norgay's arm. "I'm coming?" he said, glancing up at Norgay.

The bot gave a slight nod. "If you leave the specimen, I will prepare it for analysis. I do not have all of the sensors and equipment Armstrong carries, but I believe Zheng He possesses duplicates of the critical aspects."

"Thanks, that'll be good. Also, if you guys can run an estimate on the total population of the dragons and their global distribution, that would help."

"Indeed." Norgay delicately lifted the broken wing tip as Johari climbed down. "I will also correlate our data to see what we can learn about the sea monsters." A pause, then he spoke again with wry humor. "Armstrong is now in an excellent position to make observations."

"How long can he last without his nuke-pack?"

"Given the strain of an undersea environment and the necessity of scanning for further dangers, he will be unable to power down to a minimal level. His on-board batteries, assuming they are fully charged and in working order should give him approximately thirty-six hours."

Johari folded his arms. "Assuming? Why wouldn't they be?"

"You may recall asking some questions about Fleet concerns. One of their concerns is the useful lifespan of the colossus. The loss of the Delta Five brings this concern into focus. Each of us has been performing nano-inspection as a background function. Certain components appear to be breaking down faster than would be ideal." Norgay lifted the wingtip on the palm of his hand and examined it, various sensors moving, whirring and focusing.

"You're telling me that your batteries are dying."

"Under ordinary circumstances, they recharge with at least moderate efficiency."

"And underwater?"

Norgay's gaze re-focused out to sea. "Thirty-six hours is a generous estimate."

Johari's stomach churned. He reached out and tapped Norgay on the foot. "Find out what you can about those sea monsters. When I'm done with this convo, you and I are going after him."

Norgay's flex-metal mouth curved upward.

Johari darted past him to the vestibule of the larger shelter, backed up and triggered the suit lock. He clambered out into the dull glow of the tent interior.

"It's about time." Shawntelle lounged against a supply crate. She took a bite from a protein bar, scowling as she chewed on it. "Maybe we do need to upgrade our proteins." In person, she exuded the soft scent of spices he couldn't quite name. He couldn't decide if the scent was intriguing or distracting. If Maya reminded him of ancient Mexican sculptures, then Shawntelle was more contemporary — a gymnast maybe, with her compact, muscular strength.

Maya was on her feet as he came inside. "What happened out there? Where's Armstrong?"

Emm raised their hands in a placating gesture. "Let him sit and breathe, at least for a little while."

"Right, sorry. Shawntelle told you about Tolui? He should be able to visit the Realm when the sled reawakens him —"

"And a good thing, too, because Fleet's been calling."

"We have to tell them to stop." Johari paced into the group and settled cross-legged. "The dragons were drawn here when Armstrong sent the pulse. He made himself a target so they wouldn't wreck the camp." A wreck of dragons, floating on the sea until the monster swallowed them down. Johari shuddered.

Emm reached into the nearest supply crate and tossed him a blanket. He gratefully cocooned himself as he described the battle, the sea monsters, the last sight of Armstrong as he sank into the churning waters.

Maya's mouth hung open until she shut it with a start. Even Shawntelle stopped chewing. When he had fallen silent, she said, "So he's probably low on conventional weapons. But he'll have the machete at least."

"If I can get his pack down to him, then he'll get out of this just fine, but we don't have much time."

Emm raised their pale eyebrows. "You are suggesting infiltrating a dragon's lair? Assuming it even preserved the pack and carried it home."

Johari managed a smile. "Easier if it didn't. Then we just track it down by its radioactive signature, retrieve and deliver." He snapped his fingers, but the sound was weak. His hand trembled. Infiltrating a dragon's lair. Yep, that's what he'd just signed on to. "Look, we're down by two bots and Tolui might be carrying alien bacteria. If anything else goes wrong, we're fracked."

"So we're ditching the planet? We get Armstrong and we get out of here?" Maya asked, her face bright with hope.

Leaning forward, Shawntelle picked up a portable and tossed it toward Maya, figures and charts cascading down the screen. "Like we're gonna find a better alternative. You've been analyzing the files, same as me. We've got eighty-seven percent correlation on this rock. Even Johari's home world only had sixty-two. Eighty-seven percent. We claim this sucker, and then the five of us get to live like Fleetcom."

"It does sound appealing," Emm said, "to have a view other than endless stars."

Johari wet his lips. "I think the dragons are intelligent."

Shawntelle turned to stare at him. "You did not just say that. Eighty-seven percent, Johari!"

"Tearwing didn't attack the base until Armstrong and I were both watching her accomplice out to sea — and she couldn't even see us."

"Lots of things on Earth hunted cooperatively: wolves, whales, what are those cats with the furry heads?" Shawntelle waved her hand to indicate a mane. "Wait a minute — 'Tearwing?' You named a dragon?"

"And referred to it as 'she'," Emm pointed out quietly, their expression tight and worried.

"I had to call it something, if only in my own head. It was tending or defending the nest where Tolui broke that egg."

"We need to stay objective about this," Emm said. "If you have to call the animal something, give it a number, and enter its image and characteristics into the database."

"When we're not trying to fight it, Emm, I will totally do that!" Johari collapsed onto the cushioned floor, scrubbing his hands over his face. His subvocalizer hummed a familiar sequence. Fleet was calling — and he couldn't avoid them any longer.

Johari triggered the Realm and slammed open the door. The dog jumped up, wagging its tail at him and he ignored it, going straight for the wall where Fleet's urgent message flashed. The Fleet logo showed a colossus like Norgay in a dramatic pose against a backdrop of Earth, framed by gigantic ships ready to take off for parts unknown. Or maybe known at last? If Armstrong or Shawntelle had their way, they'd wipe out the dragons and begin the colonization process. If it were up to Maya, she would simply take off and search for someplace less dangerous. This was their job, facing the danger so the colony didn't have to, assessing the risk and making the call. His job. He tapped in the response sequence.

A door swished open on the opposite wall. On this side, a suburban house full of fake sunlight and pseudo-woodwork. On the other side, the ready room of Fleet Commander Roxanne Shen. Fleet's flagship, once the Spaceliner Galactica, retained the luxury of its former life, converted into command's headquarters after the Ruin.

A sleek environment of gray metal and plastic, tasteful red and blue checked cushions on the seats of the handful of chairs, it centered on a long slab table etched with a map of earth. The tapered surface led the eye naturally toward the single porthole, a tall, narrow one with a peaked arch at the top. From his immersion in the history of human cultures, Johari recognized it as an emulation of a church window, turning their quest for a new home into something holy. The table had the same shape, mirroring the view of endless darkness and stars.

At the point where window and table met stood the Commander herself. Stern and strong, she resembled a portrait he had seen of the Pan-Asian Protector-general from the First Climate War: someone who was used to taking charge. Did she really look like that, or did she manipulate her avatar to make an impression? Inside the Realm, the kids had assigned avatars who resembled them, but outside of it, even in Shawntelle's crazy little world, anything could happen.

He took a pause of respect, then walked in, swallowed hard, and announced, "Commander, we have reason to believe the wildlife is sensitive to our long-range communications. Until we've done more testing, any communications should be brief."

Her eyebrows rose a little. "Thank you for informing me promptly, Johari. Then I will not ask you to make yourself comfortable. The initial pin beams we received indicated this planet has a significant probability for colonization, and we were concerned to receive no other communications."

"Our comm seems to agitate them. The reaction is interfering with our work." To say the very least. Should he just tell her? His team would reap all kinds of rewards if they found the New Earth, and if they chose to land too soon, the colony might pay the price. "My assessment so far is that the planet will be very difficult to colonize. There's a large species of flying amphibians — we've been calling them dragons — and they've shown signs of intelligence."

Her scowl, at least, was painfully human. "What level of civilization?"

He shook his head. "I don't know yet. Tolui's been injured and Armstrong is damaged. Until we handle that situation, I can't —"

"Damaged?" She absorbed that with a recoil. "What are their prospects for recovery?"

"We're still assessing that. Tolui's in a recovery sled, but he should be coming around soon."

"I'm glad to hear it. Tell me about the hostiles. There's no satellites or transmissions — architecture? Organizational structures? Ritual behavior?"

Her dismissive response to learning of Tolui and Armstrong's injuries worried him. If he told her the dragons were responsible for the damage, what then? The Armstrong solution: annihilation. "None that I know of, but —"

"Johari," she interrupted, then gave a gesture of apology. "I'm sure you saw the update. Intelligence has been down-graded as a criteria."

What did it mean to downgrade intelligence? He should've read the rest of his messages before taking the meeting. "We need more time to assess these creatures." He spread his hands. "If they're on the verge of a breakthrough, if they have other forms or culture — music, art, I don't know —"

Commander Shen strode toward him, her concern settling in deep lines that framed her mouth. "Johari, you are the first offspring of former explorers to be admitted into the Colossus program. Some felt that to place you as the team commander, the civilization officer, might be a mistake. Others felt that you, more than anyone, would know what is at stake. You are the only surviving child to be born on a planet in nearly two hundred years."

Johari absorbed that, a perspective on himself he'd never really considered. The only *surviving* child. "Commander, if we don't know enough about these creatures before landing, we're condemning our own colony to death. I'm trying to stop another colony from being destroyed. "

"Of course you are, your first duty is to the Fleet and to her colonies. 'To discover potential colonization sites and to explore them with all due diligence,'" she said, quoting from the scout's oath.

"Yes, sir." He continued the oath, "'With respect to the ecosystems of such new worlds such that humanity is never again an agent of the destruction of worlds — '"

As he spoke, the scout's oath scrolled in greenish light across the air between them, ending abruptly after "all due diligence," and Johari's voice trailed away. He scanned the words again, half of them were missing. "The oath has been changed?"

She did not walk toward him, but was suddenly there, inches away from him, her dark eyes searching him.

"Our resources are increasingly depleted, Johari." Her hand on his shoulder conveyed a palpable weight and an almost tingly intensity. "Humanity needs that colony. We cannot afford to be concerned about the mating rituals of mythical creatures. In all honesty, the Founders were idealists; we could never afford that concern. When they rallied the ships that became the Fleet, they hoped for an egalitarian system, an interstellar utopia. Under the circumstances — it just couldn't be. Without rigid command structures, we wouldn't have survived the Djikstra Revolt, or even left the solar system."

Her touch warmed. "Your training naturally leads you to adopt a similar idealism. Don't allow that to overwhelm the needs of your people. If this is a struggle for you, I can name an alternate Civs officer."

Johari shook that off. "Don't worry, Commander, I will see this through."

"I certainly hope so. We will have access to team records, Johari. If Fleetcom suspects that you are obstructing the future of humanity in favor of this unknown species... Well, Colossus Norgay has had other partners, and he will have again, perhaps sooner rather than later. Do you understand?"

"That won't be necessary, Commander."

She breathed out a sigh of relief. "If these creatures are potentially hostile, and operate at the level of pack hunters or beyond, Fleet must regard them as an enemy. I am enacting military protocols for all further explorations, as of now; all dealings with this hostile species should be handled with utmost care. You're sure of their intelligence?"

"We're still studying them, Commander. They're intelligent, but I'm not sure at what level."

"In that case, you have discretion to investigate. We need to learn their weaknesses before they learn ours, but under no circumstances must they have direct access to our technology, especially the colossus units. Treat all encounters as possible mission-level threats. These orders will be appended to this communication in order to minimize the dangers to your crew.

They will be broadcast only on your local, low-resolution channel. Anyone who breaches these protocols will be considered a traitor to the Fleet, understood? There is to be no support given to our enemies, no aid or comfort."

Johari's throat felt dry, his spine rigid. Traitor: the very worst kind of outlaw. It had been concerns about treason that triggered the shift to martial law after the Ruin. Then came the Djikstra Revolt: A group of nihilists decided the universe intended for humanity to be destroyed and began working toward that end. Two ships had been lost, four hundred and seventy-five people died. When the cell was uncovered, dozens of other citizens got caught in the sweep, people who hoped their loved ones could be drawn back from the edge. People whose stupid mistakes or ill-placed loyalty allowed Fleet's enemies to get too close.

Fleet didn't feed outlaws, it ate them. Fleet needed this planet — and he needed to retrieve Armstrong before Fleet could assign blame. Tolui's rash action had placed the whole team in jeopardy, including the partner who had come to his defense. In his eagerness to claim the planet, Tolui might well have lost his own future.

"Yes, Commander." Words like two stab wounds to his throat.

"I knew we could count on you." A radiant warmth spread through the chamber as she gazed at him, a hint of the honor due to his team if they succeeded. "The planet, what have you named it?"

Neil Armstrong, the first man on the moon, landed in a feature called the Sea of Tranquility. Two hundred years later, his namesake became the first bot beneath an alien sea. "Tranquility."

The Commander beamed at him. "Excellent! That's perfect. This could really be the one — You've seen the vids from before the Ruin, Johari. Can you imagine the effect it will have on our people, to finally have a home?" For a moment her eyes took on a haunted quality. "To have enough for everyone. To have as many children as we want. Not to have to choose." She gave a quiet chuckle, a more human sound than he expected from her. "With his allocation, your friend Tolui could be the first father on a whole new world."

Taken from the bot who raised him, and given the chance to raise a child of his own. If they survived, and Fleet never found out that Tolui had caused the trouble to begin with. "He'd like that, Commander," Johari said around the lump in his throat.

She gave a little salute, and he stalked from the chamber. The door slid shut behind him, and he stood again in the hallway of the Realm. A whimper came from nearby, then a soft muzzle poked up into his palm. Absently, he stroked the head of the virtual dog, making its tail thump against the floor.

Shawntelle's door stood open as he walked by, and her voice called out, "Come on in, Johari! Don't let Fleet crap get you down!"

It wasn't crap that got him down. On the contrary: Everything Commander Shen said was true.

"In a while," he answered, and kept walking toward the stairs.

The image of Tolui's family lingered with him. Tolui, the child of outlaws, would never have been selected for an allocation without the scout program; now, he could lose it all. Johari stood on the brink, and his choices could, quite literally, change the course of all mankind.

On the floor above, each member of the Saturn Five owned a room to use as they required. His door, which opened only to his hand, revealed a sound studio: egg crate bumps on the walls and ceiling, and an array of instruments on stands around the room. He moved toward the cello and stroked his finger across the strings, releasing a series of low, clear notes, slightly off. His room, his rules — at least within the bounds of earth-reality. He chose to let his instruments get out of tune. Now, he took the cello by the neck and sat behind it, bracing it gently with his knees as he began to tune it, a reprieve from the strained reality of his mission.

Would it be his mission much longer? If he pressed the point about the dragons, he could lose Norgay, lose everything he'd ever known, including the chance to walk the world, Tranquility or any other, with his helmet off and the wind blowing through his hair. Why not let it go? Study the dragons, discover their weaknesses, and prepare for Fleet to take control, subjugating the native species into farm animals to feed a growing population.

Johari drew his bow across the strings. He'd been working on an arrangement of the "Asteroid Miners' Hymn" for cello. He conjured the sheet music into the air before him.

The door chimed softly, and Johari wilted a little. "Who is it?"

"It's Maya," she paused. "If you're playing, can I listen?"

The polished surface of the instrument glowed warmly below him, the neck settling into his hand. The warmth of Maya's enjoyment settled into his heart. "Sure, come on in."

The door opened and closed and Maya stepped past, moving to sit cross-legged to one side, respectful of the music before him. "Sorry," she whispered, then, "Thanks."

Johari set his fingers on the strings and cued a metronome that ticked at the back of his head.

Taking a deep breath, he took his position, and began, the notes echoing deep and mellow, filling up the belly of the instrument and swelling out into the room around him, but his fingers felt soft and weak, failing to press or hold, his bow-hand alternately sawing or glancing off the strings. On an especially feeble downstroke, Johari pulled back and swept his bow through the air, slicing away his music as the last notes died.

Maya let out a breath and they sat in silence for a long moment. "I like it." She wove her fingers together in her lap, curls falling forward. "Am I distracting you?"

"It's not you." He cradled the cello against him. "Do you think Founders' Day is stupid?"

Her curls popped back up again. "Of course not! That's Shawntelle, isn't it? Is that what's bugging you? I mean, I could tell in the music … "

"Not exactly." He turned the cello against his hand. "Commander Shen. She said the Founders were idealists, that their ideas couldn't last, but before we left there, the things that inspired the Founders had been around for hundreds or even thousands of years, in spite of all kinds of adversity."

"Like the Constitution, you mean? That Usian thing — they had it for like four hundred years before the Ruin."

"That's one of the younger influences. Have you read their papers? In her arguments for the Articles of Union, Dr. Andra cites her feeling that the Climate Wars offended the concept of ahimsa, the principle of nonviolence and compassion, which goes back to the Vedas — and Understeward Tuore spoke about the beliefs of his ancestors, that the land itself was alive and everything was part of it, and that belief probably goes back before we even had means to write."

"Johari, is this about the Founders, or about the dragons?"

He struggled to articulate what worried him, the weight that dragged his bow and distracted his fingers. "The Founders are what we aspire to, right? That's why we celebrate. The stuff they believed in was the heart of humanity for as long as we've been aware. Even the 2235 Grant of Military Governance is meant to be rescinded in favor of the Articles of Union when we have a permanent colony."

Maya took a deep breath and put on her grown-up expression. "Okay, so the Founders wanted to roll back human culture to before the Ruin, before the Climate War and forget everything in between, right? That's why they sealed the records for so much of that period." She shrugged. "I mean, maybe Shawntelle's right — not about Founders' Day being stupid, but that we should be looking ahead, not behind. Making new things, not worrying so much about what people used to be. Like... we don't even have a planet any more. That changes us. It should change us."

He straightened away from her. "It shouldn't make us forget the things that matter."

Maya hugged herself, lips pinched. "But who gets to decide what matters? If it's up to me, then we leave, we keep looking. If it's up to Armstrong, we kill everything." She gave a shudder. "But at least we get a planet, right?"

"It's not supposed to be a judgment call: that's why we have an oath. Had an oath," he amended under his breath. He remembered Norgay's words about his own priorities: *Humanity, Fleet, and you.*

A knock sounded on the door, then a voice hollered, "Johari — it's Tolui. Where's Armstrong? Why can't I find him?"

10

J OHARI FUMBLED THE CELLO back into its stand. Maya gave a little clap, her eyes suddenly wide. "I'll let you guys — yeah." She vanished.

"Tolui?" He yanked open the door. "How are you? How do you feel?" He reached out, but Tolui backed up to the wall, shaking his head violently. Johari pursued him. "We're in virtual space. Even if you're infested, you can't infect me from here, right?"

Two windows framed him, their sunny day and treetops contrasting his dark skin and fearful stance. "I don't know. There's been some weird shit inside my head, Jo."

"I hope you're speaking figuratively. Do you want to go to your room? Where do you want to talk?"

"I want to talk to Armstrong." Tolui tipped his head, and Johari caught a glimpse of that distinctive haircut, resembling Armstrong's helm. "I got the new orders from Fleet when I woke up. Military protocols and warnings about treason? I screwed up bad. Is that why Armstrong's not talking to me?"

Thinking of how Norgay always handled bad news, Johari modulated his voice. "Armstrong got hurt. He landed in the ocean after taking on the dragons."

Tolui pushed off immediately, his hands balling into fists. "I can't believe I was such an idiot. This whole thing is my fault."

"You were excited, man, of course you were." He lowered his voice. "But you do get a little obsessive about protein sources."

"I don't want to have to eat anybody else's parents, okay?"

Or anybody. Period. "Believe me, I get it. I came in here to meet up with Fleet, then Norgay and I are going after Armstrong. Zheng He and Eriksson can stay here on guard."

"Armstrong is in trouble. I can't just sit here."

Anger was a step up from despair anyway; Johari would take it. "You can access the Realm, so I need you back on bio. We've got all kinds of footage from the dragon raid and the fight. Norgay brought back a sample. Tell me everything you can about these things."

"You need information about the enemy. I can do that."

Movement caught Johari's eye out the window and he frowned, distracted. Randomly generated birds sometimes flew among the forest of pine and maples, but this motion wasn't familiar. A shadow bulged and receded along the treeline, like the VR environment was flickering. Had Shawntelle's programming interfered somehow? Now, of all times, they couldn't afford to lose touch with Fleet or with each other if she botched up the Realm. "Shawntelle?"

Her voice echoed through the house. "Yeah, what?"

"Have you looked out a window lately? Something weird is happening with the trees."

Tolui, standing shoulder to shoulder with him, gave a grunt. "I'm glad it wasn't just me."

"Unless it means the system is failing."

"It's not my fault," Shawntelle replied, her voice growing nearer as she mounted the steps and turned the corner. She cocked her head as she stared out the window with them. "Huh."

"Nothing to do with your code?"

"No way!" She paused, tugging on her lip. "Well, I don't think so. I'll check. Meantime, how about you guys come downstairs and share with the class?"

Tolui chuckled. "She's not civs, where did she pick up that phrase?"

"Beats me," Johari answered, but he thought of Commander Shen telling him she could get someone else for civs. Tolui was the obvious choice, but he'd be graduating. Putting Shawntelle — who thought of all things Earth-based as worm crap — in charge of finding a suitable home seemed insane. She trotted down the stairs, her blue-tipped dreads bouncing against her back.

Tolui started after her, but Johari tapped his arm. "I named the planet 'Tranquility'. I wanted to tell you first."

"As in 'Sea of'?" Tolui half-smiled. "You've got some sense of humor, man."

"Hey, the Eagle has landed! One small step for man and all that."

When they reached the first floor, they turned toward the living room, a space big enough for ten to lounge around on couches carefully programmed to be worn-in. French doors opened out to the lawn, with the trees beyond. Whatever the disturbance had been, Johari couldn't see it now. The dog lay in the middle of the floor, lifting its head and flopping its tail as they entered. Maya occupied one of the couches, sitting in the middle, her fingers knotted together and head bowed over them. On the opposite couch, Emm sat beside Zheng He's avatar.

In the Realm, the bots wore human-sized versions of themselves: metallic people with variations in facial features and body structures. Zheng He, who worked botany and ecosystems with Emm, affected a slightly green complexion, an experiment with chlorophyll-based energy production. He chose a rounded face and low bridge for his nose, patterned after a portrait of his namesake, a fifteenth-century Chinese explorer. When he was examining something closely, small half-spectacles appeared as an indication of his focus, a sort of bot "do-not-disturb" sign.

Eriksson stood behind Shawntelle's couch. He had experimented with Viking style a few years back, but she vetoed that. Now he looked simply utilitarian. Humanoid, but unabashedly bot. He maintained his personality overlay, but otherwise might have just stepped off the factory floor. Was it possible for a bot to have hurt feelings when his partner didn't like his mustache?

Norgay's avatar paced near the French doors, his metal tinged toward dark steel, a suggestion of collar and lapels at his shoulders. When Johari entered, Norgay turned on his heels and gave a slight bow, his face giving off a faint glow. Kind of embarrassing, then Johari noticed Tolui's stricken face as his gaze scanned the chamber. No Armstrong. No Earhart. At least he and Norgay still had each other.

"Push over, kid," Tolui said gruffly, walking toward Maya's couch. She started, then scooted a little to the left, faintly blushing. Tolui had to know, didn't he? Maybe it was time for Johari to clue him in. After all, his own parents had been scouts together.

"Officer on deck," Shawntelle announced, and Emm threw a pillow at her. Over the fireplace, a wide screen hung empty, waiting for orders. Johari accessed his files, and filled it up, displaying the fight where Armstrong had fallen. He approached the screen, and Norgay gave a nod, taking up a position opposite. "I'm planning a mission to locate Armstrong and his nuke, and reunite them, so he can join us and make whatever repairs are necessary. We can't use long-distance coms because the dragons appear able to sense them, so that hampers a coordinated approach. Thoughts?"

"You're nuts." Shawntelle said.

"Agreed." Eriksson gestured toward the French doors, which opaqued to show a jagged chart of depth soundings. "According to our preliminary scans the ocean ranges from one hundred to two hundred thirty meters deep in the area around those pillars."

"With my thrusters at full, I could raise him — but not without attracting notice," said Norgay. He tapped the screen, zooming in on the ocean's roiling surface. When the first dragon fell, its frills lashing in distress, those ominous waves rose up, then the spines and whatever creature wore them. "However, this creature appears entirely capable of severely damaging one of us."

"We've been monitoring increasing restiveness among the dragons," Zheng He offered. "Unable to state with certainty whether that results from our communications, or from Armstrong's activities. So far as we know, the only intruders they are aware of are Armstrong, Tolui, and Norgay himself."

Tolui said, "They occupy a high-level, but not apex predator position. Those three pairs of eyes tell me they are ready both to hunt and to defend."

He turned his hand in the air, conjuring a three-dimensional image of a dragon's head into the air between them, actual size, its gill-fronds waving gently. With a gesture, he rotated the image, displaying the eyes, but the rotation ended with the sharp face staring at Johari with a close-set predator's gaze, back-curved teeth glinting in the slightly-open mouth.

"Our guess is that they open these third eyes when they're ducking under water, so they can snag their prey without fully immersing. These divots —" Tolui pointed to a series of small indents along the dragon's jaw and brow —" are probably some other kind of organs, scent maybe? They could be specialized for underwater, for hunting, and maybe for defense or warning. The sea monsters tell us there's at least one predator higher on the chain."

Maya put her hand up tentatively. "If the sea monsters are that powerful, is it possible they've already, ah, caused further damage?" She darted a glance toward Tolui who sat down stiffly beside her.

Hating that she was right, Johari gave a slight nod. "We have to be prepared for that, as well as for the chance that Norgay and I join the food chain as well."

Maya shrank back, pulling her feet up under her.

"In that case," Emm asked, "given the recent Fleet communications, it's unwise to risk one bot to rescue another. We could at least wait until Earhart arrives."

Tolui shut his eyes running a hand over his densely curly hair. "His battery might not last. We all know the chances of getting him back if he's already —" he broke off, and his throat bobbed with the word he swallowed. *Dead.*

Shawntelle said, "I'm with Emm on this one. We're already down by two. We let Norgay go after him, we don't even have enough capacity to get us the hell out of here."

"Fleetcom ordered us to prevent alien access to our technology," Johari pointed out. "Abandoning Armstrong isn't an option, even if we wanted to."

Tolui's eyes flashed open. "If we don't get Armstrong back, I'm not leaving here."

"Oh, hell." Shawntelle's bravado deflated.

Maya's small hand crept toward Tolui, then she touched his arm, resting her palm there.

"What has Fleet been told?" Shawntelle asked.

Johari squared his shoulders. "They're desperate, as you'd expect. They've eliminated any consideration of intelligence or native ecosystems. The only criteria for denial of a colony is active civilization. We're it. If we lose our bots, we're the last scout mission that ever flies."

"At the rate our technology is failing, we'd better act fast," Tolui said.

The last scout mission ... without them, humanity wound down its days in space, preventing their children and eating their dead. Johari struggled to calm his heartbeat. The dog trotted over, dark eyes rolling uncertainly, and Emm settled before him. "How are you doing?"

"There's a big difference between 'you guys might score big and find a new home for humanity' and 'if you guys don't find a new home for humanity, the human race is frackin' screwed!" He dug his fingers into his hair and stared down at the dog resting its chin in his lap. They sat on a planet that was, so far, eight-seven percent compatible with human life. A planet he had named Tranquility. He wanted to laugh or cry or hit something: Tolui, for risking it all, Commander Shen, for changing the rules. "Sorry, sorry. Just ... give me a minute."

He felt the gentle pressure of a hand on his shoulder, and caught the scent of something spicy, though Emm remained a short distance away. Shawntelle, it had to be, using her skill with the software to send him a touch that nobody else could see. The Realm seemed suspended, like the moment before a dive. Tolui's VR dragon head still hovered, but from this view, its expression turned bleak, the last instant of a dying thing. "Maya," Johari said, raising his chin.

"Yes, sir? I mean, Johari?" She scooted forward on the couch, literally on the edge of her seat.

"We know the bots are starting to break down — that coupling Earhart lost for her nuke drive, Armstrong's chemical battery — what percentage of the Fleet, or more to the point, the colony ring, depends on those batteries?"

"Oh, gosh. Most of the hab units, including this one. I mean, they can re-charge with solar sails and things like that, and if Zheng He's chlorophyll charger works, maybe that can be modified? Mostly, they count on the mini-nukes, like the bot's backpacks." Her eyes widened. "I'll bet Armstrong's power couplings are failing as well, or else it wouldn't have been so easy to dislodge his pack." She stood up and walked toward the screen, dispelling Tolui's dragon into digital mist as she zoomed in on a different section of the playback, trying to clarify the interaction between the dragon's claws and Armstrong's back.

"The entire operation has been flying for nearly two hundred years," Eriksson said, his voice rough and low. "Things are bound to fail."

"You guys must have known them — the other bots. I mean, the teams change all the time — used to, anyway," Johari said, glancing from one to another of the three bot avatars.

"We knew them, some better than others," Zheng He confirmed.

"We've been serving together since before there was a Fleet," said Norgay, his voice hard and low.

Eriksson flicked him a look. "We are not creatures of the herd or pack. We experience something like emotion, but nothing like yours."

Johari blinked. Something like emotion — and if he didn't read it all wrong, the emotion right now was anger. "You're saying that you might be one of a handful of bots left in the entire universe — the last of your race — and you don't care?"

"It's not a relevant calculation. *We* are not among our own priorities." Eriksson stood at parade rest, staring straight ahead, and Johari dropped the question.

Norgay watched him quietly from the other side of the fireplace. Johari desperately wanted to subvoc, some way they could talk privately, but not with the dragons — what, eavesdropping? Encouraging the dog to move, Johari pushed to his feet. "Okay, so Plan A, Norgay and I go for Armstrong, is off the table. We can't risk another bot. Plan B. Eriksson extrudes the mini-sub and I go alone. I confirm Armstrong's location and the damage, and track that nuke, even if I have to go into a dragon's den to get it back."

"But that's even more crazy! You can't go alone," Maya protested.

He swept this away with both hands in a wide gesture. "Maya. We're expendable, the bots are not. We all knew that going in. When Fleet had dozens of bots, they were scarce and valuable.

Now, they've got five — or fewer. This planet is actively trying to kill us." Norgay could get a new partner, just as Commander Shen had said.

Johari met Norgay's stare, half-hoping the bot would refuse to allow him to go. "What are we here for? Why put kids inside these amazing machines?" Johari swept his gaze around the room, to each of them in turn.

"Because the bots stopped caring about Fleet," Shawntelle said. "They didn't know why it mattered that they pick a comfortable planet. They stopped caring about people."

"Because it's hard for them to be flexible," said Tolui. "They have all this decision-making circuitry, and sometimes that gets in the way of seeing these planets for what they could be. Like Eriksson said, they've got specific priorities. How do they choose among them?"

Maya added, "And sometimes, they need our help. External micro-maintenance is easier with fingers."

Zheng He nodded. "I also value the additional perspective into the behavior of biological entities." Emm gave a smile and a nod of their own.

"Because you remind us of the value of home." Norgay's resonant voice sank through the room, warm and ringing. "I despise Plan B." He paused as if for breath, then continued, "But I will enable it because I trust my partner. And you —" he aimed a hard, steel finger at Eriksson —"will make sure that submarine is the most secure vehicle since the Popemobile."

Tolui laughed out loud, but Maya looked mystified. "What's the Popemobile?"

"Look it up." Shawntelle rose from the couch, more serious than cynical for maybe the first time ever. "We've got work to do." To Johari, she added, "I'm gonna see what's up with the Realm, what those shadows in the forest are. If it's my program, I'll shut it down."

"I would hate to see it go," said Emm.

"Not as much as I would!" Shawntelle vanished from the room rather than go through the motions of walking around in the house.

"Emm. You and Maya collaborate with Zheng He to process the files more quickly. Fleet needs an answer, we've got to be ready to give it to them," Johari said. "Norgay? After you've inspected the sub, you can experiment with comms. See what range the dragons are aware of, and find a way to get information to Fleet. We need to shorten the timeline on all of this."

"And hopefully keep Fleet off your back a little longer," Emm said softly. They squeezed his shoulder and set out with a deliberate stride, drawing Maya along with a wave of the hand.

"I'm on dragons," Tolui confirmed. "Anything I can work out. What about Eriksson?"

Eriksson put on a convincing glower with a flash of his yellow eyes. "The sub is currently integral to my upper left leg. I will be occupied with reconfiguring myself in case we need to fight our way out of here."

"Yikes." Tolui shrank the VR dragon head until he could bring up an image of the dragon entire. His hand followed the line of the dragon's neck almost as if he were petting it. "Johari. This means a lot. My screwup got us into this mess, and you're covering my ass." He continued to work, drawing out a rough estimate of the internal structure of the beasts Johari was about to face. "Maybe Fleet thinks you're expendable, but I don't."

"Thanks." Johari started for the door. Instantaneously Norgay was there. Johari walked right into him, but the avatar went translucent until Norgay's image enveloped him and his skin buzzed. He couldn't tell if the effect were real, or just the VR system trying to improvise a sensation that could not be.

"You are not expendable, Johari. Not to me." Norgay's voice moved through him like a wave, a surge of strength that carried him up to face the dragon's den.

11

A DEEP GREEN-GRAY SEA lapped against the tumbled blue stones at the base of the plateau. Eriksson sat to one side, his rounded metal feet sticking slightly into the water, the mini-sub tethered to his right foot, charging up. To the other side stood Norgay, tall and still, and faintly radiating warmth. Norgay had always been more demonstrative than the other bots. Johari shifted his feet. He rested one hand on Norgay's ankle, providing a direct link for any further instructions or ideas.

Eriksson folded his hand into an enormous thumbs-up gesture, visible in bluish tones in the display surface of Johari's helmet. "I guess we're ready."

"We will speak more when you return," Norgay told him. He sent a measurement of the sun's height over the ocean, confirming. "Zheng He should be in position now. Once we hear the static burst —"

"I should get ready to go," Johari finished. "Thanks for not saying 'if.'"

"If," Norgay replied, letting the word hang, heavy, in the air between them for a long moment. "If there is any way that I can bring you home, Johari, I will do so."

Johari tried to laugh this off. "I thought your priorities were humanity, Fleet and me, in that order?"

"Approximately forty-nine hours, thirty-two minutes and seventeen seconds have elapsed since then."

Johari leaned into the contact a moment longer, then stepped away, mounting the steps and crossing down Eriksson's foot to enter the top hatch of the mini-sub.

Sleek and rounded, the craft had space enough for one, plus a bit of gear. It could extrude a limited range of attachments for gathering samples, examining or testing any natural phenomena it encountered. Phase-treated translucent metal formed the sub's nose-cone and a long strip down the center, giving him a decent direct view, and an array of cameras studded other areas of the craft. Given that he'd never piloted the sub before, he would need all the view he could get.

With a short wave, Johari slipped inside and triggered the hatch. It hissed gently down after him and sealed with a soft whine. He slid into the lounge-like seat and checked all systems, then allowed the servitor to remove his helmet, keeping it ready just over his head. He forced himself to breathe normally. Ironic, if he got his wish to breathe freely on an alien planet, only to have that happen a thousand feet below an ocean as the sub's containment failed and he gulped his last breath.

He peeled back his gloves as well. He considered ditching the whole suit: if he had to evacuate the sub in an ocean home to dragon-eating sea monsters, slim chance he'd reach the surface as anything but ambergris. Then he imagined Norgay's reaction, and he kept the suit. One more layer between him and his doom. Why not? What could it hurt?

Zheng He's static burst flared through his implant and the sub's own communication system and Johari winced. Underneath the burst intended to draw off any dragon attention, Shawntelle's voice said, "You good in there, Jo?"

"Fine — it's a lot like the skimmers we used in the swamp."

"You got it! By the way, that problem with the forest? Some kind of interference. Maybe something in the rock of the cliffs around here. Still seeking the cause — but it's not my fault."

Johari grinned. "In that case, hack away!"

Norgay's voice interrupted. "You have not yet launched, Johari, is something the matter?"

"Nope. I'm gone." The sub's visual controls hovered to his right, and Johari slid his fingers in the pattern to unlock the tether and commence the dive sequence. With a series of clicks and a final thunk, the sub dropped free of Eriksson's control and slid into the ocean. Johari confirmed the ocean conditions and his initial direction of travel.

Eriksson's voice rumbled through the local channel, barely audible in the static burst. "You should be more circumspect when the flesh-people are present."

Johari opened his mouth at the sound of the voice, then closed it again. Flesh-people? The message wasn't meant for him. His hand hovered over the control yoke.

"Fleet has been lying to him," Norgay replied, in a similar tone.

Eriksson gave a little grunt that Johari had always interpreted as a chuckle, but not of the pleasant kind. "No more so than you have."

The burst fell silent, as did the bots. Eriksson accused Norgay of lying to Johari. What the dark matter was that about? Didn't matter now: he had a job to do. When — not if —he returned, he could ask Norgay about it, from the comfort of his own habitat. His home. Johari punched the accelerator and the mini-sub sped forward into the unknown.

The first thirty meters into the sea featured a landscape of tumbled stones from the fractured cliff edge. He keyed a series of automatic processes for scanning and analyzing the water around him, recording everything he saw.

Small creatures flitted in and out among the stones: long, thin fishes with blinking spots and broad, flat creatures that curled up from the surface of the stones to swaddle the other ones as they swam overhead. Tiny threads rippled on the surface of the flat ones, resembling a build-up of algae. They camouflaged like flounder, but lay on their backs instead of their stomachs. The proximity alarm dinged, and Johari flinched, clutching the yoke, his hands sweaty.

He made himself relax — no way a sea monster big enough to eat him could come this shallow. A thick-bodied creature swam up, its broad, flat head moving side to side, thin whiskers brushing against the stones. It approached a slab and set its lower jaw onto the surface, scraping up a cyclone of algae then snapping its jaw around one of the upside-down flounders. The sides of its throat rippled as it ground and swallowed its meal. Tolui would love that footage.

Before long, the water deepened below him and the stones and their denizens fell away into the ocean's murk. Long strands of seaweed tangled upward, deep purple fronds straining to reach the sky. If he kept the sub toward the surface, he had enough light to see without turning on the sub's externals, and the sub could remain cloaked. But if he hovered too high, that layer of bio-luminescence triggered, sending green flares across the surface like a beacon that followed his every move.

It would take two hours to cover the distance, and he hoped to spend some of that time viewing Tolui's dragon information, but he couldn't do that if he had to make sure a few inches leeway didn't reveal him to the dragons. Unless ... Johari called up an image of the sea monster, the bits of it that had broken the surface in any case. Then he brought up a display of the sub's capabilities and located a series of broadcast antennas and rod sensors. Johari selected everything that stuck straight out and reconfigured them into a line down the top of the sub, superimposing the sea monster image to match the spacing of its spines. His imitation might not hold up to close dragon scrutiny, but it should keep the curious away if he rose a little high.

Setting course for the sea stacks near Armstrong's last stand, Johari settled in. He pulled up Tolui's notes about dragons in a section of the right-hand screen. Tolui's voice came on, with an image of a dragon, annotated. "Dragons we've seen range in size from twenty to fifty or so meters from wing-tip to wing-tip, and their length appears about half that wingspan, giving them a significant sail to weight ratio." A diagram of a bot overlaid this, showing the comparison, with the bot standing about forty-five meters.

"The sample you guys brought me shows their bones are some kind of silicon lattice, super light-weight, probably on the fragile side, but they have sinew woven through —" a close-up in cross-section — "and the liquid moving in the hollows. It's not blood. There's blood in the vessels inside the wings. This stuff is something strongly acidic. It was tough on Norgay, trying to preserve the stuff — he's okay, though!" Tolui rushed to reassure him. "I'm guessing those claws at the tips of the shaft are poisonous based on this scene. Zheng He caught it at a distance, more or less by accident."

A video started in the window. Over a forest canopy, two dragons flew. They beat strongly for the sky, their long bodies slithering through the air as those huge wings thrust them upward. When they had dwindled to the size of seagulls, the wingbeats stopped, and they fell, plummeting downward.

One swept its wings forward, as if clapping the other. The second dragon's wings swept outward, jerking it upward in the sky like a parachute, then it plunged downward, and repeated the clapping maneuver. They curled around each other in the sky, then a wing-clap caught the other dragon. The wings throbbed, and both dragons quaked, then the assailant pulled its wings back, breaking off. The second dragon convulsed in the air, its movements uncoordinated. Johari winced as its neck tossed up and down, tail lashing.

Tolui's voice returned, softly as if not to interrupt the behavior. "It could be a nerve-toxin, from how the subject flails and just falls from the sky."

The subject. The victim. Had that been what they were trying to do to the bots, when the one got its wing caught in Norgay's hand-armor? Thank god it wouldn't work. Then Tearwing tried a different tactic, ripping for the backpack. Evidence of higher-level intelligence, or just of a killing instinct that allowed for a variety of prey animals?

"They've been seen eating these large-bodied sealbirds," Tolui continued, and the footage shifted to a scene similar to the one Johari had witnessed. A dragon scooped one of the sealbirds from a rock while others scattered. Gripping the creature in its hindlegs, the dragon proceeded to skin it with the large claws on its forelegs, then gulp it down head-first, discarding the skin into the ocean below.

The proximity alarm chimed, and Johari froze the presentation. The eerie groan and whoosh of water against the submarine grew louder with the chop of deliberate movement. The rear sensors picked it up, the signal growing steadily larger. Water boomed against the sub, resonating as if Johari huddled inside of a drum. The creature spanned his entire scanning range on that side. Johari wiped a sweaty palm on his knee. He wanted to believe it could be a school of smaller creatures, but he didn't. The rear sensors lost contact, the forward ones a little later as the creature out-paced him. Finally the noise subsided. Gone.

The ocean floor rose into a plateau beneath him. Blocky spires thrust up like a city of termites. The rough surfaces flickered with gossamer filters that swept particles from the water, then sucked back into the towers. Flattish stones protruded from the formation, the water swishing around them. Then one of them moved, a pair of flippers at the back propelling it. A half-dozen claws scrabbled out from the front, scraping over the towers and shuttling whatever they collected back toward the underside. Claw-turtles.

Fascination overtook the tension of the sea monster's passage. All activity ceased as he drew nearer, the turtles clinging with their claws, tucking their flippers in tight. On a lower level of stone, strange, pale cups rested in the shadows. Jagged cracks broke the structures, and bones jutted from the insides. Tiny creatures moved among the shattered shells, striping any last bits of flesh that clung to them. The turtles must be about the same size as the mini-sub, and something in this ocean cracked them open.

Baroque-era landscape painters hoped to reveal the sublime: that striking blend of wonder and fear. Beneath the seas of Tranquility, he flowed between those poles with the movement of the ocean itself.

Temperature readings fluctuated in sync with columns of bubbling smoke that emitted from the sea floor. Vents surrounded by mineral growth, the start of those vast chimneys of stone that towered from the ocean floor not far away. As the vents grew larger, the temperatures more extreme, Johari steered alongside, keeping out of their chemical swirl.

Smoke roiled up in shafts of shadow, like a miner's headlights beamed across an asteroid, fading to a grainy darkness. Their beams captured the dance of motes and microbes, turning the spaces between into dark slits like the bars of a cage. Soft-bodied creatures inched along the accretions, sending out spiral feelers into the ocean, while stiff-legged arthropods stalked among them. The bases of the towers swelled to the size of redwoods he'd seen in ancient videos, then the size of rocket launching stanchions, finally breaking the surface of the water above. High above, they became the chimneys he had seen earlier, spewing mineral smoke into the sky, forming that permanent storm Maya picked up.

Through the gaps, he spotted a flash of something brighter. Johari slowly turned back and proceeded between the towers. Something gleamed down below. This close to the smoking, heat-generating vent, so much activity should conceal his own. He aimed his external lights to penetrate the darkness.

Broad reflector eyes glinted blue. Long, thin fishes rippled over the vast metal helmet. Armstrong's stern face stared into the alien sea like a Greek statue found in an Aegean shipwreck, its noble countenance still visible. Johari's heart leapt. The bot appeared intact, but his body receded into the shadows between shafts of the vent. Johari steered closer, emerging from between the pillars.

Unfortunately, the bot's position would make it hard to view any damage to his back — he had placed himself in a defensive posture, fists raised, back to a pillar of rising stone. Johari slid his fingers over the controls, preparing a tether for direct communication. The reflector eyes rippled, shifting from subtle blue all across, to the gray blankness of a power loss. Was Armstrong dying before his eyes? Johari punched the sub forward. Then the ripple came again, top to bottom, as if the bot were looking down.

Shifting the angle of the sub, Johari leaned forward. Armstrong's body vanished into the murk just below his arms. In the lights of the mini-sub, the drifting particles swirled and churned, then rushed aside.

Johari kicked the sub into reverse as the monster lunged straight toward him.

12

T HE SUB'S ENGINES STRAINED to force it upward and backward, two directions foreign to its design. Something ground as the lower back of the sub scraped against stone.

Below, thick, green flesh rippled and surged. Dozens of fins along the creature's sides propelled it toward him. The near end opened broadly into four-pointed jaws lined with jagged edges of bone surrounding a pulsing red gullet. Tentacles lashed out alongside, hurled toward the sub. One of them slapped the viewing window, a thousand tiny suckers straining to reach him.

Johari slammed the yoke sideways and jerked back, tearing away from the grasping thing and shooting sidelong over Armstrong's head. His left hand fumbled over the touchscreen conjuring nets, air hoses, a drill — jabbing his fingers, he selected it and the sub's arm extended, the drill head whirring.

Tentacles flailed after him, and the creature surged upward again, sucking down a great mouthful of seawater. Blasting the seawater out from a dozen orifices on its sides, the creature met him half-way, hideous jaws plunging toward the sub. Johari's drill-arm pushed forward, grinding on the ridges of its mouth, and the creature recoiled.

Armstrong's fist lashed out at the creature's middle, with his own array of tools bristling from his knuckles. It tore into the monster's side, and the creature thrashed free, careering off the next pillar, costing Armstrong precious amps of his dwindling power. The sub's communications array signaled a pin beam. Source: Armstrong. A status-check scrolled open down Johari's screen. Then a single word roared through the comms. "Run!"

Lurching above the bot's head, the monster trailed thick liquid from a half-dozen wounds along its side. Its fins paddled hard against the stack, then it shot toward him again, a twin rank of spines shifting upward from its flesh.

Johari hauled on the yoke. "Come on, come on!"

The engines whined and cycled as they pushed hard, harder than they were meant to. A klaxon blared at him. A tentacle whipped against the belly of the sub, but failed to gain purchase.

Johari slewed the sub between two narrow pillars and shot up along one of them, pressed back into his seat. He burst from the water in a spray of glowing green bacteria to match the stars in the night sky above. A haze of mineral smoke swirled around him. The surface wasn't safe, wasn't far enough. In his mind, he replayed the images of battle: The dragon splashing down to the water, screaming, struggling to rise, as the monster latched onto it from below.

Keeping one hand on the yoke, Johari yanked his helmet back on and latched it with a hiss as the air supply connected.

Something fleshy smacked the sub's underside and he dodged away between another set of pillars. A crevice opened into one of the biggest stacks. Waves rushed and sucked through the jagged hole. Deep enough to cross without crashing? One way to find out.

One of the propellers snarled and whined as a tentacle shredded through it. Tentacles recoiled and lashed.

Johari rocked left, compensating for the clogged engine, keeping the second prop in contact with the water. The sub rolled halfway under.

The green-gray bulk of the monster filled his view, then the sub scraped through the opening: a rush of stone cut across his view. Tentacles smacked the stone and reached through the opening as the sub slewed in a circle, ending with its prop against the far wall, its nosecone aimed toward the inlet, barely submerged.

As the water rose and fell, the tentacles snaked around, and the upper jaws broke the surface, that hideous maw sucking and spewing as if enraged by its failure to reach him. He knew the danger of anthropomorphizing, attributing emotions to anything non-human, but that mouth — bands of muscle and rigid membranes opened and shut, cycling as if it were already chewing him down.

The sub's arm extended before him, holding out the spinning drill, a penknife wielded against a giant. For a time, the tentacles continued to creep through the narrow gap, then receded. The jaws slowly sealed. The blunt head sank down, with a last glimpse of spines as it curved back under the sea.

Water lapped against the basin and the submarine. One propeller churned, waiting for orders, while the other thunked, blocked by the thing that would have dragged him in. Johari killed the engines and sat there, shaking.

The craft ticked and hummed into stillness, mostly submerged, his horizon a rough edge of stone in a cracking chimney. Still alive. The sub largely intact. He keyed in the commands that drew back the feeble arm with its tiny drill and let that, too, power down. Johari gulped down a breath, then another. With a shaky hand, he called up his own files, and slid his finger across the speaker. Soft strains of synthesized cello music rose up around him, part of Thanh's 2193 *Symphony for Lost Instruments*. Still alive. So far.

Johari lay back against the seat, willing himself to relax. The tones of the cello reminded him of Norgay's voice, low and resonant, and he wondered if Norgay had modulated his voice to match on purpose, or if, conversely, Johari had been attracted to the cello because of that reminder.

He was here, in the sub, in the middle of monster land, so that Norgay didn't have to be. So that Fleet wouldn't lose another explorer-bot, part of their last hope for a new home. So they could get Armstrong back, and salvage the mission from a catastrophic mistake. So that Tolui wouldn't have to be alone.

Just at the moment, he knew exactly how his friend must feel: isolated from the only family he'd ever known, fighting off aliens and the creeping dread that, in the end, he had to lose.

Straightening in his seat, Johari recalled the file Armstrong had sent him. He refused to lose. At the very least, he would go down fighting, like Armstrong had. According to the scans, his battery had about twenty-one hours of life remaining. Johari started a countdown timer to run at the edge of his vision. Would the monster return there, or skulk off deeper into the sea to tend its own wounds? Johari had to assume it, or another one just as fearsome, would be there when he got back. So he needed to not only find the nuke pack and get it down there, he needed an assault powerful enough to hold off a dragon-eating fiend while Armstrong performed the repair.

The chimney of stone trapped his sub unless he planned to face the fiend again right now. He declined. Instead, he popped loose his safety harness and opened the sub's interior panels, locating a toolkit and a net for carrying samples. He loaded the tools into it, along with the stash of emergency supplies he had brought along, and an antenna that could extend the scanning capability in the suit. He found a diver's knife, sheathed, and slapped it against his thigh in case he needed it later.

He dare not reach out to the Realm from this distance, but his implant could store and track more information by allowing it to link with the suit. The sub contained a personal prop, meant to help a diver maneuver under water. It weighed more than Johari liked, even granted the lower gravity on Tranquility, but he'd need a way to transport the nuke pack. Cutting free the only cargo net inside, Johari fashioned a sling for the prop, and hung it off his back.

He triggered the sub's tether, and it slithered out, then flopped without a recognizable surface to connect to. He'd have to anchor it manually from the outside. Finally, he powered down the sub completely. The control panels blinked out and the internal lights dwindled to darkness, leaving Johari with the faint illumination of his suit's display, and nothing more. The suit contained an excellent climate control system. The chill he felt had nothing to do with reality.

Reluctantly, he approached the hatch. Had the mini-sub been as secure as the Popemobile? Close enough that he hated to leave it behind. He had gone from the extended family of the Saturn Five, to the close comfort of Norgay's presence, to the confines of the sub, and now he must stand alone.

Hopefully, the dragon dropped Armstrong's pack nearby, and he just needed to elude the monsters long enough to retrieve it. He pushed out of the hatch and scanned his surroundings. A little steam still hissed up between fallen stones in the basin of the chimney, but it had crumbled from the top down, like the tower of an ancient castle. It still rose thirty meters above, a jagged hole open to the night. One of the planet's moons peered at him over the edge.

Once he left the sub, his own suit power would be limited. Twelve hours, maybe less if he had to do anything strenuous. Like climb up thirty meters of stone to scan for the nuclear signature.

Johari climbed out of the sub, keeping a hand on the external rail as he edged over to the tether. It wouldn't quite reach the wall. He settled for a huge chunk of debris with one end above the algae zone, and triggered the suction mechanism. Golden light from the moon showed monster flesh oozing from the damaged right-hand propeller.

Johari squatted and dug out the shredded bits of tentacle. Tolui might like to have them as samples, but Johari hadn't the time or place to store them properly. He tossed them aside, and rotated the prop inside its frame, searching for more tentacle.

Something slurped.

Johari scrambled backward up the slab of stone. In the shallow water next to the sub, something large moved. He turned up his headlamp. A creature lay in the shallows, munching down the bits of sea monster he tossed aside. A pair of wide-set eyes took turns looking back at him. Another set of eyes gleamed wetly. A third set, centered on the narrow face, remained closed. Frills backed its neck, and two powerful legs framed a tail that waved softly to keep it in place in the water. It resembled the giant salamanders that lurked on the edges of medieval manuscripts and were said to be impervious to fire. Tolui should be out here, not him. Tolui would make connections to the animal realm rather than to old books and worm crap.

The creature stopped chewing and blinked up at him, its frills glowing faintly.

In his hand, Johari held a strip of muscular flesh as long as his arm, its miniature suction threads hanging limp. He tossed the strip downslope. The salamander lunged for it, catching the flesh in a mouthful of teeth and chomping it down. It lay now partly on the slab still two meters below him, clinging with powerful front limbs. Okay, probably not a larval dragon then, despite some similarities. Was it eying him hungrily, or was he anthropomorphizing again? Maybe daylight was a better time to take care of the sub.

Johari scooted backward a little further. The salamander blinked its eyes in alternate pairs so they were never all closed at once. Awesome.

Johari bumped the sidewall of the chimney and slid himself up to standing. He shifted his gear. The salamander wriggled, its gills flared, dots of light pulsing down them. His implant hummed and Johari winced, reaching for it instinctively. Yeah, the thing was a dragon alright, in some form. Or a product of convergent evolution with a similar communication system. Converging to resemble a predator species? No doubt, a dragon could snap a salamander like a hotdog.

Johari edged sideways. The salamander humped sideways as well, until it encountered the edge of the stone and floundered off with a splash, frills dazzling. It squealed, and Johari laughed. The creature appeared so startled, then annoyed to have lost its balance. Patches of water lit with murky spots that grew brighter by the moment.

His laughter choked off abruptly. Four other salamanders emerged from the depths, nosing around the first one, their frills radiating color. His implant buzzed. Johari grit his teeth and tried to block the sensation. It meant something, as if he were able to hear the high-frequency squeaking of bats.

Five faces stared up at him, their large eyes glinting in the moonlight, their tails rippling the water behind them. Johari's throat went dry. Time to go — had to be. He scanned the rim of rocks and the inner surface of the chimney. The exterior surface would have a better slope for climbing, but if he fell, he'd be a monster munchy for sure. Would it be any better to fall on the inside and be a salamander snack?

Armstrong needed him. The Saturn Five needed him and Armstrong both, and Norgay assured him he was not expendable. Johari pushed himself into motion, amping up the friction of his boots and gloves.

He clambered over a series of tumble-down slabs and boulders against the far wall. After that, he dug in his fingers and toes, counting on balance, strength, and high-tech to keep him moving the right direction. The prop and supplies net hung in an awkward balance. Hand over hand, feet pushing hard, he followed a series of cracks and rough grips up the chimney. His muscles strained by the time he reached the top. His head crested and he dimmed his light, then carefully sat on the broad lip of the tower, a perch about as wide as he was tall.

The full moon hovered in the sky like a great eye. A second moon, a bare sliver, showed higher up, and unfamiliar stars scattered the darkness above. An edge on view showed a trail of brightness with a sprinkling of stars, the plate of the spiral galaxy, and Johari perched upon its arm like a hawk to its falconer, waiting to fly. If he could name that, too, he'd call it the Dragon's Tail.

The vault of the heavens wore constellations no man had ever seen until now. What heroes would they be named for? What great stories would be remembered whenever mankind looked to the sky? Johari tilted his face up, tracing a pattern of stars like an arrow aimed at the brightest moon. Armstrong would be that one, bold and direct. Where was Norgay? There: a cluster that glowed warm at its heart. Darkness swept over the stars as if the hand of God scooped them all away. The stars swept back again a moment later, with the arcing, scalloped edge of a dragon's wing.

Johari flung himself face-down on the ledge, his helmet rapping loudly. His heart raced, sending up an alert to flash in the helmet's display. As if he needed another danger sign; whoever programmed that thing should be spaced through an airlock. Something slammed into his back, jolting him, but it didn't catch as he slid a few feet along the stone. The tail slapped and slithered alongside for a moment as the creature gained altitude. In seconds, it would swing about for another try. The dragons ate their prey head first: grab with the hind legs, lift up, grab the head and strip the skin.

He scrambled toward the higher edge where the stone grew rough again, hoping it would give him some cover, then one hand hung over nothing.

Could he survive the drop into the ocean? If he did, would he survive the monster waiting there? At the moment, he didn't see a choice. The rough water meant less surface tension. Tranquility's lower gravity should help. If he crossed his feet, he could — the dragon screeched, and Johari's implant flared with pain. A call for backup? Oh, shit.

Johari scrambled up and jumped over the edge, crossing his legs, crossing his arms close to his chest. Holding his breath — stupid, stupid. He sucked in a breath as he plunged downward.

He jerked in the air like a loose puppet and his head swam as he pitched suddenly upward.

The dragon carried him, his head dangling down. The sea stacks dropped away, and his leg felt like it was caught in a vise. The dragon tossed him back in the air. Johari pinwheeled, screaming.

It snatched him again. Its strength bore into his left leg and pinned his right arm to his side. Its head lunged toward his. Johari triggered his headlamp, full power, and the dragon shook its head, but it did not let go. He grabbed the knife strapped to his thigh, a hefty blade as long as his forearm, and as tiny as a thorn compared to the beast above him. The wings beat hard as it soared over the row of sea stacks. Any minute now, it would go for his head, to skin him and swallow him whole.

Through his link, Johari shut down the suit warnings, and popped the pressure gauge. Normally, the suit clung to his body, pressurized to match the level of the atmosphere and move more easily. Now, he blew the pressure and let the suit go limp, the bulges of its systems and storage creating gaps around his body. With his left hand, he fumbled toward the latches at his neck.

The forelegs beat him to it. The dragon pulled him up toward its belly. Its head swung down, snuffing out the stars with a crunch of teeth. Saliva streaked the faceplate of his helmet.

A claw scraped his arm as he and the dragon reached for his throat. Johari peeled himself back as much as he could. The claws tore into his suit. As the dragon yanked upward, Johari pulled his head down and curled into himself. He sliced at the claws on his right, sliding his sweaty arm out of the suit. The helmet cracked and the suit ripped.

Johari folded forward, shaking free of the suit, gasping for breath. Praise the Fleet that Maya's calculations were correct and the atmosphere was breathable. How high was he? Over water or stone?

Johari kicked and struggled. The dragon spit out his helmet, still latched to the tattered suit.

The shadows of stone towers jutted up alongside them. It still had his leg. Stab it and fall — or — or what? Johari wrapped himself around the dragon's leg, holding on for all he was worth, his leg bent back and throbbing. The dragon's skin felt both rough and pliable. For a moment, bright eyes peered back, then the head swept forward again. The dragon released his suit and it tumbled down, still clinging around his foot. With a crash, the personal prop slid free and fell onto stone, tumbling down into nothing.

The helmet's light waved below him in the darkness, a wild beacon flagging their location. It flashed over stone pillars, mounds of shells, bright, staring eyes backed by the crackling gleam of dragon frills. Heads lifted and swung to follow his passage.

The dragon jerked and shook its leg. It pulled its legs inward, forelegs reaching down, and Johari jabbed with the knife, forcing it to straighten out again. He had both legs wrapped around it now, and clung with his right hand, his head tipped back into the wind, his hair flicking over his shoulders.

Ahead and below, dozens of dragons framed by the constellations of their flickering gills. They perched on the sea stacks, hot mist billowing up around them, illuminated like silent storm clouds by the dragons' own light.

13

T HE SULFUROUS WIND stung his nostrils. As the dragon dipped through the roiling smoke, his eyes burned, and he shut them tight, but the air cleared a moment later, and Johari squinted into the breeze. His captor dipped closer, and one of the dragons among the flock darted its head upward, jaws open, reaching for him. He wriggled toward the inside, dodging the snap of the jaws. The teeth caught his suit and tore it free, tossing it down. Too many eyes glared at him. His captor emitted a piercing cry, and brought its other leg close, scraping viciously downward.

Johari glanced down, and leapt free, yelling as loudly as he could, triggering his implant to broadcast on the same frequency where he'd been feeling the dragons scream.

The huddle of dragons broke apart, rearing back their necks, their frills sparkling. Johari tumbled to the ground among them. He bounced up again, knife in his shaking hand. His arm burned, the skin gouged by the dragon's claw. His feet, clad only in light-weight socks, met a warm surface and he stumbled as he turned about. He roared fiercely in each direction. Dizzy already from the flight, he turned as much to keep his balance as to confront the monsters all around him. He was among hostiles now for sure. *Treat all encounters as a mission-critical threat.* Sure, but what could he do about it?

Breathless, his throat seared, Johari finally halted. He swayed on his feet. He was alive. Exposure to the atmosphere hadn't killed him, nor had the fall. Nor had the dragon.

The dragons before him edged aside, opening a gap in their number, wings held high. The dragon who had brought him landed there with an echoing thump. Whatever they were standing on didn't feel or react like stone. They must be atop a vent chimney, sealed off somehow. A slight chemical tinge stung his eyes and nose.

His captor regarded him with its forward-facing eyes. Its teeth glinted in the moonlight. Small mandibles wriggled at either side of that mouth, as if they wanted to catch him.

The floor bounced a little, and Johari swung to face the disturbance. A smaller dragon with a streaked muzzle crept a little nearer. "Don't you dare!" He shouted at it.

It hesitated, and the gills to either side of its neck pulsed with light.

"If you kill me — if you eat me — you're all gonna die. My friends will show up here and nuke you to dragon dust." He brandished his knife. Fight or flight, the instincts said, and flight was no longer an option. "You are not going to eat me. I'm not prey, you understand?"

He turned again, more slowly this time. His left knee buckled, and he dropped to the floor, trying to catch his breath, more like prey than ever before. It didn't matter if he knew they were intelligent, what mattered now was that they knew it about him. Assuming they had any respect for intelligence in other species. Unlike Fleet, for example. Would he rather face a tower topped by dragons, or a roomful of officers? What was the difference, really?

An eerie light flickered through the air and Johari got his focus back on the threat at hand. His captor's frill flared with a scintillating pattern, and one of the others launched itself into the sky. For a moment, light beamed across the floor: his helmet! His suit lay crumpled at the edge of the chimney cap some ten meters away. If he could get to it, he could reach the team.

The tail and legs of a new dragon broke his view. It lifted its wings and dropped into the space allotted. Those wings spanned the sky overhead and bits of moon and stars gleamed through a series of jagged holes on the right-hand side. Tearwing. She leaned in toward him, gills waving, two sets of eyes staring intently.

Johari sagged. "Yeah, I know, we killed your baby. I wish it hadn't happened that way."

She lowered her head, examining him, or so it seemed. Her gaze focused down and to his right, where blood streamed from his arm. She hadn't eaten him, not yet — nor had any of the others, but he wasn't naive or crazy enough to think they understood his warning. His eyesight flickered, his blink taking too long. How much blood had he lost? If he fainted right now, he wasn't making it down from there alive.

Taking one edge of his ripped sleeve in his teeth, Johari held it while he cut off a ragged strip, the dragon watching.

He set the knife down near his feet. They probably didn't recognize it as a threat, but his hand felt smaller without it. Tucking one end of the strip under his arm near the top of the wound, Johari started wrapping awkwardly. It wouldn't be the blood-loss that killed him, after all, it would be the alien bacteria driven in by the slice of an alien claw. He wrapped as tightly as he could.

The suit had antiseptics as well, a first aid kit in a pouch at the side. He leaned, trying to see around Tearwing to figure out how much of the suit remained intact. Tearwing leaned as well, matching him. Johari straightened, regarding her. She had been the first to make contact, reacting to the loss of the egg, then she had pursued them all the way to camp, using another dragon as a decoy. When Armstrong fought back, she apparently rallied the others to swarm him, and had torn off his nuke pack in the assault. Was she already a leader, or did her loss energize her to take action? Anthropomorphizing again.

Back in the Ring, hoping to be approved for the Saturn Five, Johari took classes in all kinds of things, mostly focused on human history and culture, but also protocols for interacting with other intelligent species, protocols Fleet now apparently wanted him to ignore in the absence of the two biggies: technostructures, and radio signals, things they had never yet encountered in the vastness of space.

Fleet moved a thousand light-years away, hoping to get the all clear to settle. Either the dragons were just animals, in which case the military order would be rescinded, and it didn't matter what Johari did in his effort to get Armstrong up and running, or the dragons were the enemy, an enemy he had already engaged with. One way or the other, Fleet needed to know as much as possible.

So. Protocols for contact. First up, exchange of greetings. Johari gave a laugh. Their greeting had been to grab an egg, and break it. Not the best start. He settled himself as comfortably as he could — his left leg ached, the joints torqued by the dragon's snatch-and-run, and his arm still burned. "I'm called Johari, Colossus Norgay. My people are the human race, and —" he stopped short of "we come in peace." *And we come to fry you all so we can move in*? His throat ached as well, and Johari coughed hard.

The dragons dipped their heads, apparently intrigued. Excellent. What had he just accidentally "said?" His suit also included a water reclamation and desalinization unit. He could really use a drink. Unbidden, the creamy heat of mocha filled his mind. Johari propped his forehead in his palm. He had never felt so tired in his life — nor been so very far from rest.

Tearwing gave a snort, and the dragons shuffled as she turned away, rooting behind her. Light shifted and flashed as Tearwing nuzzled his suit. Johari scrambled to his feet. "Hey! That's mine — please don't —" He scooped up the knife and dodged between the dragons. She swung her head toward him, mouth open, those little mandibles pinching at the air. Johari stopped short, staring back at her.

He edged forward in careful steps. Every protocol for a first-contact situation had been chucked out the airlock the moment the dragon grabbed him out of the sky; he had to salvage what he could. Starting with his suit. Then Armstrong. He breathed in little gasps, expecting the lightning-strike of that enormous head as it snapped him in two. Then his foot nudged something that rolled, and he grabbed his helmet. Hugging it to his chest with his left arm, he gathered up the suit with his right hand.

A meter away, the edge of the chimney sank out of view into the darkness below. No, not darkness. Lights bounced toward him up the side, with the scrabbling of claws. A group of salamanders rushed up the stone, their frills waving madly and every eye reflected a tiny, distorted image of him.

Johari stumbled back and fell, sprawling, the helmet bruising his chest. No way was he letting it go. Ever. The flooring beneath him bounced and jiggled.

Salamanders hurried past, their claws scraping and frills bobbing. Each as long as the mini-sub, they took a little while to pass. One of them stopped near his head and stared down at him, opening each set of eyes in turn. The lowest eyes resembled those of a frog, optimized for underwater sight. The salamander cocked its head to stare at him from only one eye — an eye as big around as his helmet. Grooves and furrows marked its face, transforming the skin into an ancient script or the topography of an unknown land.

The dragons loomed overhead, the salamanders rippling in between. They hunkered down alongside tails and powerful hind legs. Some of the dragons ruffled their wings down, stroking the salamanders, and their frills flickered and shone above and all around him: a sky full of fireworks. His implant buzzed and Johari's shoulders tensed, the sound/vibration setting his teeth on edge. They were communicating alright. Did it qualify as language?

The salamander staring down at him gave a full-body shake that tremored the floor beneath him. Is this what the dragons had been waiting for, until their young arrived and they could enjoy a proper feast? He would hardly make a mouthful. Something thudded down beside him, and the salamander stretched its neck and forelegs upward. Then it shifted away a little bit, moonlight gleaming on its moist eyes, its frill shimmering a soft pink.

Johari dragged his shoulders back down, and released his clenched arms around the helmet. Not dead yet. He swallowed hard. Whatever had fallen lay beside him, knocking lightly against his knee. Slowly, he moved up onto one elbow, and took his eyes from the salamander's rumpled face.

The personal prop lay beside him, dented from its fall, the net stripped away. Had it brought up the prop because it belonged to him, or because the dragons made a collection of curiosities? Who knew — but he had it now. He glanced back at the salamander. "Thank you."

Its frill flashed, blue, pink, a cascade of yellow, and he felt a pulse of sound that jabbed at his neck.

With a cry, Johari slapped his hand over his implant. Being around the dragons made him feel like a sonic pincushion. Awesome.

The salamander bobbed its head, and its frill went pale. Another pulse, smaller this time, but no less painful.

The smaller dragon that had tried to snatch him earlier ducked its head in. Its frills arched out to either side and its jaw gaped, then it emitted a tone that shot through Johari's body as if the beast were tearing his head off. His body rocked in pain, his back arched as he screamed. Tears streaked from his eyes.

With a hiss, the salamander whipped around, rearing up on its hind legs. It clapped its forelegs around the dragon's frills, wrapping them against its head and dragging it down. The dragon thrashed against this grip. The salamander grappled it down and swarmed on top of the dragon's head and neck, still hissing, but the dragon had fallen blessedly silent.

Johari curled on his side around his helmet, panting. He scrubbed the tears away against his shoulder. How was he ever going to talk to them if it hurt so damn much?

The spectacle of the salamander's strongly muscled body curled atop the dragon's neck filled his vision. The dragon's eyes blazed beneath its captor's grip, glaring at Johari as if it meant to shred him, but it would torture him a while first. Fury, Johari dubbed it. And the one on top? Savior.

"Thank you," he whispered again, his throat hoarse from the screaming.

The "chatter" among the others died away during the struggle, and now rose again, the buzz at the back of his neck. It felt like a language: rising and falling, units of different lengths. He couldn't distinguish recurrent phonemes yet — if that was even the right term. Fury twitched its wings, and Savior hissed. One of the other salamanders rumbled closer. It bowed its head deeply, bringing together its frill with Savior's. Lights twinkled too fast for Johari to catch them. Maybe it wasn't the lights that conveyed meaning, but the electrical pulses that carried them?

The second salamander — call it Gandhi, the peace-maker — separated itself, but did not go far.

Savior unwrapped from Fury's neck, and eased backward. It sat, propped on its arms, between Johari and the dragon. Fury's neck arched up and its frills spread, but they remained dark. With a powerful downstroke, the dragon launched itself into the air, flapping hard up, up, until it shot out over the sea like an arrow. Johari desperately wished he already knew what they had been saying. He had a terrible feeling that his life and those of his friends might depend on it.

14

J OHARI PULLED HIS SUIT into his lap. He still felt shaky, but he had
no time for terror. Armstrong, and the Fleet, were counting on
him. Time to get to work. But first ... he rummaged through the
suit's compartments, finding the first aid kit, a stash of protein
bars, and the tube for the water reclamation system. It contained
maybe half a liter, but that would be a start. He drank greedily,
then found a hypo full of antibiotics and another with an immune
system booster, and stabbed his thigh to release the medications.
His relief was more placebo effect than anything else, but he'd take
what he could get. This done, he munched down one of the bars,
the chewy kind that emulated fruit, sweet and sticky. The
salamanders watched, their frills blinking from time to time.

Johari could hardly wire himself up for electric pulses, but
lights, he could do. Johari triggered his suit to link up with the
implant — the link shut down automatically when he wasn't
wearing the helmet. Or at least, it was supposed to.

The system blinked a transmission symbol. He pulled on the
helmet. Apparently, his abrupt separation from it had set up some

kind of black-box recording loop. Well, he didn't need to worry about the dragons knowing he was already there, but he also didn't need Norgay scanning the channels and finding an endless loop of him screaming. Johari powered down the function.

As he ate, he called up the video of his first encounter with the salamanders. He zoomed on the face of the one he had fed, then scanned the salamanders around him, and performed a correlation search. Those ridges and spots around the eyes formed a distinctive pattern, matching Savior, and not quite the same as Gandhi.

Johari programmed the names and faces, studying them carefully to make sure he would recognize them again, with or without his technological back-up. Savior leaned in toward him, shifting its head from side to side, apparently studying its reflection in his faceplate. Its frills rippled through a spectrum of colors.

So. Some kind of hierarchy allowed Savior to intervene against Fury, and the other dragons acquiesced. Now, Savior recognized itself in its reflection, a sign of higher intelligence among Earth species. Cats and dogs often attacked their own image, while dolphins and chimpanzees acknowledged it. Commander Shen's voice echoed in his memory, *"Intelligence has been down-graded."* Humanity cohabited on Earth with dolphins and chimps for thousands of years — when they weren't eating them. Here, the food chain would go in the other direction.

Johari took another bite, chewing meditatively. He swallowed, cleared the displays from his vision, and held up the bar. "Eat." He took another bite, exaggerating his movements, chewed, and swallowed. "Eat."

Savior's frills rippled. Behind it, the sun edged pink and blue into the sky, a visual reminder that he was losing time — or rather, Armstrong was. Some of the dragons spread broad wings and soaring away. A few curled their wings high as they flew, turning and pirouetting into the sunrise.

Savior spread backwards, pushing against the floor to stretch out along the platform as more space opened up. Some of the salamanders wriggled back over the sides of the chimney, while a few, including Gandhi, settled down as well. The cap over the chimney warmed with the rising steam from the vent far below, making for a comfortable perch, almost too hot for Johari. He'd been thinking of the salamanders as a larval form, but in what species could a child reprimand an adult? If their metamorphic cycle went the other direction, that would mean they lost their wings as they matured for a return to the sea. Damn, Tolui should be here — he'd understand so much more of this.

The first time they met, Tolui descended in the palm of Armstrong's hand, fully suited, helmet tucked under his arm, like he stepped from one of the original Saturn V launch movies a few hundred years ago. He was an eleven-year-old god coming down from Mount Olympus, a boy barely older than Johari who'd already been a scout for two years.

"Colossus Norgay." Tolui nodded, another too-mature gesture.

"Tolui Colossus Armstrong. May I present my new partner, Johari." He curled his own hand open and placed it on the ground. "Johari is a person of compassion and intelligence. He has absorbed all of the lessons of civilization so far presented. I believe he'll be an asset to your team."

"All the lessons of civs ..." Tolui looked him over. "Okay, then, what's your favorite culture?"

Johari blinked. "Excuse me?" His mind raced, wondering what answer the older boy wanted, the kind of small tribe or clan structure that made a good analogue for the team of scouts? Maybe one of the cultures that influenced the Founders, or one of the organizations arising in Fleet itself: the ring-farmers' distribution network, the miners' covens, the anonymous ritual groups that grew around the allocation lottery, developing chants and superstitions they believed could help them gain some advantage? But one of the basic principles of civs was not to view any given society as inherently superior to another. Tolui frowned at him, drumming his fingers on his helmet.

"An orchestra," Johari blurted.

"Like a musical group?"

"Sure, listen, there's dozens of different instruments, they have a leader — a conductor — and they follow the music — but they all work together to make a symphony. Each instrument and every player has their strengths, and each orchestra takes on its own character. But if they lose one member, if they're missing anything, their collective effort — the music — suffers." Did that even make any sense? Johari's palms sweated.

Tolui's frown deepened for a moment, then he flashed a grin. "Never thought about it like that." He stuck out his hand, and they shook, warm and human. "That's what we need. Somebody who can make us think like we never did before."

If Tolui ever regretted that moment, he had never let on.

Johari keyed the helmet to run a full diagnostic on suit capabilities, then started his official record. Talking with dragons, take one.

Flipping up the faceplate, he fiddled with the heads-up display, redirecting its projection capability. The salamanders' glowing frills gave them at least three modes of communication: colors, movement, and electricity. Plus they had body positions, gestures, and tails. The dragons added wings to that array of options: wing positions, wing coloration changes, or even aerial display. So far, their vocal range seemed limited, more like exclamations than conversations. Aside from the one that deliberately tortured Johari when it figured out how to use the sound against him. Another sign of intelligence. Fan-tastic.

It wasn't Tolui he needed most, but Shawntelle, with her quick mind and formidable programming skills. She could analyze patterns in the colors, movements and electrical output of dragons and salamanders both, cross-correlating them and searching for how they related to the real world.

The suit chimed, and his retinal display scrolled the results of the diagnostics. Life-support damaged, battery at forty-seven percent, long-range transmitter damaged — probably when Tearwing yanked his head off. Commence repair: Y/N? Johari thought about that for a long moment. The planet itself wasn't killing him, and the suit couldn't protect him if the wildlife chose to. Commence repair: N. He might need all the power he had left to locate Armstrong's nuke pack.

Savior's frill rose and twinkled.

"Oh, hey, sorry. I don't mean to ignore you." Johari smiled. Might as well let them get used to his voice and his own expressive range.

Much as he wanted to just delve into the mysteries of dragon-speech, Johari set that aside. Armstrong was dying at the bottom of the sea. What did he need in order to communicate his urgency and his mission, right now? Savior had already delivered the answer.

Johari pulled the personal prop closer to him and hugged it, smiling broadly. "Thank you." He patted it and kept it close against his side, trying to convey his gratitude and affection for the random piece of metal. Too bad he didn't have more tentacle — he could offer a reward.

Triggering the new projection system, Johari queued up the video sequence of Savior accepting the tentacle bits — surely a moment of gratitude if there ever was one.

Savior jumped up, shaking the whole platform, frills blazing.

Johari's implant flared to life and he cried out.

Savior reared over him, hands scrabbling at the air, revealing the nascent claws at the inside of each hand.

Cutting the playback, Johari gripped the helmet with both hands, barely breathing.

The other salamanders recoiled, focused on the spot where the projection had been. Slowly, Savior sank down to all fours, though its back remained humped up, as if prepared to strike. Johari let the helmet settle into his lap, his hands leaving outlines that reminded him of cave art. Had he "said" something that mortally offended the creature? Maybe not this time, but next time could be his last. Note to Fleet: If the kids were considered expendable, maybe they should send more than five.

Savior swiped a hand through the air where the projection had been. Gandhi and the others drew closer, piling against Savior's sides and back, matching its movements like a virtual crowd generated by a crappy algorithm. At last, it brought its eyes up to his, staring at him with the predator gaze. It gave a single pulse of blue-green light that nudged Johari's implant.

He winced. "Yes, I hear you. I have no idea what you're saying, but yeah, I felt it, okay?" Then he froze. Idiot!

He thought of it as visual or auditory, but the mechanism of the projection had its own frequencies: the salamanders didn't know what was intentional and what wasn't.

He touched the back of his head, where the scar from his implant hid beneath his hair, then pointed to where the projection had been. Savior watched warily. It had punished Fury for deliberately triggering Johari's pain, and now Johari had apparently done something similar to it. He shifted the helmet out of his lap and leaned forward, resting his head, one ear to the floor, at Savior's feet, inviting the same punishment. Close-to, the material that capped the chimney revealed gaps and overlaps. Smooth, gently sloped units like giant fingernails formed the whole. Some kind of shells?

A shadow loomed over him, and a raspy breath warmed the back of his neck. The rising sun glowed faintly through the translucent material of the frills at Savior's throat. The nearest eye shone golden-green, flecked with bits of brown around the depth of an oval-shaped pupil. Savior lifted an enormous hand, six fingers, slightly webbed, the two innermost fingers opposed to the others. From the second of these glinted the curve of a killing claw. The slightest whim, and it could clench that hand and tear through his skull like a punctured balloon.

Savior's fingers curled. The thumbs tracked along the back of his head, down to the implant scar. The fingers curved across his face like a football visor. Veins in the webbing pulsed against the glow of the sun. Warm and heavy, the hand lingered over him, then lifted and settled back to the ground. The fingers flexed, a little scratch that resonated through the shell covering the chimney. Johari jerked upright, the sound echoing in his head.

Savior's frills ran in small pink dots, echoed by some of the others, dragons and salamanders alike, and Johari had the distinct impression they were laughing.

Savior's scratching resonated through the shell-material — what if the helmet's sounds had done the same? With its head resting on the surface, Savior might have felt as much as heard the sound that offended.

Talking with dragons, round two.

Johari kept the helmet in his lap. He pointed to the surface where he had projected before, and Savior started to hunch up. Johari quickly waved his hands, as if he could erase the tension. He tapped the back of his head, then made a terrible face as if it hurt him. "Pain," he said, then repeated the action. "Pain."

Cushioning the helmet in his lap, he said, "No pain." He gazed up at the sharp face, too many eyes trained upon him. "Not this time. I'll be careful."

He took a deep breath, and started the sequence, the clip of Savior receiving the tentacle pieces, and the pattern of colors that followed. Savior sat completely still, colorless frills drooping slightly.

"Thank you," Johari said, gesturing toward the image, then toward the prop Savior had brought him. "Thank you." This was way too complicated. He should go back to "eat." Then, at the very least, he could say, "Don't eat me" next time the dragons returned.

When the playback finished, Johari waited. The salamanders' frills began to flicker, elevating as if the electric charge animated them. The accompanying sound/sensations echoed slightly in his implant, and he wondered if they were whispering for his benefit.

Finally Savior darted its head forward and tapped the projection space.

"Again?" Johari asked.

The frills gave a pattern of orange and yellow, then fell "silent" again, devoid of color.

They watched it half a dozen more times. Savior lapped its hand through the image, letting it project onto its palm, or trying to watch through the webbing. A few of the other salamanders dozed, while the dragons rotated out — some of them soaring off as others returned. The newcomers spread their wings wide, their pulsing veins in distinct patterns against the light. and Johari began to capture individual images.

One of the new dragons arched its neck over the salamanders, peering down at him, and Gandhi swiveled about, its frills in a static display of deep purple. The dragon withdrew, and for a moment, Savior and Gandhi leaned closer, their frills commingling.

Savior turned back to him, and re-created the pattern shown in the video. It swiped a foot toward him, and Johari flinched, but the salamander scooped at nothing and brought the empty hand to its mouth. Its frills brightened and darkened. Eating? It was pretending to eat?

Fumbling into his meager supplies, Johari found a protein bar and peeled it open. He took a big bite, chewed and swallowed. "Eat."

Savior repeated the pattern of bright and dark, the frills writhing around its face.

Eat. Johari knew a word! If word was the right ... word. He grinned and took another bite. Savior imitated his actions. Breaking bread with an alien species. If only Norgay could see him now! Then, as if it had taken the exchange for a command, the dragon lunged toward him, jaws wide.

15

WITH A SHOUT, Johari tumbled backward, holding his helmet up like a shield. The dragon snatched the helmet from his hands, huge claws curling around it and yanking it away. It pulled the helmet in close to its chest and swept out its wings.

Savior emitted that terrible pitch, the one that clawed at Johari's implant. He yelled, and the salamander's noise broke off abruptly. The dragon — Fury — lunged toward the edge of the chimney, Johari's helmet clutched like a game-winning football. What the hell did it want with his helmet?

That helmet represented everything he had, and everything he needed: the ability to search for the nuke, to reach out to the bots, to communicate with the locals. Commander Shen's orders echoed in the back of his head: if they were intelligent, under no circumstances could he allow them access to Fleet technology. If he let his helmet go, he was as good as dead, in more ways than one.

Johari sprang to his feet as Fury's wings beat downward. He ran toward it and launched himself, wrapping his arms around the dragon's hind leg. Fury gave a jerk of its legs as it soared from the chimney, but it did not shake him loose. It peered back at him, then stared resolutely ahead, frills waving with color.

Two more sprang afterward, their frills pressed along their heads, radiating blue. In moments, they had left the chimneys behind.

Johari clung for all he was worth as they swept through billowing sulfurous smoke. His eyes watered and his mouth burned, then at last, they broke free, so close to the ocean's waves that the occasional wingtip dipped into the spray.

Separated from the suit's battery pack, the helmet's juice wouldn't last much longer. Using his implant, Johari triggered the emergency beacon, broadcasting on tight beam for as long as the battery lasted. The dragon's grip shifted and its leg jerked again. It stroked hard, turning upward, breaking away from the ocean's swell. The air around him crackled with energy, stinging through his implant. The dragon brought up its other leg and clawed against him. Johari tried to squirm out of the way. His injured arm gave way and he fell.

Johari plummeted toward the water, tensing in anticipation of the impact — then of the sea monster's bite. The world spun around him — the smoky blue of the sky, the too-green frothing of the sea. He landed on a smooth, flexible surface, then rolled to the side, striking a bony ridge. A dragon's spine beneath its rugged, leathery skin.

A huge bluish wing swept up into his line of sight, extending into a plane that made, for him, a new horizon. The wind rushed over, ruffling his hair. Johari's mouth went dry. He was riding a dragon, not as a prisoner, nor as a stowaway. His leap of daring had, apparently, earned him a ride.

Terror gave way in an instant to awe. He huddled along the dragon's spine, just behind its powerful shoulders. The dragon pitched beneath him, tossing him a bit to the side before it righted itself. Johari sank down lower, trying to spread his weight. Up above, Fury still carried his helmet, but at least this dragon kept pace. Wherever they were going, they went together.

With every stroke of its wing, the dragon bore him further from any world he'd ever known. The wind whipped tears from his eyes. Who cared what happened next — he was flying!

He had flown his entire life inside the chest of a giant robot, insulated from the twisting paths of hyperspace and the atmospheres of alien worlds. Together, they had soared through nebulae where stars were born, and through the methane clouds of a watery globe. Out here, he had neither control nor partnership. He lay on the back of an alien beast, the wind battering him, the creature's powerful body transporting them both. Its skin twitched in response to his presence upon it — a presence that, to the dragon, must be just as alien.

"Johari —" a voice echoed at the back of his skull, strangely resonant.

"Shawntelle? Can you hear me?" Without the broadcast antenna or signal boost of the helmet? He clung to the leading edge of the dragon's wings, but it flicked and pulsed, energy buzzing under his hands.

"— emergency beacon — can't track you clearly, but your biorhythym's off the chart! What are you doing? My algorithm's building mountains — mountain ranges! It's beautiful!"

"Where are you?" Emm's voice, cutting in.

"Flying! I don't know!"

A metallic noise disrupted the moment, and Johari glanced around. It came from his helmet — the chime of the search pattern he had input hours before: they had just flown over the chemical signature of Armstrong's nuke pack. The ping emanated from a half-toppled chimney that leaned onto its neighbor. He made out nothing more before the location vanished again behind them.

"What can you see?"

"Hang on." His leg throbbed and an edge of blood seeped along his bandaged arm, drops dashing away in the wind. He cleared the tangle of hair from his eyes. Mountains loomed up, one in the distance smoking softly. Tranquility's tectonic plates must be colliding down there, creating the vents that made the chimneys, and, as they marched up out of the sea, becoming mountains.

"Mountains! Where the volcanic action stops."

The dragons dropped beneath a layer of soot from the offshore chimneys.

"Emm?" Nothing. *"Shawntelle?"* Whatever crazy miracle connected them had broken — interference from particulates in the air, maybe.

Low clouds of burnt sienna smoke cast an apocalyptic tinge, dulling the colors. Dense foliage climbed up the lower slopes. Thick-stemmed flowers taller than Norgay loomed up and reared back from the dragons' approach, the colossal cousins of those around the nests. Gaudy purple and red blooms lolled among the vines, then something more substantial appeared among the greenery, a stone pillar, half-crumbled into ruin. A petrified tree, perhaps? Dozens more marched across the saddle between the chimneys and the peaks. Johari stared down at them, blinking to trigger his cam.

A few dozen dragons perched atop these columns, holding themselves erect like Shaolin monks practicing balance. On some of the taller, more narrow columns, the dragons clung with all four legs, tails wrapped. These dragons ... looked wrong. Even on their pillars, they perched a wingspan or more apart, their heads swung upward as the newcomers arrived. The first two locals launched immediately, soaring ahead and vanishing to his view as his own captor turned. The one carrying him pitched sharply, and Johari fell again, crashing into a plant that spewed liquid all over him, then sliding down the stems until he rolled across the ground.

He lay still a moment, performing a diagnostic of his own. His leg throbbed; even with his exercise regimen, his bones remained on the weak side. Bruises and scrapes, currently streaked with alien debris. Hopefully the shots he'd given himself when he still had his suit would hold off infection for a while. Sticky plant spew all over his clothes, but at least this plant didn't have passengers. If Tolui were infested, so was he — might as well bust him out of the sled, and have a colony of two, assuming Johari lived long enough to get back to camp. All in all, he felt like a hot mess.

When the wings swept overhead, with that distinctive whoosh that signaled a landing, Johari scrambled up and ran, hoping to gain the safety of the dense foliage and see if he could spot Fury with his helmet.

The sharp, terrible screech shot through him, not from a single voice, but from a dozen, from all directions. He clenched his jaw, staggered by the pain. There was no injury, only pain — an internal blaring, like a fire alarm falsely triggered. Johari stumbled between pillars, his shoulder ramming into one of them. The sound broke off, and he leaned for a long moment, catching his breath. Fury perched on a pillar a short distance away, watching him with a predator's gaze. The helmet rolled in its palm.

They didn't want him to run. Maybe they preferred prey that would fight back. Fine. Johari limped toward Fury, head high. "That belongs to me. Give it back." He pointed toward the helmet, and himself. Fury's hand paused, the helmet gleaming dully in the low light. It gently tossed the helmet away, down into the formation of columns.

Johari started walking, step by step, through the dragon's shadow. He forced himself to breathe, calculating how quickly the dragon could pounce and snap him in two. His foot knocked against metal, and he bent down, taking up the helmet with a shaky hand.

The faceplate showed a crack from ear to ear. He turned it upright and made sure it was recording. The cam in his implant might survive inside a dragon's digestive tract, but he couldn't picture the others sorting out the shit to find it — and if Norgay tracked his signal to a dragon's stomach, there wouldn't be enough left of the dragon to analyze.

If he ever got out of this, Johari would apply for a teaching position at Fleet. First contact protocols meant nothing in the real world. He cleared his throat, lifted the helmet, and said, "Thank you."

Fury stared down at him, then thrust its head forward. Johari stumbled a few steps back. Its frills glittered. Fury leapt to another pillar, closer, then watched him again. It repeated the gesture. He stepped back again, in control this time. Fury hopped to another pillar, with a powerful sweep of its wings that rocked Johari. Other dragons moved forward in a ripple, some launching ahead, leaving an opening where Johari stood. Might as well accept the invitation.

The footing grew uneven, with heaps and sticks. Long, thin, pale gray. Logs, he thought, the remnant of a forest fire that leaves a scatter of downed trees and broken limbs. They blocked his path and forced him to turn or slide beneath. Smaller sticks tumbled out of his way, and a few very small indeed cracked beneath his feet. He paused by one of the largest, tempted to hide there, but a toothed jaw snatched it up and carried it away. Its receding shape showed a ball at one end, its length extremely smooth, slightly twisted. Very strange tree. His heart thundered and he turned about. He was navigating through a field of bones.

He had broken free of the pillars and the last of the trees. Bones all around him. His chest strained with every breath, the atmosphere getting to him. Making slow progress, Johari had come down the slope of the saddle. A fine ash of some kind filtered down over him, sticking to his damp clothes and making his eyes water. Four dragons hovered, their mighty wings beating up the dust that stung his face. Others perched on the pillars, reared back from the plain of bones.

Johari's gut clenched. If this weren't a trap for unwary groundlings, what could it be? But Fury hadn't meant to bring him here, only his helmet, as if it were another item for the boneyard. Any one of the dragons could have eaten him when he arrived, or dumped him into the sea before they ever got here. Why would they allow him to reach a place so precious or so frightening to them?

Away down the slope, something rattled. Johari froze. Bones clicked bones. The ground beneath his feet trembled as ponderous steps approached, claws grating over stone. He stared up slope at the dragons, but they were no longer looking at him. They raised their necks.

With a shock of wind, every one of them spread its wings, forming a pale blue and black and green translucent wall streaked with the pumping darkness of their veins, silhouetted against the angry orange of the sky. A shadow moved onto the field of bone where his own pitiful shade lay over the dead. It was a trap, but not merely a game for the dragons he knew. That danger lay before him and he had no idea what lay behind.

Darkness grew as the footsteps approached — then with a slap of sound, shadow-wings unfurled, a ragged form encompassing him, smothering his shadow with jagged shapes like giant teeth.

Johari's helmet fell from his nerveless hands. Somehow, he found his breath, and turned to face his destiny.

16

T HE WINGS THAT SPANNED the narrowing saddle of stone showed tears from edge to bone. Between the six long digits, the membranes hung tattered and rippling, with no pulse of life or light. One wing had only five digits, shortened and broken off at an angle. Fracture.

Tolui's rash action began this adventure, but everything since then had been Johari's choice. He had inserted himself into their world, to take whatever consequence might come. At least the promises Fleet used to get new scouts excited weren't just hype: he was seeing things no human had ever seen before. Johari's knees trembled, but he refused to fall.

Fracture's angular body tilted toward the broken wing, twisted by years, maybe centuries. Scars raked the leathery hide. It carried its head off-center as well, lowering toward him, then away, drifting from side to side. Scars marked its neck — great pits of smooth flesh behind the gill slits where layers of frills should have been. Nostrils opened along its sharp muzzle and it sniffed at the air around him. The wings folded in slow-motion, a careful drawing together of the bones across that torn flesh. Imagining the pain, Johari winced.

The scars ran deliberately, those piercing its eyes and muzzle, and those crossing the void where its frills should be. He envisioned a pair of clawed six-fingered hands gripping the dragon's head, holding it down and digging in against its struggle. Other hands tore away its frills, stripping Fracture of its voice. Had its wings, too, been deliberately torn? How many had it taken to do this? Blinded. Silenced, made flightless.

Johari faced a terrible mystery: a creature of extraordinary strength and will-power if it had survived long enough for those injuries to heal. But was it a great hero who had sacrificed for its tribe, or a dread villain, suffering this most terrible punishment?

He glanced back at the ones behind him, and realized what made them strange. Most of them had been shorn of one or both frills. Some lacked eyes as well, but none lacked every sight-based organ. Fury sat among the others, the only one intact. Its forward facing eyes stared at him, but the others were closed. Johari stood as a supplicant before a creature who couldn't even see him, much less understand his plea for life with no way to communicate —

Johari straightened. The great, damaged dragon lacked the light displays, and the means to "read" them, but light wasn't the only component of those messages. Still, in order to put his idea into use, he would need to be closer, to touch the hide of the monster. The video he had taken of Savior's gratitude display remained queued, the question was, did he have the rest of the information it transmitted? What he needed was Shawntelle, and Tolui. What he had was a damaged helmet with barely enough juice to do what he wanted to try.

He dropped to his knees, sucking a breath against the pain. He worked fast, calling on his implant and manipulating the direct inputs of the helmet to cross-reference his other instrument readings with the images, locating the series of electrical output spikes and valleys. He isolated that segment of the recording and changed the output. Instead of projecting the image of Savior, he could project the sensations: the electric frequencies associated with the color shifts. Gratitude might not be the most appropriate message to send, but it had been well-received by the others.

Besides, it was the only thing he had to work with, aside from "eat," and that was the last message he wanted to send.

Bones crunched as Fracture moved closer, taking a sidelong approach, its head and tail held low. If it had been a cat, it would be stalking him. If a dog, it would be submitting to him. What did this posture mean to a dragon? It crept ponderously up the slope. Running gained him nothing except (maybe) his life, and that only until some other fate caught him up. Staying, speaking, in whatever form that might take, risked everything. What he might win if he succeeded? Adrenaline buzzed through his system, and every sense felt heightened.

Fracture came toward him. Johari's muscles tensed with anticipation, his breath coming in little gasps. Bones clacked and rattled. Fracture's feet pushed them aside, preserving the bones.

Fracture's head swooped just over his own, its scarred jaw revealing stretched skin over ridges of bone. As with Savior and the others, Fracture's skin bore a pattern of bumps and pits, altered by scarring, but still present: the pits that Tolui described as sensory organs.

Johari brushed his fingers against the underside of the dragon's muzzle, the left side of its jaw at a series of narrow indents. Rough and warm beneath his touch, the dragon gave a shiver down the length of its body, and stopped abruptly. The enormous head cast him into darkness.

If he lifted both hands and spread his arms, he could just reach the hollows where its amphibious eyes should be, if he chose to embrace the monster. Keeping his touch light, letting the electricity flow over his skin, Johari closed the circuit and sent. It tingled over and through him, ceasing almost as quickly as it began.

Fracture's gill slits and throat moved slightly as it breathed. Maybe his transmission wasn't strong enough. Johari pulled his hand back, reaching inside the helmet.

Fracture moaned, a low sound that vibrated through Johari's chest. It dropped its chin lower, and he ducked. His bony seat shifted and Johari slid flat on his back, still bracing the helmet with one hand. He reached up by instinct. The moment his fingers touched, Fracture stopped again. Johari dare not move.

That massive head filled his world. It shifted a little, settling its jaw against his touch, his fingers closer to the pattern of pitted skin.

Johari sent again, at the same low level.

The ground and the bones shifted around him. Fracture tipped its head as if to see him better. Johari's hand hummed, his bones transmitting the dragon's answer. The vibration stirred him, flesh and bone, and his own eyes stung. The dragon had answered, and he had no idea what it said.

In his peripheral vision, Johari caught movement. Fury hovered nearby, beating a breeze. Fracture shifted its head, prodding at him. Johari scrambled to his feet, then gasped as his leg twisted beneath him. Pain throbbed from hip to ankle.

Fury's head snaked toward him. Johari grabbed a bone off the slope, long and thin, pointed at one end and knobbed at the other. A dragon's wing tip, unless he was mistaken.

He thrust it in Fury's direction, and the dragon withdrew. "Good — that's right, you stay back."

Fracture turned away and started down the slope, a long process during which the shattered wing swept over Johari's head with a fluttering sigh like a flag of surrender. "What happened to you?" he breathed.

Fury gave a soft burst of light that crackled Johari's implant. Its side-long eyes opened, one of them turned toward him, a huge, luminous orb like a star in the making. Not a predator's gaze, but prey.

Warily Johari lowered the bone's tip to the ground and leaned on it, taking the weight off his injured leg.

Something nudged him from the other side. Fracture's tail, a thick, muscular obstruction with a pattern of spikes, whorls, and pits in its gray-blue hide. Pits ... The tail rested against him, and hummed into him, this time making his teeth ache.

Fury sprang into the air and hovered there with great sweeps of its wings. No — not hovered, it edged a little forward, and a little back — but always more forward than back, keeping pace as Fracture started walking. The dragon stood leaning forward, its tiny arms held to its chest and tail elevated, but wavering. It reminded him of Tyrannosaurus Rex reconstructions he'd seen in the database, but T. Rex was meant to walk on those legs, with a tail properly made to balance its weight. Dragons most definitely were not.

With Fury as careful escort, Fracture walked toward the sea. Johari set his helmet on his head, shoving up the cracked visor. The lower half broke away and fell among the bones. Fracture shuffled down the slope, and Johari limped alongside. He stepped over bones, and sometimes under them. He cataloged them in his mind, fitting them together in the diagram of the dragon Tolui had been making when he left. Here and there, he saw other bones, smaller species, maybe even salamanders.

They reached a crest where the view opened up in the clearer air down below. Bones littered the downslope, all the way to the churning tide. Trails curved through the field of bones where Fracture must have walked before.

A sound like wind through the VR trees followed them downslope, and Johari glanced over his shoulder. Dozens of dragons swooped back and forth over the field of bones. Occasionally, one darted down and rose up again with a bone in its mouth. They resembled a flock of enormous seagulls picking at a school of fish. Carrying their prizes, they soared upward, their wings making eddies through the murky sky.

Down below, something splashed, then another. Beneath the bones, rough old lava formed the slope, humped and rippled in the patterns of its violent emergence. The slope leveled out where it met the sea, and a series of pools marked the shore. Bones dropped from the sky above into these pools, splashing down, then bobbing up again. The dragons disturbed the swirling clouds above as each of them delivered another bone.

They couldn't be far from the equator, which would ordinarily make for lower tides, but the planet's three moons changed that, too. Maya would be working on those figures. At times, though, this entire slope could be submerged. Johari examined the area as Fracture processed down the slope. No algae or other growth touched the base of the slope near the pools, either from the chemical make-up of the water, or the inhospitable nature of the stone. A dragon's length down from where he stood, bits of stone and scraps of sea wrack collected in the hollows of the bones. Johari rubbed his forehead beneath the helmet's frame. No, actually, that made no sense. If the tide reached this far up, it would suck the bones into the sea.

Fracture stayed on its path, weaving down among the bone deposits until it reached the pools. Its wings and tail remained lifted, not touching the bones as it passed. Johari tried to be just as cautious. He limped a few steps down, letting his bone-staff take his weight. As he walked, he eyed the patches of bones. All sorts of bones lay here, some flat against the slope, others sticking up or propped and piled together. Had the lava itself engulfed the bones, or maybe overtaken a number of creatures here, like the pyroclastic explosion at Pompeii back on Earth?

When he reached that section of human history in his studies, the image of hundreds of skeletons crammed into tiny rooms, clinging to each other, gave him nightmares. Fleet took it as a positive sign that Johari became so invested in his role as humanity's ambassador and the scholar of civilization. His nightmares became something to be proud of.

When he reached World War II, and saw images of concentration camps — video footage of the haggard prisoners, documentation of their graves — he begged to leave the service. Worst of all was knowing mankind had done this to each other — just as they did during the Climate Wars. Pompeii had been a natural disaster, followed by two thousand years of man-made horrors. What else would he see? What more must he know in order to fulfill his role? Those visions made Johari grateful the records of the Ruin remained locked behind a firewall: he couldn't imagine witnessing the devastation of their entire world.

Norgay had enveloped him, transforming the habitat into a nest of comfort. He introduced Johari to the rich mocha drink his mother had loved. He extruded his first stringed instrument, and encouraged Johari to play.

Johari paused on the rough ground, resting his head against the bone staff, and squeezed his eyes shut. He was not dead, not yet. Fleet willing, he would see Norgay again soon. His chronometer popped into his retinal beam, displaying the countdown to Armstrong's death. Johari swallowed hard and pushed himself to continue. He hummed a selection from Beethoven's Pastoral Symphony as he moved. His leg ached with every step, but at least his arm had stopped bleeding. When he stopped again, he turned uphill, stretching out his calves. The saddle between the chimney and the mountain stretched up before him now. It hadn't looked so steep when he started down.

From this vantage, the bones formed clumps. Johari pulled his helmet off, rested it at his feet, and scrubbed his hand over his face. He stood too close to see the patterns clearly, but still ... the bone clusters at the top resembled Egyptian hieroglyphics, or maybe Japanese kanji characters, made three-dimensional. For a moment, he forgot to breathe.

The bone-constructions might be art, created for alien needs, but given the repetitive structures and patterns, they resembled words and sentences. Paragraphs, chapters splayed across the slope around him. Johari stood in the middle of a miracle, surrounded by it, moving through it: language, spelled out by alien minds beneath an alien sun. It was the moment he had been trained for, raised for, maybe even born for, to recognize artistry in the works of an alien mind.

How did the bones adhere to the slope, or to each other? He did not know, nor did he dare intrude even further into this extraordinary space. He did not know what it meant or how it could be read, if a human would even be able to do so. His presence in the bones could rewrite the dragons' religion or cosmology. It could force them to change their entire social structure.

In almost two hundred years of searching, scouts had found no other intelligent species — and few other planets containing all they needed for life. Mankind had ruined their own planet, wrecking the environment, driving each other to war, exploding into environmental catastrophe while those few who worked in near-space watched in horror.

The Founders established the scout corps to seek a new planet, giving them an oath meant to guarantee the Fleet didn't just show up and ruin someone else's world. Fleet butchered that oath, downgrading intelligence, preparing the way to destroy another world.

Was Johari going to let them do it?

17

JOHARI GRIPPED THE DRAGON BONE in both hands, images flashing through him: dragon flight, Savior's rough, curious face, the tingling rush of knowing he was getting through — speaking — to a creature no man had ever even seen before. *There are more things in heaven and earth than are dreamed of in your philosophy.* Shakespeare dreamed that up. A student of a hundred, a thousand human cultures, he stood now in the presence of another dreamer. He felt still as stone himself, burning with revelation.

Humanity needed a world like this, it didn't have to be this one. They had the capability of finding and settling another place. Even without the bots, without the scouts, Fleet would go on, as it had since the Ruin — the dragons had no such refuge.

They had to leave, as soon as possible. Earhart would be in orbit soon, and Armstrong's pack had been found, they just needed to get it back and make repairs. Johari had activated his beacon, such as it was. Now he added a message, with extreme urgency. "Norgay. The dragons took me to the edge of the chimneys, at a volcano. Come get me, ASAP. Be —"

Even as he spoke, the lights winked out, and his helmet went unresponsive. When Norgay or one of the other bots got close enough, his implant alone would give them a signal to follow. Johari coughed, spitting up a bit of orange-gray dust. Then he remembered: their long-range sensors couldn't pierce the clouds generated by the chimneys. From Norgay's perspective, the beacon must have gone dead from the moment they soared beneath the clouds. Johari had to return to the open air before they could even find him.

Facing the ocean, Johari surveyed the area before him. To his left, the first chimney, a huge tower of mottled black and red rose up from the saddle, obscuring his view. To the right, the shelf of lava curved around, becoming a swath of rubble, and vanishing into the jungle that crept along the slope of the volcano. A long finger of water pushed in that direction, bordered by a thin strip of land on the far side. Definitely, he could see more clearly in that direction, but it would be rough going. Now that he had some idea what they were doing with their bone heap, though, Johari needed to do one more thing before he left.

He limped down the slope, staying to the path Fracture used, studying the bone arrays as he went. Something white and nearly bone-like joined them and merged them with the slope in the places where they stuck out. None had been broken, at least, not in any way related to their construction. A few of the jutting pieces showed signs of wear or had jagged tips as if battered by the sea. A distant sound, like a sonic boom, caught his attention briefly. Could be Norgay on the way, tracking the beacon.

Johari grit his teeth against the pain in his leg as he hurried downslope.

Fury and a few other dragons perched on knobs of stone that jutted up from the water. Fracture walked at its stately pace into the largest pool, where a few bones bobbed on the water. It stretched out its neck and lowered itself into the water, pressing bones beneath its bulk. One set of eyes and nostrils remained on the surface. It tossed back its head, flinging a spray of water and casting a bone onto the shore. In a moment, it tossed another. Gleaming water swirled through the air, reminding Johari of the showerhead spraying in zero-g. It selected three or four bones. Ponderously,

Fracture arose from its little pool, taking the bones in its mouth and carrying them uphill. It pulled itself into a squat, tail smacking against the stone. When it withdrew, a clutch of flattened shapes remained: floppy, ill-formed eggs. It leaned down, prodding at the egg mass with one of the bones, then settling the bone where it thrust away from the stone. The dragon emitted a soft rumble. It scraped against the eggshells with the next bone, dragging the white material along to place the new bone a little distance from the first. The final bone, a thin, flat shape that might have been a scapula, it fitted against the first one. Again, it rumbled. Finally it returned to its pool as Johari completed his precarious journey to the ledge. Not "it," "she," the egg-laying member of the species.

Fracture rooted around in the pool, swamping more bones. The next emergence showered Johari with salt water. He barely managed to turn aside, protecting his broken helmet. The dousing drenched his hair and washed down his clothes, erasing some of the flower sap, blood and dirt from his ordeal. His scraped skin stung. A huge vertebra clattered to the stone beside him.

Fracture paused, head turning toward him. When she was submerged like that, water carried a variety of signals to those receptors. Which of her senses recognized his approach? The question made him think of the bots with all of their sensor arrays and computational capabilities. Both had senses he could only imagine and try to emulate through technology.

"I brought you this," he said. He tossed the bone he'd been using as a staff into the water. Fracture's ruined wing flapped a few times, drawing the bone closer then forcing it under the water.

Fracture's blind face stared at him a moment longer, then submerged with a rumble. She lay in the pool, her back humped up and tail curved around to fit within the confines of the space. The pool had smooth, regular edges, suspiciously symmetrical. Likewise, the channels between the pools, and from them to the sea took slightly curving paths. Six of them. Dragons made this place, carving or refining the pools and channels both.

Fracture remained submerged for a long time, and Johari let out his breath, moving away. He set his back to the dragons and walked toward the next pool. His leg hurt less on the level, but still slowed him down. Water whooshed behind him, and Johari looked back to see Fracture fling up her head. The long, thin bone spun in the air and clattered against the stone where Johari had been standing. His bone. Fury's eyes found him across the distance, but the dragon made no move to stop him. Joy and peace soared through him, and he grinned as he faced the path. Who knew what it meant — any of it — save that he had brought his bone, and Fracture had chosen it, had, in some strange way, chosen him.

Johari took a few more steps, longing for a chance to lie down. He already missed his bone staff. The wind shifted with a sweep of wings, then a dragon wailed.

He slapped a hand to his implant, doubling over. His leg twisted beneath him, and he staggered, barely keeping his feet. Johari glanced back, expecting to see Fury there, resuming its earlier attitude. A strange dragon dropped heavily into the water, keening and thrashing. Where it struck the water, darkness spread. Spines broke water a few lengths away.

Fury and the others sprang from their perches. Two of them dove for the injured dragon, snatching at its neck with their hind legs. One of them caught hold, but lightly, and its wings strained as it hauled the downed animal toward the ledge. Fury plunged toward the ocean, dashing the surface with one wingtip. The spines surfaced again, closer to the beach and its spreading stain of blood.

Fury turned a tight circle and dragged the tip of its tail along the water. The spines swung back. For a moment, the sea monster's head broke the water and Fury shot upward, beating hard. The monster lunged, tentacles lashing. Fury's frills shot brilliant gold, its wings and tail flaring with sudden light. The tentacles recoiled and the beast dove under.

Fury's assault stabbed at the back of Johari's skull and he cried out.

By the time he mastered himself, the wounded dragon lay stretched upon the shore, its blood streaming into the pools. Fracture shook herself free of the tainted water and cast about. The wounded dragon's frills sparkled, messages of pink and gold that Fracture could not receive. Fury swept up its wings and landed in front of the newcomer, rocking slightly as if the defense had weakened it. Fury's neck drooped as it watched the downed dragon's frantic light display.

Fury answered in an aurora of colors. The injured dragon rolled onto its side, its wings unfurled up the slope, brushing the bones and revealing a dozen holes in the membranes. Long gashes marked its throat and side and carved through one leg. One of its frills dangled in a mess of blood, barely lighting. Black parabolic streaks framed the wounds. These wounds burned as well as cut. The furrowed wounds resembled artillery strikes, glancing shots at the wrong angle. If it had been broadsides those furrows would be holes blasted in one side and out the other. Johari's stomach churned. The dragon had flown directly at its attacker. Its attacker, the robot. Which one?

Fracture shifted, half-emerging from the water. She rested her head along the head of the newcomer. She reared back her neck an instant later, scenting at the air, lifting her chin to turn its receptors. Fury lifted its muzzle, sides still heaving and frill hanging limp. They stared at Johari.

Fury launched, a half-dozen others soaring with it. The lead dragon shrieked. The pain shot through Johari and pinned him where he stood. The back of his skull felt as if he, too, had been shot down by rockets. Johari swayed on his feet. He wished he knew how to apologize.

18

ROCKETS FIRED AND FLAME EXPLODED across the sky. One of the dragons punched sideways, streaming blood as it crashed against the wall of bones. No. Johari gasped for breath, and cried out, "No!"

Fury's squadron turned sharply, rushing to meet the attack. Pricks of fire in the sky expanded into blossoms of death, their contrails twisting. Another dragon spiraled out of control, sliding sideways into the water where the monsters waited. Fury's wings lit with inner flame. Light streaked along a thousand pathways and outlined its eyes with pits of glory.

A bomb twisted into range and exploded short of its goal. Shots thundered across the inlet. The air battered at Johari's ears. He jammed on his helmet, hoping it would dampen the effect, then he ran — straight back toward the dragons. Fracture, at least — Fracture must live! His leg spiked with pain at every step. His feet slapped the stone, his hands bunched into fists. He ran as if he could punch the bullets from the sky.

With a deafening roar of engines, Norgay slammed into view, arms extended, shoulders and forearms bristling with armaments

Johari had never seen before. His chest tightened. "*Stop shooting,*" he subvocalized. "*Immediately! Norgay, don't kill them!*"

Norgay kept firing. More dragons swept down over the saddle of stone, shrieking, jaws agape, but the dragons of the enclave were not warriors. They had no frills and produced no golden fire — they lacked the ability to generate that level of power. It wouldn't have mattered; Fury's attack had changed nothing.

Johari clenched his jaw and stumbled on. If he couldn't stop the rain of bullets and blood, he could at least shield the artist. Bullets hissed along the water and shattered against stone. The shrieking overpowered Johari's implant. His voice grew hoarse with shouting, but his subvocalizer only whined.

Three dragons together crashed into Norgay, pitching him off-course, shoving him toward the chimney as if to crush him against the stone. The bot tipped away from them and excreted a sheen of oil. Their claws skittered across the smooth metal. One, then another pulled up, flapping desperately to escape their own trap. The third one cracked its wing against stone and slid until it grabbed the rough surface with its hind legs, tail wrapping to hold it steady.

Johari reached Fracture's pool. The blind dragon shifted, raising her head, scanning as she had before. The wounded one lay still. "Stay down," Johari rasped, knowing it wouldn't matter. He staggered the last few feet to the narrow shingle between Fracture's pool and the crashing sea. He waved his arms, snatching off the helmet to extend his reach — anything for Norgay's attention.

Four sets of spines stalked the ocean. One of the wounded dragons tumbled into the sea and two huge maws snatched at it. Tentacles flailing, they broke the dragon between them. As the winners splashed down, water surged up. The wave smacked Johari off his feet. It hurled him against Fracture's unyielding side. Her head snapped toward him. For a moment, he felt the tingle of her touch. The wave sucked him back again, scraping against the stone, mouth full of water as he tumbled from the ledge into the sea.

Green. Trails of bubbles rushed past him, streaking over his face. Johari fought his way back to the surface, clawing at the water. Water, in space, was an elusive element, carefully tended and preserved, now it surrounded him, forcing its way into his nose and mouth, ripping his breath away.

For a moment, his face broke through and he gulped at the air, arms pumping to try to stay afloat. Saltwater seared his torn skin and poured into his mouth. Something slick stroked his ankle. Johari kicked wildly. A tentacle slapped the water near his face. As he sank again, the sky went dark.

Golden fire streaked. The tentacles sucked back again. A dragon's head plunged into the waves, snapping. Fury, its frills ablaze. The water around Johari buzzed.

A massive silver fist slammed into the dragon's head, knocking it aside.

Gagging and choking, Johari struggled toward the surface. Already exhausted and wounded, he clawed upward. His legs weighed a thousand pounds, dragging him toward the deep. His vision narrowed to a black tunnel that stung his eyes.

Sudden brightness cut the narrowing path. The silver span of Norgay's arm thrust into the water, fingers spread. Norgay scooped upward, gathering Johari into his palm. Johari collapsed as the water drained away. Coughing wracked his body. He vomited sea water, and coughed again. He curled convulsively into the metal hand that carried him.

Norgay drew him close against his chest, his hand already warming, the surface metal softening. Johari wrapped his arm around Norgay's enormous thumb, hugging its warmth. Ever so gently, it stroked the back of his head, and the fingers enfolded him.

"Johari Colossus Norgay," the voice thrummed inside of him. *"I have you, and I will not let you go."*

"Stop fighting," Johari breathed. "Please. Stop." He couldn't hear his own voice. Blood pounded in his ears and his lungs couldn't expand all the way.

"I have achieved a primary goal," Norgay answered. *"You need treatment."*

Johari let his eyes stay shut. He shuddered with every breath. He gave up on his voice entirely, but forming the thoughts and the words to subvocalize only drained him further. *"What's happened? You — attacked. Killed them. You didn't get my message."*

"I heard your scream. They were attacking you."

He heard nothing but the gentle hum of Norgay's systems and the comforting baritone of his voice. *"Sometimes. In part. I spoke. I know how to hear them. The ones at the chimney."* The staccato phrases of his panic.

Norgay said nothing.

Johari shifted a little off his wounded arm. His breathing eased enough to release some of the pressure at his chest. *"Norgay. What have you done?"*

In answer, he felt the nudge of his implant to a VR request. He accepted. For a moment, a hundred data streams rushed through him, making him queasy, then the channel narrowed to video only. Cams forward. Through the VR feed, Johari and Norgay became one.

Soaring through the sky, Johari's scream replaying in Norgay's head. Eriksson taking the lead, his leg oddly formed without the minisub, jury-rigged from other components. Scanning, pinpointing the location. They turned, not going supersonic, not yet. Sound bursts arrived at intervals, and sent. Private bot communications. Norgay provided no translation.

They slowed over the ocean at the first cluster of chimneys. Norgay spotted the minisub inside one of them, detecting evidence of damage, and battle. Another com-burst, and the bots split up, forming a search pattern.

Dragons hovered, dipped, and flew away from a taller chimney some way off. A few soared toward the sun, the direction Fury sped with Johari clinging to its leg. From the position of the sun in the sky, this must be an hour or more after they had left. Johari imagined the debate. He was expendable, they weren't. Norgay hadn't wanted him to go, Eriksson warned about the dragons, Zheng He waited for more data. Shawntelle performed a signal boost, and the helmet's distress call flared, only to fall silent again almost immediately. He briefly made contact, full of joy, then vanished again.

One of the dragons swept closer to the search position. It flared its frills and bated its wings, then abruptly cut away and shot back toward the chimney. It gave a shriek of alarm as it flew. Eriksson extruded guns and powered up. He wavered a little in the sky, compensating for the changed aerodynamics of his repaired leg. Another com-burst, then another. Norgay's arms stretched forward, weapons emerging.

According to Fleet, they were exploratory bots, created for scientific purposes. Each had some sort of armament, but not arm cannons, not like this. Every system scan, every diagnostic, every schematic Johari had ever seen of his partner showed only a minimal complement of weapons. Back when they were launching the minisub, Norgay remarked that Fleet had been lying and Eriksson had replied: *No more than you.*

The knowledge hurt, but he didn't have time for hurt. Johari focused on the playback. Norgay sped up, and the two bots flew side by side, fists forward.

A handful of dragons occupied the chimney, though most of these launched at the bots' approach. They spiraled above the chimney, interleaving their wings in an elaborate pattern like dancing, effectively blocking the approach to the cap. The wingless salamanders remained on the chimney cap. Some began to scramble downward, making slow progress with their claws gripped into the stone. The remaining salamanders tossed something among them, something dull silver, heavy.

The video jumped into a zoom, magnifying the scene. One of the salamanders dropped the personal prop and took up the torn suit instead. It wriggled headfirst over the side. Norgay's vision shifted again, some kind of scanner overlaying the scene, picking up traces of — what? Biochemical spatter thick with genetic evidence. Johari's blood.

Another com-burst, this one from Norgay, then the flare of rockets launched. The first volley tore through the thicket of dragons, spraying blood and shredded membranes. One of them fell and bounced off the chimney with a crunch that left its neck dangling. Two others tumbled aside.

A scatter of smaller rounds chipped into the side of the chimney, and the fleeing salamanders froze, their frills gone mad with color like a lightning storm inside a nebula, but this fire would birth no stars.

A second round of rocket fire, and the protective spiral of dragons scattered. One of them turned about and soared directly toward the bots. Norgay split right, Eriksson to the left. The dragon hit hard against Eriksson's side. It lit up with gold and Eriksson's body jerked, tumbling side-long, the dragon's claws grappling with what it could not see. With contact, then, a dragon's electric assault could fell even a bot. Norgay flipped a new weapon from his shoulder and fired.

Bullets struck the dragon's body as if implanting a series of new biosensors. Ammo pinged off of Eriksson's metal sides, leaving little divots, but not penetrating. Dragon blood smeared his surface. He arrested his fall and rolled more slowly, the dragon dropping free and splashing at the base of the chimney.

The bots overshot the chimney cap. Three dragons remained in flight. One of these dropped to the cap, wings spread over a pair of huddling salamanders. It frilled and shrieked, daring the bots to come closer. But they had no need for proximity. They spun and circled back with startling efficiency. Eriksson's arm cannons thundered. The dragon and its wards vanished along with a good chunk of the cap. Shards of shell flew outward.

The salamander with the suit changed course, running madly around the chimney, forcing the bots to track it. Eriksson stopped short, taking aim. Norgay swung about to the other side, strafing the chimney. The suit tumbled away toward the sea. The salamander doubled back, curled and shot straight upward, choosing a path midway between the bots. Bullets spat blood from its back and sides, then broke off as Eriksson dove for the suit, snatching it from the air.

The salamander reached the top of the chimney and reared up onto its hind legs, reaching upward. Its frills glowed a deep green and it emitted a low tone. Blood streamed down its sides and it struggled to stay erect. Dancing on its hind legs, arms upraised, pleading, for all the world like a child hoping to be gathered to its father's breast.

Norgay's sight zeroed in, closer, closer, magnifying the salamander's head and overlaying the view with a targeting tracker. Savior's head.

19

JOHARI'S THROAT BURNED and tears slicked his face. "No," he moaned, but all of this was in the past. The slaughter had already happened, and he was now carried in the palm of the killer.

The image jolted suddenly, the tracker fizzling and lurching sideways. Norgay's vision leapt back to close range. A dragon flapped away from him, then swooped back, building up a golden charge, claws extended. At the last minute, it pulled back its legs and let its tail smack the robot's arm, delivering a shock that sent streaks across the playback.

Norgay soared upward, firing at the dragon's retreat. A second dragon swooped into view, jaws wide, coming straight for him, its frill glowing an ominous gold. Norgay fired, and the creature lost altitude, struggling to pull out of its dive.

A com-burst from Eriksson. Norgay hesitated in the air, one arm extended and tracking the flight of the dragon as it dwindled into the distance. That one, at least, survived long enough to tell the others.

Norgay soared around the chimney to find Eriksson clinging to a nearby broken chimney with one hand, the suit extended in his other. They exchanged a flurry of com-bursts, at the end of which, Eriksson, hanging low in the sky and twitching to the side with disturbing regularity, turned back toward the plateau where they had made camp. Norgay rose slowly higher and higher — but not before Johari caught a glimpse of the salamander splayed across the chimney cap while down below sea monsters fought over the dead.

"We have to go there, go back." Johari's eyes snapped open. *"If Savior's still alive, we have to go back!"*

"Negative. You need treatment. Your vital signs suggest severe dehydration, and you have several small stress fractures to your left leg, not to mention exposure to an alien atmosphere. I detect numerous abrasions and contusions." Norgay sounded like a family physician on some old tv show — maybe on purpose. "Johari, I will not allow you further contact with the enemy."

The mother-hen routine started to grate on Johari, and it wasted time. *"Norgay, open your hand."*

No response.

Johari slapped the inside of the nearest finger. *"Open your hand — I'm not gonna jump."*

The fingers unfolded, just enough for him to peer between. He made out their location, not far off shore. *"Come on, it's hardly even out of the way. We can check for survivors then head back to base to rendezvous with the others."*

What had Maya and Emm heard about all of this? Tolui would surely be just as furious about the wanton destruction of life. And Shawntelle — if she'd been inside Eriksson at the time, he gave no sign. Johari suspected the bots had undertaken this action all on their own, leaving behind the kids who were to serve as their conscience. He felt ill, no longer able to distinguish between the effects of his ordeal and that of the video he'd just been watching. *"I thought Armstrong was the only warrior."*

A long pause, then, "Negative."

Johari pushed himself to a seated position, leaning against Norgay's massive thumb. Bits of wind reached around the fingers, starting to dry his clothes and tease the water that dripped from his hair. With his good hand, he pushed back his hair. *"What else have you been keeping from me?"*

The fingers closed just a little.

"Norgay, they are people," Johari said softly, wanting to hear it said aloud, even as the words stung his throat. "Like me. Like you. They have language, culture, art and ritual. We have to go there."

"No one regrets this more than I do." Norgay's carefully modulated voice sounded almost pained.

"Look at me, Norgay, come on!" Johari's voice gave out. "*Why? Why won't you do it — you just said you regret it, now's your chance for some kind of redemption!*"

Norgay slowed to a crawl, then stopped altogether. He raised his hand before him, and the fingers uncurled, placing Johari before those vivid blue eyes. "You are compassionate and empathetic, Johari."

Johari's heart ached, but he didn't know why. He stroked his hand across Norgay's thumb. "*That's what you taught me, Norgay. You raised me this way, so I could lead as well as serve.*"

"That is not how I was raised." Norgay paused. "I do not think I can be redeemed."

Johari absorbed the words like a blow. "*Because you're a robot? That's insane. It's Fleet, isn't it? They're doing this somehow — making you do this — what's going on?*"

Norgay lifted his head, staring straight as if his eyes would level the world. "Fleet has activated military protocols, Johari," a pause, "Colossus Norgay." He spoke as if pronouncing a sentence. "You declared that the aliens are intelligent. You have been a long time among them."

"*Yeah, all day and all night. I'm exhausted, I — oh, shit.*" He knotted his fingers into his hair as Norgay's voice finally pierced his own emotions. Among alien beings who, under the provisional military protocols, were considered the enemy. If he didn't submit to Fleet interrogation and pass, he'd be declared traitor. "*Oh, shit. I'm sorry, Norgay, I didn't understand.*"

"You have no need to apologize, but you must now understand the urgency of returning to our base." Norgay's motors whirred back to life. Johari stilled him with a touch.

"*The dragons were going to eat me, Norgay. Savior stopped them. I can't leave it there alone, not if it's still alive. I was learning to talk to it.*" He almost smiled. "*It taught me the meaning of 'gratitude.'*"

"I cannot allow you to have further contact. You were abducted. The sooner they review the evidence of coercion, the more readily you will be cleared of suspicion."

"We're running out of time!"

Norgay's head pulled back, just a little. "Johari," pause, "Colossus Norgay. I serve humanity, Fleet, and you."

Every time Norgay spoke Johari's official title, the bot's voice hitched, as if he ran a thousand calculations in the interim, trying to be certain Johari still owned the designation. It hurt like a sliver jabbed beneath the skin. Johari swallowed. *"In what order?"*

"Fleet and humanity are one."

Oh, shit. And if Fleet reviewed the evidence, they might forgive him leaping onto a dragon in an effort to retrieve his helmet. But inviting Fracture's touch? Joining in an alien ritual, when he didn't even know what it meant? If he told Norgay any of that, would his partner feel a duty to protect him, or to turn him over to Fleet's idea of justice? Johari felt cold in spite of Norgay's comfort, and the last protein bar he'd eaten soured his teeth and tongue.

The fingers began to close and Norgay accelerated.

"Wait, wait, wait!" Johari banged his hand on Norgay's thumb. *"Fleet only has five bots left, and one of them is at the bottom of the ocean. Rescuing Armstrong has to be a higher priority —"* Norgay's acceleration increased, pressing Johari against the metal, and Johari talked faster — *"that's gotta be a higher priority than my interrogation, right? Fleet needs him, and I know where he is."*

"Without his nuclear pack, he is —"

"I know where that is, too. You've got," he checked his chronometer, *"Twelve hours and twenty-three minutes to get the pack, get him repaired and get him out of there. Put me down on the chimney, there's no way I can escape, right? I've already been exposed to whatever they're gonna do, Norgay, brainwashed or whatever. The damage is done."*

The huge hand shivered, a barely notable vibration, one maybe only Johari would have noticed. "I cannot violate Fleet commands."

"I'm not asking you to. But you can determine the optimal order of Fleet priorities. You just did, right? Humanity, Fleet, and me." Johari stared up at Norgay, the bot's head tipped back, displaying

a smooth expanse of metal sculpted to resemble a man's throat. If Norgay had been a man, a well-placed blade could claim his life just then. *"You've got to choose Fleet, Norgay, you have to. Put me down on the chimney. I'll tell you where to find the nuke. I'll direct you to Armstrong."*

The chin notched downward. "I have the capability of locating him without your assistance."

"It'll take time that he doesn't have."

"Johari. What are your priorities?"

"Fleet, humanity, my team. My partner." A short hum of acknowledgement, then Johari continued, *"You said Fleet and humanity are one, but you're wrong. I'm supposed to be your conscience, Norgay, to remind you of what's important, because a bot can measure the readouts and analyze the atmosphere. You can study the ecosystem and find the proteins we need to survive. But humanity means more than just biology. I study art and music, literature, history."*

He gave a short laugh. *"They used to call it 'humanities', but the definition doesn't end there. It also means benevolence, empathy, the spirit inside the form. Fleet is how we survive, Norgay — humanity is why."*

20

THE HAND SUDDENLY SHUT, caging Johari as Norgay burst into motion. Johari started to slide, but the contours of the hand shifted to cushion his body. It didn't matter — he might as well fall to his death. He had failed. If he couldn't convince even Norgay of his truth, how would he ever survive Fleet interrogation?

As quickly as it had begun, the acceleration slowed, and Norgay's fingers peeled back, his hand lowered to rest at the edge of the chimney cap, what was left of it. Savior sprawled across the surface, its tail dangling over the broken cap. As the giant hand touched down, Savior's prey-eyes slid open, then shut. Still alive! Hope rushed through him as if newly flown from Pandora's box.

"Thank you." Johari worked his way across Norgay's palm, and the bot gently tipped his hand, letting his partner slide carefully to the surface. Pain sizzled up the injured leg, and Johari gripped the top of his thigh as if he could stop it.

Norgay's face loomed over him like a second sun. "You need treatment."

"Leave me the medipak, the generator, the evaporator."

Norgay's body shifted, his hand lowering as he retrieved the items. "Emergency shelter?"

"Negative, I ..." Johari tried to think of an excuse, but flicked a glance toward the injured salamander, blood seeping along the grooves in its skin.

"The use of Fleet medical technology on enemy combatants violates —"

"Frack off! If you're that worried, then don't give it to me." Johari lay back on the shell, taking control of his breath, slow and careful. One of the ways to control his pain. One of the things Norgay had taught him.

The bot's hand placed a few items next to him. "Johari, this is not easy."

"You're the one who said you weren't raised for compassion."

"That is why I have you. You are the spirit within my form."

Johari ached, inside and out. *"Armstrong is standing with his back to a submerged chimney. There's a broken chimney protruding about five klicks from here, that way —"* he pointed, but also transmitted the coordinates from his implant. *"Biggest sea monster I've seen yet is down there, hanging around his legs, maybe hoping the salamanders will investigate. I parked the submersible in the broken chimney after a run-in with Moby Dick."*

Wearily, he let that hand flop down, and raised the other, pointing in the opposite direction. The ragged bandage he made of his torn sleeve unraveled and pooled at his elbow, except the end that stuck to his dried blood. *"The nuke pack appears to be inside of, or maybe on top of, another chimney, close to the route between here and where you found me."* He sent those coordinates as well.

Norgay's eyes zoomed and focused on his injured arm.

"You'll know where to find me." Even without speaking aloud, his lungs worked too hard. He might have ruined them forever, breathing in the tainted air of Fracture's enclave. He rolled onto his side, reaching toward the supplies, and Norgay reached as well, turning one of the silvery cases and triggering the set-up function. The evaporator folded out of its casing and began to hum, drawing in moisture from the air around him, analyzing and filtering it. How long would it be before he could get a drink?

Norgay's hand descended once more, a cluster of manipulators protruding from one finger as he offered a plastic bladder filled with water. When Johari didn't respond, he lowered it to the ground in easy reach. His motors hummed as he took off, and flew away alone.

After drinking a third of the bottle — careful not to chug it, despite his urgent need — Johari triggered the medipak. It unfolded into a broad shelf and drawer selection of items. He released a debriding nanite swarm and let them scurry all over his body, removing foreign matter from his many scrapes and cuts. Their work tickled, and sometimes burned as they scoured him, removing whatever his dip in the ocean had not, and whatever the ocean had left behind. He hoped. The nanites chirruped, requesting to shave his head, and Johari waved them back into their casing.

He found a smartcast and dragged it over his leg. His leg tingled as the cast wrapped around him, configuring an artificial joint to either side of his knee and running a thin strap under his foot. The materials conformed to his leg, quickly producing a soft, cushioned interior and a solid support structure at the outside. He would be able to hobble, but not to run. During that process, he fished out a dose of painkillers and pressed the auto-injector into his thigh. Happy chemicals rushed through his body, buoying him with waves of numbness. Follow that with an antibiotic chaser and he'd live, at least for now.

After applying skinknit to the cuts on his arm, Johari turned his attention to Savior. Throughout his arrival, the salamander lay still panting softly. Its eyes stirred from time to time, shifting behind its eyelids, opening a slit, then sliding shut as if weary from the effort.

Just as he'd been trained, Johari began his primary assessment: Breathing, yes. He had no idea where or how to check the creature's pulse, or even how much intervention it would accept from him. Blood oozed from a series of wounds along its side. Most of these furrows showed angled hits that didn't fully penetrate, but at least five penetrated the hide, and two of those showed exit wounds on the other side as he limped over there.

Despite Norgay's warning, he pulled open a few more compartments in the medipak and found the largest bandages they had. Antibiotics and surgical bots designed for humans could easily do more harm than good. So, stick with the basics: keep the insides in, and the outside out. Johari applied bandages to the most egregious wounds. Savior twitched and rumbled as he worked, and once —

when he brushed against a bloody elbow — it swung its head about quickly, frills flashing, but not rising very far.

"Sorry, sorry." He put up his hands. "I wish I could get you some tasty tentacles. Maybe later, okay?"

Savior's huge forward eyes gazed at him, then its head settled again, in a position where it could better keep watch on him. Except that its eyes immediately began to close. The frills flashed again, then again, a little more dully, like a tired chaperone succumbing to a nap while continuing to issue warnings for good behavior. Salamander blood, thick and purple, marked Johari's hands and knees, and his leg ached beneath the cast.

Grabbing a few more items from the pack, Johari found a comfortable position and switched on the generator. Solar panels whirred out and rotated, tracking the sun until they found the sweet spot. He connected the evaporator, just in case Norgay returned unexpectedly and wondered what he was up to. Finally he triggered the component he really wanted: the antenna booster, a handy emergency feature in case a scout got stranded. Narrowing the transmission as tight as he could, Johari pulled on a sleep mask and sent the command series for his implant to sync with the booster. When it gave him the handshake, he sent a direct message to Shawntelle, requesting permission to enter her VR chamber, her private domain.

He got the pingback immediately, but took a moment to call up his avatar off-the-rack, not allowing the image to update. VR blossomed across his vision, then his avatar floated in Shawntelle's crystalline dream-space. She flowed toward him, her blue-tipped dreadlocks forming a nimbus around her head. "Johari — is Norgay with you? Eriksson showed us the battle, but he didn't know where you were."

"I told Norgay where to find the minisub, so we should be able to get Eriksson's leg back to spec soon. It's lightly damaged, but nothing Emm and the bots can't handle."

Her glance roved over him. "Way to dodge my questions — what are you, some kind of an outlaw?"

"Nope," he said. "Not yet." He tried to make it sound like a joke.

"What happened to you?"

"Bunch of stuff. For now, I need your help —"

"Shut the frack up." Shawntelle's finger prodded his chest. "I'm not doing anything for you, with you, whatever, until I know what's going on. The bots went off without us, Johari. They heard your — ah, distress call, and they took off, leaving Zheng He behind, but it sure feels like he's on alert. They don't tell us a thing, even Norgay who's usually the chatty one, and now you show up on my private channel. What do you expect me to do?"

He owed her the truth, or something like it. "Fleet wants me for interrogation. I spent a long time with the enemy, and some of it was voluntary interaction."

"Shit, Johari, I shouldn't even be talking to you." She recoiled as if he had slapped her. "You're halfway to traitor already."

He started to follow her, the impulse so strong that it drew twinges from his injured body. His breathing hitched, and he scrambled to make sure his avatar didn't reveal any of his automatic responses. "That's why this had to be private."

Her narrowed gaze swept over him again. "You remember how this place works? Biofeedback? Yeah, Johari. Look around you."

The malachite veins keyed to his vital signs broke and spiraled. They rippled like waves against a rockfall.

"You're either hurt or terrified, Johari. You're hiding something, or at least, you're trying to. Whatever drugs you took are starting to work, but I've already seen it." She planted her fists on her hips, lips compressed as if she might be about to cry. "Go on, Johari. Keep lying." The naked betrayal on her face hurt him in turn.

For a moment, he bowed his head, letting it rest against his palm.

"We're a team, Johari," she continued more gently — more gentle than he had known she could be, "You're the one who's always saying that — a frackin' orchestra, isn't that your metaphor? I know I'm a shitty team-mate, but don't you start following my lead. You're what the rest of us are trying to live up to."

The words stunned him, and he drew himself up to face her. "You're not a shitty team-mate, Shawntelle. You're here now, aren't you?"

"Convince me to stay."

He nodded. "Okay, give me a minute." He paused his VR presence and slipped off the sleep mask, then found the generator's landing drone, and flicked it on, aiming the camera toward himself, joining its transmission to his own. Pulling the mask down, he slid back in.

Inside the glittering geode, Johari froze. Tolui, Emm, and Maya floated there as well. Shawntelle stood behind them, her arms now folded, her sharp eyes aimed at the ground.

"This is meant to be private, Shawntelle. What are they all doing here?"

"What's going on with you is too big to hide. If I'm a part of this team, I'm in it all the way, just like you. If our whole damn world is falling to pieces, we all need to know."

"Jesus, Man, you look like you took a deep dive into an asteroid belt," Tolui muttered. Johari followed his stare. Against the geometric precision of the background, a clear patch showed a view of Johari lying on the chimney cap, the sleep mask over his eyes. Flecks of blood rimmed his nostrils, and a long scrape marred his cheek. His mouth gaped a little to breathe, and every breath caught short. His normally warm brown skin looked gray and wrong, aside from the dozens of scrapes and bruises, and that was before noting the sealed gash down his arm or the full cast on his leg.

"Asteroids might've been easier."

"Johari!" Maya pounced on him, wrapping him in her arms, and he returned the embrace. After a moment, Emm crossed nearer, and placed their hand on his shoulder.

"You are still alive, and that is something," they told him.

"So far." His throat tightened. "Listen. I need your help. I came to ask Shawntelle for a favor." She stared back, chin lifted and eyes damp.

"You took me to task for going EVA, Johari, and you're not even wearing a suit anymore. What kind of microbes are you carrying?" Tolui expanded the screen. Maya glanced up at the zoom of his injuries, and shuddered, burrowing closer into his chest. "And what's that?" Tolui indicated a large, dark area at the side of the screen.

The form shuddered even as he waved toward it, and they all flinched, then Tolui lunged forward as if he could leap into the video. "It's alive. Oh, wow, that's one of those creatures, the ones that hang out with the dragons! Is it some kind of symbiotic relationship? What do you know about these things?" He produced a tablet and started making notes, glancing from the bit of Savior he could see back to the screen in his hand. "Can you re-focus the camera so I can see more of it?"

Johari's friends released him. "Before this goes any further, you need to know something. Fleet's worried that I've been compromised by the enemy, and that's before they question what happened to my suit. I bought a little time with Norgay, but when he gets Armstrong up and running, I'll have my Fleet interrogation, and it's not likely to go well."

Shawntelle gave a hard laugh. She pointed at the screen. "You applied bandages to an alien. That's the frackin' definition of aid-and-comfort. If they think you're sympathetic to an enemy of Fleet, you're gonna be protein bars."

"I hope they choke on me. You all know the oath we took and all those Founder ideals about intelligent life and cooperation? They downgraded intelligence as a criteria against settlement. It doesn't matter anymore if the resident population has an evolving civilization. The only thing that matters is whether they can fight back. We're not explorers any more. We're the vanguard for an army."

21

"THAT'S GOING A LITTLE FAR, don't you think?" Tolui said. "We need a colony, Fleet does, anyway, so they don't have to live in the Ring any more. So they don't have to allocate who gets to have children, and send kids like us out here to — Humanity didn't evolve to live in a box."

Tolui, who was about to graduate and win one of those coveted allocations himself, had finally come to a place with biology worth studying. Johari replied, "And you think we should settle, regardless of how we do it? We should just destroy the local ecosystems because we need their resources?"

"There could be a middle way."

"Unless they're dangerous." Maya gestured toward Johari's battered face on the screen. "Like, maybe it's better for them to be contained."

"We need to at least talk to the natives before we open the planet for colonization. When we invade their home and endanger their young —" he aimed a look at Tolui, who remained absorbed by what he saw on the screen — "they have a right to fight back. Imagine you're enjoying a fine afternoon, and suddenly some creature you can't even see starts messing with your nest. And they have language, art, ritual behavior — this amazing construction from bones and eggshell. They're not just a protein source, they're a nation."

That brought Tolui's head around. "A nation?" He gestured toward the salamander. "They're some kind of amphibious reptiles. That's cool, but that's not people."

Johari took a deep breath. "You have African ancestry, so does Shawntelle. We all do to some degree or another. When Europeans first landed in Africa, they didn't think Africans were people either. The Founders knew that whoever we met wouldn't resemble us or live like us. They don't think like us or talk like us; it doesn't mean they're not people."

"The same happened when Europeans conquered America and killed my people," Emm said.

"Cut the rhetoric, Johari," Tolui said. "You'd condemn humanity to drift in space for another hundred years for a bunch of glorified frogs."

Every time he spoke, it hurt: their shared mission, their years together, fractured by an impassable divide. "You're the biologist, you should know what separates people from animals."

"You're claiming they communicate — prairie dogs did that." As Tolui spoke, Shawntelle frowned, then looked up and left, some kind of trigger. An image of a prairie dog town full of cheeping rodents appeared. "Now you say they make constructions of found objects. So did the African Bower Bird." A new image, showing a display of blue litter in front of an elaborate nest. "Humpback whales could sing, and wolves hunted in packs — nothing you've said proves culture! Where's their architecture? Their tools — their science?"

"I don't know," Johari fired back. "I need you to help me prove it —" He looked to Shawntelle. "Or disprove it."

He focused on Tolui. "Come on, man, you've got to be curious. You think I'm biased because of all my time studying civilization, hoping to find one. Alright, yes, I want this. How about you? Up until now, all of your studies, every hour you've spent on animal behavior, has been theoretical. Now we've got these creatures: living, breathing, interacting. You've got to be curious."

He spread his hands. "Tolui, you want the colony, I get that — we all do, but at what cost? Do you really want to abandon the best chance you've ever had to study complex non-human systems?" He stepped toward his friend. "If you want what I'm saying to be wrong, then let's get the evidence. That's science. I make a hypothesis, we gather data. Maybe I'm wrong. Let's find out. Together." Johari extended his hand.

Tolui used to be one of Johari's anchors. An anchor prevented drift. By holding you down. He traced Johari's face, down to his hand, back again. "You realize what you're saying. If these things are just animals, they're not an enemy. And you're not a traitor. It's not just about me, what I want, or even what Fleet needs. If you're right, Johari, it's your life on the line."

His hand drew back, just a little. His blood cooled, the malachite swirl around him turning in knots. If they were animals, Fleet would kill them. And if they weren't, Fleet would kill him. What price to save a nation? He felt again the hum of Fracture's answer. One way or the other, he might never know what she had said.

Johari's head rose and he lifted his hand, open and unshaking. "If they are a people, then they deserve our respect. Everything we do here has consequences."

Tolui winced, a micro-expression gone as soon as Johari saw it. He put out his hand and they shook, once, with the brief formality of the introduction at the start of a duel.

"Where do we begin?" Shawntelle asked.

Johari pointed toward Savior, up on the screen. "I started trying to communicate with this one. I call it 'Savior' —" Maya opened her mouth, the question already furrowing her brow, but he shook his head, and she kept silent. "They have at least four modes of communication: vocalizations, gesture and posture, bioluminescence, and the electrical impulses that produce those lights. From what I've seen, the last two are primary."

"That makes sense." Tolui brought up his wire-frame reference dragon, which had gotten a lot more detailed in the last day, especially the area of the wingtip. "The part I dissected had all kinds of electro-receptors right at the end. A lot of Earth-based animals had receptors like that. Carrier filaments run throughout, like some kind of nerve/tendon hybrid that lights up when they make their displays. I'd love to know if the frills are the same kind of fibers. I'll ask Eriksson to bring me a whole one."

"In the video, leviathans devoured the corpses as soon as they hit the water," said Emm.

"The living, too, when they can get them," said Johari. Leviathan. He should've thought of that name. "Dragons can generate enough of a shock to startle a leviathan into backing off."

"Electroreceptors explains a lot." Like how Johari's implant had been able to broadcast to them while he was clinging to a dragon's back.

"More than you know. You wanted me to figure out the VR interference?" Shawntelle moved through the couch, dissipating it with her stride. "It's the dragons. Something happens when they're close enough to our generators. Or the bots, or the comms. I don't think they do it on purpose. If they're transmitting and receiving these pulses, that would account for the patterns I'm seeing."

"I think they could do it on purpose."

Shawntelle performed an exaggerated turn to face him, and her own hair sent out little bolts of lightning. "Seriously."

"Then they're definitely an enemy," Emm observed.

"I tried two different approaches to communications. With Savior, I played back video of an earlier interaction, one that seemed relatively simple."

"How many times and on what level have you interacted with these creatures?" Emm, with a question straight from the Fleet script. Just doing their job, observing his mental states.

Johari plowed ahead. "There's a leviathan guarding Armstrong, and the sub got into trouble. When I parked the sub, I met Savior and a few others. I think they're like a ... a larval form isn't the right word. They're clearly related to the dragons, but I don't think they're juveniles."

Tolui stood inside his wire-frame dragon. "Is Armstrong okay? He shouldn't have to die because I got over-excited."

For a moment, Johari didn't feel very sympathetic. If the bots were people, so were the dragons; did Tolui not see that, or was he willfully ignoring it? "I succeeded in finding his nuke pack, though I wasn't able to retrieve it. Once he's repaired, Tolui, he'll be fine. Norgay knows where they are; he'll take care of it." A hint of softness returned to Tolui's face.

"Then he'll go back and take care of you, right, Johari?" Maya asked in a small voice. "I don't think the medipak is enough."

Shawntelle tilted her head, and their eyes met. She mouthed, *"Take care of you."* Johari nodded. The words had more than one meaning, but he didn't like to think about the other one.

Tolui said, "You were telling us how you communicated."

"I started working on the word for 'eat' because I had some bars, and I was starving. 'Eat' is an easy word to learn because it has clear physical references, though you have to make sure you're not naming the food substance, or your hand, or whatever. I'll need to do more work to disambiguate."

"Great — now you can tell them to eat you," Shawntelle said. "What was the part you isolated from the video?"

"Something like gratitude." He put his hands up to forestall her questions. "I met another dragon, a blind one, so I rigged the electrical pattern of the lights to pass along my skin and I played that for her."

"Her?" Shawntelle's eyebrows rose.

"The blind dragon lays eggs. Her. Okay?"

Emm's avatar began to grow. It grew around them, stretching through the space until the others broke off and stared up at them. In an instant, Emm resumed their normal contours. "Argument serves nothing. We need to find the facts, regardless of what we decide to do with this knowledge."

"So you had to touch it." Tolui's eyes grew large. "What was that like?"

Johari smiled faintly. "Her skin is rough, but supple, not like the hardness of scales. And she has tiny divots all over her face, mostly on her chin, which I figured are the receptors?"

"Like a platypus or a dolphin — they're for finding prey when you can't see."

"So the dragons repurposed them for communication."

"Says you."

"She answered me. My skin tingled and warmed up, but I'm not sensitive enough to understand it. That's —" he faced Shawntelle — "where you come in."

Her dark gaze tracked over him, flicked to the video of his injuries, then back to his face. "You need a system for recording not only the three-D visual spectrum these things are outputting, but also the electrical energy underlying it, which may not always correlate to the visual. Then you want an array for yourself, so you can echo what you see and feel. Got it so far?" She was interested in the technical problem, if not in the moral dilemma.

Her interest buoyed him. "That's what I need."

"How the hell're you gonna apply it? You'd have to be connected to the monsters for any of this to work. You'd have to sync your implant to a monster. No frackin' way." The sarcastic tone returned, but without the heat, as if she were thinking through the problem.

"If we get the right kind of information, we may be able to divert Fleet's justice." Emm stepped nearer. "I can develop the implant coding and the uplink. As for being in contact, it seems that the one you call Savior may be available for a talk. If need be, we can present it as a prisoner interrogation."

The term revolted him — but it just might save his life. "Right."

"Leaving me the analysis and translation," Shawntelle said.

Johari replied, "If you can handle it."

She set one hand on her hip. "Oh, I can handle lots of things. Where's the groundwork? Show me what you've already done."

"The best vid went down when I lost my helmet. I can trigger an upload with my implant data. It'll only be partial — the stuff I saved, whatever happened since the last write-over."

Shawntelle's lips parted, then she pressed them shut. Finally, she said, "Yeah, okay. Tolui can get me everything he's got. Maybe have a beta version in a few hours, if we work non-stop."

"I'm helping!" Maya announced. "I'll do anything, you just say what you need."

Shawntelle tossed back her head and laughed. "What we need is a plausible excuse not to let the bots in for a while."

Maya frowned furiously, already working.

Johari hugged her shoulders. "Thanks, everyone. Guess I'm the one without a task."

"Sleep, you idiot." Shawntelle waved at the screen. "You think you're any good to anyone like this? Whatever pain meds you grabbed, get something stronger. That is if you don't think your monster-buddy will wake up and have a bite. I'll keep an eye on the video monitor to make sure you're okay."

"Right."

"But before you konk out, give me your access code for the vids, so we can get this party started."

"For the record?" Emm stood to center. "We are undertaking this action to further our knowledge of the planet Tranquility and the ecosystems that occupy it. This is no guarantee of our position, either individually, or collectively, about the future of colonization." Shawntelle nodded reluctantly, and Maya with emphasis.

"That's right. Zheng He couldn't have said it better. We burst Johari's delusion and clear him of Fleet suspicion in one go." Tolui slapped his hands together and his dragon model disappeared. "I want to head to my lab and pull together some ideas."

"Everybody get out of here. I'll send a ping when I need your contributions."

Emm vanished in an instant, and Tolui right after. Maya made her way to the door, chin resolutely lifted, clearly trying hard not to look back. Before he could vanish, Shawntelle materialized at Johari's side, catching his elbow. "Wait." She slid her hand to the crook of his arm, drawing him closer, holding him gently. They stood alone in her cold, hard world, with the video of him hovering in space. "Jo. You're a mess."

The virtual dog passed by the door, taking no notice of them. "Got it."

"Look at your breathing."

"I'd rather not. You want something?"

She released him, but kept her hand lightly on his arm. "Your implant. You think it only saves what you trigger, and wipes every hour with new data from the top."

"Um, yeah." He glanced back at her.

"Who told you that?" She stared at him, forcing him to meet her eyes.

"Norgay." Who was his everything. And also, it turned out, fully weaponized. Which made perfect sense, except that it had been a complete surprise.

"Just like Eriksson told me. Bummer for us, it's not true. These implants have enough memory for a lifetime or more, and the best part is, when they're implanted early, we just get used to it, storing and retrieving our visual memories from a piece of hardware. Everything's in there. It doesn't have access to your thoughts or anything, but any other recorded analytics will be included, like biometrics, location data, all of that. I can access the whole record of your interaction with these things."

He eyed her warily. "As long as you're not uploading to Fleet, go ahead and do it."

She shook her head. "Memories aren't indexed. You can set a cut-off date, but if you've accessed older information recently, that all gets linked. It's not like I can plug in a search function and go straight to the spot. It'll be like rifling through your whole life, anything connected to now. Once I download the files, I can set up a routine to scan for the dragons. But unless you haven't been thinking about anything except dragons for the last twenty-four hours, I can't guarantee I won't see other stuff."

"By accident," he prompted.

She gave him a little shove. "Of course — you think I want to get involved in your head?"

"Honestly, Shawntelle, half the time I don't know what you want. I get the feeling you don't actually want us to find a colony. You're always railing on about worm stuff any time we talk about finding a home."

Her gaze slid toward the creamy waves of agate in the floor. "We have a home, Johari, but it's out there." The stone went translucent to reveal the pinpricks and clouds of a million stars, as seen through the glimmer of a bot's viewing window. "Only place we've ever known."

"I was born on a planet, not that I remember much of it." He managed a smile. "Maybe you'll see that during your search."

"I don't know where I was born. A janitor found me wandering the manufacturing band. I knew my name, but nothing else." Her hand turned idly in the air, and the stars shifted into the habitation ring, into Fleet comm's ship, into a landing shuttle, into an inflatable hab. All of the places people lived. "That's what I was trying to find, when I learned the truth about the implants." Her off-hand brushed up along the back of her neck.

"What did you find?" he asked softly.

"Nothing at all." She tipped her head, her face lit with that otherworldly glow. "The implant's grown in, like it was there since I was one, same as you. From then 'til I was six years old, Johari, I've got no memories at all." She lifted her hand and made a gesture as if she had plucked something and flung it away to vanish in the void around them.

22

A SLIMY SENSATION CREPT UP HIS ARM. Johari shook it, then snapped out of VR, jerking upright and instantly regretting it as pain flared from his injuries.

A shelled-and-squishy thing the size of his head lay nearby, its soft underbelly flexing, spewing some kind of liquid. The liquid oozed to a halt, and it pushed itself upright with its fleshy tail or foot or whatever. On top, its shell had segments like an arthropod. Johari's forearm glimmered with traces of the same liquid around his injury and he recoiled, wiping it off on what remained of his tunic. The arthrosnail crept toward him and Johari yelped, kicking it away until it curled up near the edge of the chimney.

Savior sprawled nearby, its skin creeping with the same creatures.

"Get off him! Get off." Johari scrambled to his feet and hobbled toward the salamander. The things worked over Savior's wounds, extruding that same thick substance. The bandages he had applied lay in tatters on the chimney cap. He grabbed one of the arthrosnails and tried to pry it off. An unfamiliar salamander reared up on the other side of Savior's body. It waved back and forth, frills wildly flashing. It, too, held an arthrosnail in its claws.

Startled, Johari let go of the one he was tugging on, and tried to catch his breath, his hand rising to his chest as he struggled.

The swaying salamander grew still. It leaned over Savior, tapping the disturbed arthrosnail with one foreclaw, then carefully placed the creature it was carrying on one of the smaller cuts.

Savior lay still. Its blood flows had stopped, and the creature's breathing and eye movements evened out. As liquid seeped into the valleys and around the ridges of the salamander's skin, then thickened, the arthrosnail sealed Savior's wounds more adequately than the bandages had.

"Thanks, Doc," he told the new salamander, wishing he could play back his recording of gratitude. Doc stared at him with predator eyes. A darker band of skin marked its brow ridges — all six of them. Lucky he'd caught it tending Savior, or he might have called it "bandit" instead.

After a moment, Doc scuttled around Savior's body to collect the bug Johari had kicked aside. It rolled the creature around between its hands, and held it against its chin, then tucked it close against its side. The arthrosnail uncurled and clung there. With another glance back at Johari, Doc scrambled over the edge of the chimney. The sound of its claws diminished and ended in the soft splash of a cautious water entry.

Well. Savior's friend? Relation? Took care of it. Good. Now if only his own breathing would level out. He'd almost asked for an evacuation sled, like the one they placed Tolui inside of. The steady flow of oxygen and the specialized medical sensors would have helped a lot, but the sled would confine him, and give him no supplies to share with Savior. Norgay probably knew what Johari had been thinking because he didn't even offer the sled as an alternative. Norgay, the warrior, the carrier of secrets in more ways than one.

Edges of anger surfaced, but Johari couldn't deal with that right now. He dug out an oxygen mask and regulator from the kit. He took a few deeper breaths from the oxygen-enriched mask. His chest still ached, but already his vision grew more precise and the pain receded.

He set his implant to upload to a secure area of Shawntelle's storage, where she assured him nobody would see his memories but her. Weird, to be trusting her, of all people: not Maya, his 'little sister', nor his friends Tolui and Emm. Shawntelle, who kept to herself except when she was making wisecracks. He thought of what she had revealed, how she had been found. Yeah, that would make a kid build some armor, but it seemed like this adventure was helping her open up, her skills not only discovered, but vital to the success of their mission. They were a team; at least, they were meant to be. Damn, it felt good to act like it. They didn't agree on what to do next, but they moved forward together, every instrument performing its role, and together, a symphony.

Finally, Johari did as Shawntelle ordered. He set the medibot to calculate the dosage for a four-hour nap. He stuck a rolled-up blanket under his head, draped another over his body and went straight out.

His skin buzzed gently, and Johari's eyes snapped open. According to the chronometer, he'd been out for five hours, seventeen minutes. Longer than the meds should've lasted. Not long enough for his body. Darkness hovered over him, but he saw light in his peripheral vision, as if the sun rose to either side simultaneously. It had been eclipsed by something large, dark, and faintly humming.

He lay very still, letting his eyes adjust. A salamander's head hovered over his own. The light he saw changed color in bits and flashed, weakly. It moved its head slowly toward the equipment, and away again. What was it doing?

Of course! It sensed the output of everything around him: the oxygen regulator, the readouts of his vital signs, the working of the evaporator and the generator. He boosted the sensitivity of his implant and the buzzing on his skin took shape as a series of pulses and steadier signals. Some of these correlated with changes in light, others appeared unrelated. Not clear enough for him to read or record, but a pattern at the very least. Savior was talking to his medical equipment.

Johari chuckled.

Savior reared back its head, then wriggled to one side, to see him more directly. It tilted its head, the frills on one side glimmering faintly. They still drooped like plants in need of watering.

Johari sat up slowly and Savior retreated. It moved slowly as well, favoring its right foreleg where the bullet wounds concentrated. The arthrosnail extrusion remained in place, but its creators had gone. Johari reached up and slipped off the oxygen mask, rubbing his face where it had dug into his skin.

"I think it was talking to you, in your sleep." Tolui's voice murmured from the generator. "I have video."

Savior's head panned in that direction.

"I took over monitoring from Shawntelle," Tolui said. "And, y'know, cataloging dragon and salamander light, movement, and electrical pulse patterns. We studied some earth-analogs for the type of receptors, then she got to work on a coding structure while I started analyzing vid clips from our encounters so far, and some stuff she sent me from your logs. I cannot believe you got to fly on one! You must've been scared shitless."

Savior crept in a half-circle, examining the equipment from both sides while Tolui spoke.

Johari worked his fingers through his salt-crusted hair. "That describes most of my day, aside from some moments that I don't even have words for."

The sensation of Fracture's reply, the enormity of her presence, the moment he knew that Savior understood him, not to mention the revelation of that place — the bone archive. After Fury launched its sonic attacks and Savior drove it away, he had taken the dragon's behavior as aggressive in the extreme. In point of fact, he really had no idea what any of them wanted or why they did what they did.

Eat, drink, excrete, sleep, have sex. Presumably, humans and dragons had those things in common. Dream, plan, despair, imagine, admire — did they have those, too? Savior rose over the medipak, many eyes glinting in its rough, angular face. Savior ran a claw along the edges of the kit. Johari needed to watch out for the anthropologist's curse, that the first individual interested in communicating was likely to be an outcast or some other unusual character, rather than a typical member of the tribe.

"Another one of them showed up and peeled off all those snail things —"

"Arthrosnails."

"Yeah — good name. It stuck them all over itself and left again, after making lights with Savior for a while."

"They're employing other species for their own purposes. Doesn't that suggest a level of forethought and interaction?"

Tolui growled, "Some ant species cultivated other insects for defensive purposes."

"Or they might be attracted to injuries, and they just taste good for dinner," Emm said.

"Okay, enough chatter," Shawntelle cut in. "We have a beta version. Probably gonna get you killed the minute you fire it up, but you're halfway an outlaw. Least this way, we won't have to eat you."

"My protein's as good as anyone else's! How do I download?"

"Not so fast. Emm's developed an integration structure for the implant to carry my program, so you need to mod that sucker, and Tolui made you a puppet."

"I can't receive anything here, unless you have a delivery drone."

"It's a virtual puppet," Tolui explained, "but you'll need a projector or something, some way for the salamander to see it."

"Unless you can improvise a frill array out of cotton swabs and suturing needles," Shawntelle added. "Or we jump straight to plan B and forget the puppet show."

The casual dismissal in Shawntelle's tone alerted him. "What's plan B?"

"Create an interface on the other end and go entirely virtual."

"The other end. You mean Savior? Can't I just touch it, the way I did with Fracture?"

"That was your lady-friend, Fracture? Great naming convention, Johari. You can touch it, but it can't touch you, or at least, it can't respond except on its own terms."

Tolui said, "Language acquisition will be much faster if the salamander has the chance to get our language. If this is an interrogation, you'll need clear communications. Pretty sure it's not going to speak English with that vocal anatomy, but then you'd be screwing with local biology, and we don't even understand their brains enough to know what that would mean."

Emm whistled softly to get the conversation back on track. "There's an implant recovery kit in the medipak. I need you to find it."

Savior's rapt gaze made him feel self-conscious as he rummaged through the supplies.

"Plan B starts there, too, and the best part is, it encourages sharing! You like that, right?" Shawntelle said.

Johari pulled out an electrostatic-guarded case covered with caution signs. *"Only open in case of emergency. For significant implant reconstruction only. Inspect vials prior to use, within a cleanroom environment. In case of damage, destroy the damaged vial immediately using a non-dispersal method and commence accidental swarm release protocols. For use with new crewmembers, please see section eight, paragraph two."*

The vials. "Wait a minute, Shawntelle — you want me to infect an alien lifeform with a nanite swarm?"

"That's why it's plan B, Johari. In this case, the 'b' stands for 'bad idea.'" Tolui sounded pretty terse. "We're trying to study them — we don't need to get that close. And it would clearly violate protocols about the exposure of our technology. Not that you care."

Savior settled onto the chimney cap with a slight deflation, its face not far away.

"We need to speed this up. Johari doesn't have much time until Norgay returns, then, he's toast," Shawntelle said.

The box rested heavily in his hand, the warnings even heavier on his mind. "Thanks for the reminder." He glanced at Savior. "I think we've done enough damage already."

"I'm trying to save your life, Johari," Shawntelle said, a little sharply. "You've got the kit, Emm'll talk you through it."

Shawntelle's and Tolui's voices murmured in the background as Emm took the lead. "The vials have an auto-injector on the end. Inject as close to your implant site as possible. I can use the command channel to format the swarm. Simple. If not exactly easy." A smile glimmered in their voice.

"Got it." Johari popped the case open on top of the evaporator. Inside, three vials nestled into gray foam. The opaque vials revealed nothing but more caution labels.

"You'll feel strange while it reconfigures. You may get flashbacks or have difficulty seeing."

"Awesome. I need to feel weirder than I already do."

"In that case, fire away."

He pulled off the yellow cap, then steadied the autoinjector at the back of his neck and gave it a squeeze. A sting of pain followed, then a cold rush through his body, as if he were flying. Johari collapsed to the deck and opened his eyes to infinity.

23

FRAGMENTS OF WORLDS swirled around him, accompanied by eddies of dissociated data. Figures, facts, charts and graphs flowed around and through him. BP 96 over 60 and falling — the Mongols under Genghis Khan and his immediate heirs held the world's largest contiguous land empire — Mars colony Theta-zon rebelled against corporate control in 2118 — Push here to open — the cascading pink, green and blue of an Impressionist painting overwhelmed his vision.

The taste of something sweet filled his mouth, a juicy, red substance, slightly grainy, tinged with wonder and delight. Watermelon. When in the years of dwelling in Norgay's chest cavity had he ever tasted watermelon? Fruit of any kind? Still life paintings of fruit bowls arose and faded, succeeded by portraits of people formed out of fruits and vegetables. Another artist: Arcimboldo, the lush, round forms spilling into chins and cheeks, peaches, bananas, things he had no name for. Things he had never seen outside of paintings.

Johari reached for the watermelon. The fragment of memory expanded around him. The sensation of eating, his small hands gripping something hard, damp, and green. The rind. A woman grinning down at him, laughing.

"Watermelon, Jo-jo. It's called watermelon. It's the first one from the new greenhouse." Dark, shining eyes, a river of black hair. Johari willed himself to reach for her, but he could not.

"Are you sure it's safe?" A man's voice, his face less distinct as he walked past, carrying something, pausing just long enough. Dark curls, tightly cut, a sharp beard. He reminded Johari a little of Tolui. The memory slid sideways, and a younger Tolui emerged, a worldly-wise ten-year old at the control panel, showing Johari — no! Just as Shawntelle had said, every time he thought of something, his implant pulled up fresh associations. Johari rejected the new memory. His dad — he caught a glimpse of his parents, no way was he letting that go!

He reached for his father, the watermelon rind in his hand. A sound overhead, surrounding him, scaring him. Like a rocket booster?

"Qassim, we've tested everything about this place."

"Everything except the rain. This planet has never had rain before — it's too soon to be shooting hydro-stimulants into the atmosphere."

"We've been here five years, besides Norgay reviewed our conclusions."

"The bots aren't always —"

"Let's don't have this fight again." His mother turned back to … a table, inside a habitat, but larger than any hab he'd ever seen. Large as the model house in the Realm. The virtual dog bounded toward him down the hall, the wall panel flashed an urgent interrupt from Fleet. Maya's silhouette blocked part of his view. Not a memory, an access point to the Realm.

Johari snapped his connection, sending him back — where? Or when.

Shawntelle's face, lit by a weird purple glow. His own voice. *"Phantoms killed my parents."* She had never known hers. Fleet used orphans, so they wouldn't be missed.

Norgay chose him. After his mother. After the phantoms. The bots weren't always *what?*

Johari's head throbbed. He tore through a barrier of scrolling formulas, the updating algorithms of the implant itself. Rain. "It's just water, Jo-jo, like in the watermelon. We made it rain with technology and chemistry. Look, it's beautiful!"

Thunder, and rain. It streamed down the window of his parents' habitat, blurring the green-gray world outside. What was its name? Tranquility? No. A dragon's face carved in light rose into his vision, and Johari rejected it, clinging to the memory. "More, Mommy! Eat more!" He brandished the rind at her. "Eat, eat!"

Her grin widened, and she reached for a new slice. Her hand wafted toward him, sailing the watermelon through the oceans of memory. Was he losing it again? The memory shredded at the edges, pale smoke rippling. His mother's expression changed, her eyes widening, her grin becoming a grimace.

"Get to the safe room! Jo-jo — how fast can you run?" She waved the watermelon at him.

"Fast and fast!" Johari's view bounced away from her as he ran through the habitat. The whole place bounced and trembled.

"Noloni — what is — oh, my God."

"It's some kind of chemical cascade; the soil is reactive. Qassim, go —"

"You think the safe room is going to stop this? Call the damn robot!"

Walls cracked and shifted, and Johari dodged falling debris. A white shaft of crystal thrust up through the floor, metastasizing with the rush of water, and he tumbled. Falling knocked the fun right out of him. He screamed. A familiar buzz-whine cut his hearing. Norgay's alert signal, but not issued by Johari, not that day.

The safe room door stood open before him. He stumbled and slid, and stopped short. "Daddy!" His little arms flailed.

The bucking ground tossed him over. Like a mushroom on a crystal stalk, the safe room tore upward, then tumbled away, ripping half the roof off the house. Johari lay there, screaming, as a giant hand descended from the sky — through the water — through the wall — taking up his battered body — scooping him into its palm.

"Noloni Colossus Norgay!" the voice echoed through him, through the metal hand that held him safe. "Qassim, report location!"

Screaming, howling, silence. Panting, then coughing, Johari let go the memory. It swept away from him like his home, like his parents, broken by crystal spires that gleamed still in the heart of that ruined place.

Streaks of colored lightning cut his vision. The streams of data ebbed away, but the crashing sound continued. Johari blinked himself back to reality. The streaks of light hovered around his head, overlaid on a view of the chimney cap.

Savior's body thrashed and coiled, its limbs scrabbling against the shell covering, then into the sky as it rolled. The chimney cap bounced and shuddered with every wild movement. The salamander's seizure slammed it from side to side, the medipak already scattered. Oh, shit — the nanites! Johari pulled himself toward the evaporator where he'd left the other vials. The lid of the case lay on the ground, the hinges broken. Gouges raked the plastic. A few bits of foam tumbled nearby, but the vials were gone, yellow caps and all.

"Johari! Get out of there! Climb down!" Shawntelle's voice, shrill in a new and frightening way.

"He's in transition, idiot, he still can't hear you!" Tolui. "There's nothing we can do for him from here — for either of them. Isn't this what you wanted? This was your damn idea, I told you the biology wasn't compatible!"

"Both of you need to calm down."

The platform jolted underneath him as if he were on a sinking ship. Savior thrashed as if it were dying. Wait a minute: Tolui said this was Shawntelle's idea. This — that Savior be injected with the nanites, which would then configure its brain to communicate with Johari's. Bile stung his throat and his stomach cramped. They had to stop it, to stop hurting things.

"Emm," he swallowed and called out, "Emm, I can hear you."

Johari scanned around him for the source of their frantic voices, and spotted the medibot with its onboard camera. It lay beneath the generator, perilously close to the edge. He pushed to his feet and hobbled over. Savior's tail slapped his legs out from under him and he rolled, his cast knocking hard against shell, then stone. Johari spread himself against the roof to slow his skid and maybe stop the fall.

The translucent dragon's head appeared again, as a mask around his face. Tolui's virtual puppet, laughing at him as he tried not to die. His fingers slid over the smooth shell, and caught an edge. His feet dangled in the air, his left leg held out straight by the cast. Its sensors whined in protest of this rough treatment. He coughed hard, his chest tightening.

"Johari!" Three voices, in various states of horror. From that angle, they couldn't see him, only hear his own shouts and coughing.

He shook his head, still wracked by coughing. The edge of the shell grooved into his fingers as he clung to it and tried to haul himself back onto the platform. Finding the cracks between the shell layers, Johari crept toward the medibot and its camera. He freed one hand to pull it closer, staring into the lens. "Shawntelle. The program you uploaded, does it have electrical charge capability?"

"It's designed to transmit along your skin, but you'd have to get close enough to touch."

Tolui groaned, "You're not serious."

"If it keeps thrashing around like that, it's going to kill us both! Shawntelle, get me electric-only playback of the moment with Fracture, when she touched me with her chin."

"On it!" Shawntelle barked back.

"The medipak contains tranquilizers," Emm said. "The supply is likely to be enough to —"

"No. We've got to stop messing with them." He swiveled the camera away toward Savior where it lay still for a moment, chest heaving, then thrashed again, shaking its head violently.

"Savior got the nanites — how? Were you watching?"

"For G — you gave them to it, Johari." Tolui's voice cracked. "You were hallucinating, I think. You picked up the box — it was like you couldn't even hear us — and you held it up. The puppet activated, and you said something. The virtual frill operated. Savior snatched the box out of your hands and chomped down on it. It shouldn't have been anywhere near that stuff — Fleet is gonna be furious."

Johari thought he knew two words in their language. When he said one of them, the program he hadn't meant to trigger translated. Why couldn't it have been gratitude? Instead, it was "eat."

"Sorry. I'm sorry." He wished he knew the word for that.

"Jo — I've got it!" Shawntelle said. "I used your modulator as part of the program, that thing where you played back the electro-frequencies, and ran through the encounter with Fracture. If you're going, now's the time." Shawntelle came through loud and clear, while Tolui broke up under pressure. Thank god he had someone he could count on.

He righted the camera as best he could then waited for the next lull in Savior's thrashing.

"This is nuts," Tolui muttered.

When the floor beneath him stopped tremoring, Johari scrambled up and sprinted across. He dodged Savior's restless tail and dropped beside the salamander's body.

Tolui sucked in a breath, and came back on line. "Go for the chin. If these electro-receptors developed to seek prey in murky water, the most sensitive receptors will be there."

Three sets of giant eyes rolled and glared at Johari. He stroked his hand along the salamander's jaw, noticing the divots that marked its receptors. "How do I trigger it?"

"Gestures. Close a fist. We picked gesture because the dragons don't seem to use that."

When he closed his fist, his skin buzzed, arm hairs standing on end along his dark skin.

Savior twitched away with a low growl, and Johari stiffened, bracing for the bite that would end his life. Savior's head sank down again toward him. Finally, its chin touched his hand. Its eyes closed in sequence: predator, amphibian, prey.

For a moment, it lay there. A tremor passed along its body. The prey eyes opened, showing a watery, golden reflection of Johari's face. Its damaged frill expressed a range of colors and patterns, then settled into a pulse of white that streamed along the tendrils while they shivered as if in a faint breeze. A quiet hum accompanied this, a hum that Johari could feel from the top of his head down to his toes.

Bathed in each other's presence, at last, they lay still.

24

24

"WE DON'T HAVE TIME to relax, Savior." Johari said aloud.

Savior gave a tremendous shake, its gaze rolled back. It turned its head, stretching to look behind it, the lowest eyes examining its own body.

"You can hear me, can't you." Johari's stomach growled, and the creature swiveled again, staring down at him. Its frill twinkled.

"Gimme a minute." He limped over to the remains of his camp and found a few protein bars, and a few fruit bars as well. The cheerful pink pattern of their wrappings reminded him of the watermelon and slowed his steps to return. He kicked over one of the blankets and prodded it into a mat he could sit on a little more comfortably. His leg throbbed, reminding him how long it had been since his last dose.

Savior examined his haul along with him. Its frills sparkled and rose, and a steady rhythm of electric pulses shivered along his skin. Johari flinched. "I can feel it talking without touching it. Is that supposed to happen?"

Again, Savior reacted to Johari's voice, twitching and searching.

"Here's the deal," Shawntelle said, her voice echoing within him. *"You've both had sensor upgrades, if it worked properly for the lizard. You have enhanced receptivity to electrical conduction. The implant will be recording and sorting the information you receive, and we'll be able to do some analysis behind the scenes. There's a readout here that documents visual/spatial and electrical activity. Full disclosure, it's also transmitting what you see and hear. I'm now the ultimate spy."*

"And that's why you're inside my head," he subvocalized.

"You got it. Because Savior's got enhanced hearing. Turns out their ears are pretty pathetic. The noises they emit seem to be almost involuntary — like cursing, or shouting 'ouch' when somebody steps on your foot."

"How do you know all this?"

Shawntelle hesitated, and Johari sensed a quiet flutter at the back of his head. Maybe he'd gotten more than one new sensory input. *"Tolui dissected one, didn't he?"*

She sighed. *"The thing was already dead."*

"And we don't know what rituals they have around death."

"Speaking of, you saw the video of the two dragons attacking each other, one of them clawing at the other one's face while they're falling? We thought it was a fight, but the loser was in your footage of that bone place. Too weird."

"Like I said, we don't know enough about their culture." Johari picked up one of the protein bars and bit into it, dispelling the memory of actual fruit with a chewy, meat-like substance probably made out of former crewmembers. He moved his wrist in the way that brought up the puppet. Aloud, he said, "Eat," and the puppet's frills portrayed the word.

Savior tipped its head, bringing each set of eyes to bear. It repeated the word with its frills, and he heard a voice, as if at his ear. "Eat."

"Tolui assigned it a neutral voice for now. Nice pitch, don't you think?"

"It should take up gospel singing."

Rearing back to its hindquarters, Savior scanned the skies. It spoke for a while, frills rippling and pulses moving, but Johari recognized none of the words.

"No, they're not coming back to kill you," Johari told it, adding a silent, "*I hope.*"

"*Not so far. Norgay reports he's got the pack, and located Armstrong, but the silt and chemical content of the water interferes with comms. He did bring back the mini-sub for Eriksson.*"

So the soldiers would soon be ready for another attack. Great. A series of clicks and a high-pitched whine intruded, but Savior hadn't done anything. "*What was that?*"

"*Fleet. Trying to get through to us. Not sure they're buying Maya's respiratory ailment excuse.*"

Savior walked to the edge of the chimney cap and peered down, then up again, still searching, but what for? A dark smudge on the horizon grew into the shape of a dragon. It swept over them, then dropped lightly onto the cap near Savior. Fury. Relief flowed over him.

Fury survived the attack! He tensed, expecting the dragon to shred him with those wicked teeth. It dropped a mass of something dead and oozing onto the cap.

Savior glanced at Johari and flashed "eat," then set-to, devouring its meal with great chomps of its jaws. Fury addressed it with wings lowered, frills active, and Savior answered, without stopping its meal. Convenient, that.

Johari ate a couple more bars as well. Self-consciously, he walked to the far side and relieved himself into an alien sea. A whoosh of air nearly knocked him in as Fury launched. He dropped painfully to his knees, coughing, and Fury swept past toward the surface of the ocean. Its tail lashed and it turned sharply, beating hard to rise again. It flowed upward, sun shining through the membranes of its wings, pierced and damaged, but flying nonetheless. Flaunting its life.

"Woo-hoo!" Johari cried after it, fists in the air. Still alive, all three of them. With its nose and foreclaw, Savior arranged the remaining fruit and protein bars into rows. Johari limped over, taking a detour for another dose of painkiller before he settled gratefully onto his blanket. Savior indicated the bars with its chin, as if it had set up a game.

Johari tapped his chest and said, "Johari," then he pointed toward Savior. "Savior." Savior's response to hearing his voice lessened, and it echoed him this time with a pattern of lights. It pushed its chin toward him.

"Johari." He tapped his chest, and used the puppet to mirror Savior's pattern of light.

Savior echoed, "Johari," its frills elevating and filling with dots and streaks, mostly in green.

Johari laughed. He had a name in a language no human being had ever spoken before. The world sparkled with possibilities.

Savior showed him the pattern for the name he had assigned it, as well, a pattern upswept on the frills, with a few pulses of electricity following. It seemed a lot more complicated than a name, and Shawntelle agreed they would have to break down some of the patterns as they learned more.

Numbers came next, using the food bars as counting sticks. One. A brief pulse, no frill. For any number between one and six, he got the same expression, a ripple of pulses. Above that number, variations on the pattern of pulses. For the middle ground, his team agreed on "several."

"Wait a minute." Johari subvoc'ed. *"'Several'. That pattern's in the word it used for me, isn't it?"*

"Ah ... yes. Same pattern of lights, but without the pulse," Shawntelle confirmed.

"Okay." He pushed aside most of the bars again, keeping four, then pointed to himself. "Johari?", and to the small pile.

Savior's tail snapped up and back down. It cast about, bringing its chin down low, and sending pulses. Finally, it pushed forward some crumbled rock from the chimney's edge. It scooped aside the bars and offered rocks instead, then dropped the other loose blanket over Johari's head.

He jerked at the sudden gloom and fought off the blanket with one arm.

Savior lit up with blue, and repeated, "Johari." It pulsed over the stones, then toward the blanket in his arm.

At the back of his head, Shawntelle said, *"I think it means, dumb as rocks."*

"So helpful. It's probably something like, 'several blankets'. But that means the numbers we got earlier weren't just numbers, they referred —"

"To food. Guess you're off the menu."

Over the next hours, they counted a number of objects and named a hundred more, plus a few adjectives like good, bad, large, small, broken. Verbs came next: Savior crawls, Johari walks, Fury flies — Fleet interrupts, with increasingly annoying strings of interference.

"What is Maya telling them?"

"Emm is working on it with her. We've gotta decide soon, Johari, that's the bottom line. Fleet needs to begin their deceleration process."

Savior roamed the chimney cap, piling to one side the items they had named. It didn't know what most of them were, but collectively called them "Johari's rocks". Aside from sky, clouds, ocean, that was the stuff they had available. It pinched the medibot in one hand and sprawled over the edge of the chimney.

"Savior, no!" Johari scrambled up, but Savior flashed, "Hears," which it seemed to use as some kind of assent. It lay with its forelegs over the side, turning the medibot carefully in its... Its hands.

"Please don't drop this," Tolui said from the speaker.

Savior hesitated, turning the small bot more slowly and testing it against its chin. It spoke to the device. Johari limped over and tried to sit next to it. His injured leg slipped, and he flailed, grabbing Savior's shoulder. The salamander sat very still, head cocked as Johari eased himself down. He flashed gratitude.

Savior nosed toward his leg, then its own side, and flashed a new word.

"Hurt?"

Savior repeated the word, in its own way, and Johari's, then resumed its study of the bot.

"I think it's confused because it can hear your voice coming out of the bot, but it can't see you," Johari explained.

"It could," Tolui said. "You could bring it into the Realm. The implant makes that possible."

Johari snorted. "That's crazy. Aside from enhancing its hearing, we have no idea what the nanites are doing in there."

"Their brain structures are different, but on a molecular level, they appear to have very similar functionality."

Savior stopped rotating the bot with it upside down, the camera facing its chin.

"They have wing buds — did you feel that when you leaned on it just now? Some of that vestigial musculature in the salamander supports manual dexterity. But the age of the specimen is close to a hundred years, based on bone growth rings."

As it listened, Savior's frills emitted a few pulses, repeating some of the words: wing, dragon, feel. It slid its claws along the surface of the bot, toying with the bot while listening in on the conversation. Far above, a dragon circled, caught in glimpses through the clouds from the steaming vents. Out to sea, along the line of chimneys, waves rippled and grew choppy. Someone was coming. Norgay. Had to be.

Savior stared in that direction. With a flutter of gold through its frills, it thrust aside the medibot, letting it tumble away on the roof. Above, the dragon swooped down and dropped beside them. Fury turned its many eyes on Johari. Fury and Savior spoke in a rapid flashing and buzzing, like a fireworks display.

The chop on the ocean picked up, and Johari received Norgay's incoming ping. Savior twitched at the same time. Johari clambered to his feet between the salamander and the dragon. He knew their terms for themselves, but not what the words meant. How was he supposed to convey what was happening with the handful of words they now shared?

"Johari's rock flies. Johari's large, large, large rock." He gestured in the direction of Norgay's approach. "Norgay," he said. He pointed toward Savior's injuries, and the pierced edge of Fury's wing. "Dragons broken. Norgay —"

As he spoke, Fury reared up on its hind legs and golden light slid through its wings.

"No! No, no. You can't hurt him." Words that meant nothing to them. What did they mean to Johari — that they would be unable to hurt Norgay, or that they shouldn't, that he didn't want them to? Images of the destruction at the bone display flashed before his eyes. Dragons shattered by gunfire, wings torn, blood in the pools. They had every right. Johari's stomach churned. Norgay had been his home, his partner, his companion for all of his life. And he had never known the truth about the bot.

Fury's wings unfurled across the cap, but it did not launch. Rather, it held the posture, wings wide and body slightly hunched over Savior. Gray-green wings streaked as if lightning ran through a stormy sky. It loomed over him, and he wanted to sink back down to his knees, to see if he knew how to plead for mercy. His new senses buzzed, a sound-sensation so strong it made his teeth ache.

"Johari — what's happening?" Shawntelle's voice inside his head. *"We lost video and I'm seeing some crazy readings from your implant."*

Orange-brown clouds roiled overhead. Darker lines cut in and vanished again into the murk, small, sharp glimpses of something moving beyond. Dragon wings. Dozens, or more.

"Something's up there — all around us. Norgay's coming and they know it." He swung about to face the ocean, clumsy in his attempt to be quick.

"Norgay." He echoed the ping. *"Johari Colossus Norgay. Turn back, it's an ambush!"*

The weird new soundscape inside his skull shifted with an increasing pressure against the pseudo-receptors the implant had given him. The dragon and the salamander already oriented that direction.

The ocean curled into eddies and the air rippled from top to bottom. Norgay's head, all shining metal and piercing blue gaze, materialized before them, his broad, semi-human face impassive. The change swept down his body as he revealed himself in his terrible glory. Shoulder-mounted rockets aimed forward and up. His arms rose to either side, elbows set back, the barrels of his guns dark and ominous. He trained his guns on the dragon before him, and his cameras dipped toward Johari and rose again, a nod of acknowledgment. Norgay had hidden the truth for all of Johari's life, then assaulted dozens or hundreds of aliens without even pausing to think. The robot had been his everything.

Johari's anger fled in an instant. Norgay's hands spread and the sun haloed his head. He gleamed in the sky like a saint in a Russian icon.

Savior's injured frill rose on an unseen breeze. "Johari. No hear. No see." It lifted its head, predator's eyes focused on Johari's oldest friend. "No hear," it said again, then a few more flashes, and Johari wondered if he'd finally seen how to say, "I'm sorry."

He barely had time to shout, "Kill my implant — all my sensors! Kill it!" before the shrieking swarm of dragons plunged from the sky.

25

D RAGONS FANNED OUT in all directions, and a few swooped up from the ocean's surface. Gold streaked through their wings as they soared. They dodged up and down, then cutting across the sky as if, together, they wove a vast net with Norgay as its target.

"Hostiles, please stand down," Norgay boomed, his voice broadcasting across the air. Johari heard it as if through wads of cotton.

He barely heard the war cries of the dragons as well, saving him the agony of their power against his enhanced senses, and preventing him from communicating at all. The puppet did not respond to his gestures.

"Shawntelle?" he subvocalized. Nothing. In saving him from the sonic assault, she had cut him off.

Johari stumbled toward the medibot, hoping to get the video feed up. Wisps of smoke curled from the bot's joints and black marks scorched its surface. Savior hadn't merely cast it aside, it had fried the bot's circuitry with that golden pulse. *I think they could do it on purpose,* he had said. *Then they are definitely enemies,* Emm had replied.

Dragons dove, pulling up when Norgay aimed his big guns. Norgay's torso swiveled, the fixtures at his waist allowing him to fire in a full arc around him, but he refrained, repeating his message, then he turned back, and extended his hand toward Johari.

Huge metal fingers uncurled, spread upon the chimney cap, palm up. His shoulder guns targeted automatically, lasers pinpointing one dragon after another. They recoiled from the red dots, but circled closer, the net drawing down. Dropping the ruined medibot, Johari ran toward him, the smartcast struggling with his urgency. His knee locked and loosened so that he staggered and pinwheeled his arms. Fifteen feet. Twelve. Ten.

With a surge of muscle, Savior thrust between them and Johari smacked into the salamander's side. As he rebounded, his skin tingled, every hair standing on end. Savior's frills crackled with gold.

The jolt shuddered Norgay's arm. For a moment, flaps and hardware ports flew open, tools flicking out, then snapping back again.

The back of Johari's neck throbbed, and Shawntelle's voice barked, *"What's going on? We got a distress call from Norgay! I can't keep you damped."*

"Savior, move!" Johari lunged forward and grabbed the salamander's leg, his arms wrapping around it. It had a few electroreceptors on its feet, maybe they would be enough. The VR puppet's frills overlaid the valleys of the salamander's skin.

Its head snapped around toward him, predator eyes glaring down, and its skin gave an ominous hum. Even on all fours like this, it loomed over him. The frills that resembled whiskers or fireworks or gentle fronds now lashed and flared. The tips of its teeth glinted between its lips, those pincers near its mouth poised. "Johari move," it said, the pulse of its power sizzling along his skin.

Johari let go, his mouth gone suddenly dry. "You used me." Words for which the model had no translation. With a swift movement of his arm, he brought up the puppet. "Johari is not Savior's rock." He swept his hand toward his heap of possessions, his useless tools.

"Johari rock hurt."

"Yes, that's right. Please, stop!"

Savior answered with a rainbow of colors cascading along its frill.

With an ominous roar of engines, Norgay's guns came about, visible over Savior's back. The net of dragons screamed shut, and Johari's implant struck agony through him at the sound. He shuddered and pitched to his side, deafened, his body gone rigid with the pain.

A dozen dragons plunged downward, their frills and membranes coruscating with golden danger. They tipped their wings suddenly upward, their powerful hind legs grabbing Norgay from all directions, seizing his arms, his shoulder cannons, his head and back. The giant robot stood taller than any single dragon. A dozen of them dwarfed him.

Their claws dug into joints and crevices, a seething mass of green and gray. Their wings struck him and each other in the effort of staying aloft. They struck in silence. Norgay's eyes blazed, his guns at last spat fire. Blood blossomed into the air, one of the dragons thrashed and fell, smearing Norgay's silver skin with the stain of its death. The remaining dragons gave a single unified pulse, glowing like a new sun, the image searing into Johari's vision.

The jolt of a single dragon repelled the greatest leviathan of the sea. Eleven dragons shot Norgay with their power. His body shook. His cameras rotated wildly and his eyes flashed. The mouth he had given himself remained in the slightest smile, then melted away, his responsive metal failing.

Johari screamed. He pulled himself forward. Norgay's hand, the one that invited him, cracked hard against the chimney cap, shells shattering and falling away. Savior thrashed nearby, a wild spasm. Whatever punishment the dragons doled out to Norgay with their war-screams and their pulses, some part of it visited Savior through his implant.

What had he done? Johari only wanted to speak, to commune with these strange and wondrous beings. Norgay a warrior, Savior a saboteur. Tears stung his eyes.

The dragons fell silent. Their great wings beat long, slow strokes, keeping them airborne, but only just, the solid weight of Norgay clutched between them, his eyes vacant as they carried him away.

Just short of the shattered edge, Johari slumped down, reaching toward the void.

The mob of dragons lifted off, some of them joining the victors' flight. The rise and beat of enormous wings obscured Norgay's form until only flashes of silver could be seen, then just the receding cloud of dragons. Something moved close by and Johari curled defensively. The cap beneath him — what remained of it — bounced as a dragon landed heavily nearby. Fury gazed down on him, shutting its predator eyes, frills moving lightly, then it faced Savior.

The salamander's twitching finally ceased. A few patches of the snail-bandage flapped away as it rolled to its belly, prostrate, legs tucked against it.

Fury brought its head down low, to rest against Savior's back and its frills flickered just a little, the by-product, Johari began to understand, of its electro-pulses. Finally, Savior heaved up enough that Fury could grasp it behind the arms. Together, they soared from the chimney cap.

When they did not immediately take to the sky above, Johari scrambled to the edge in time to see Fury set Savior down in the ocean. A number of other salamanders hovered there in the wash of the waves. One of them looked up, but he wasn't sure their eyes could even pick him out at that distance. The gathering swam off in the same direction the dragons had gone, Fury keeping pace overhead.

"*Shawntelle.*" He scrubbed the hair back from his face.

"*Fracking Fleet, Johari. Are you still alive?*"

He managed to roll onto his back, staring up at the roiling orange clouds. "*Maybe.*"

Her voice felt soft. "*Holy shit, Johari, they killed Norgay.*"

"No!" His throat burned. "*I don't think it's that easy.*"

"*You call that easy? Norgay was broadcasting the battle, then the connection went dead. Now Zheng He can't even raise him. He sent us a tight beam before they — shot him.*"

Johari flinched. "*What did he send?*"

"*I haven't — I was busy monitoring you. Holy shit, Johari, that was not fracking easy. Just —*" she broke off. "*You know how part of my space is synced with your vitals and your transmissions? It's been like a volcano, or maybe a supernova. Just watching that, watching you, I feel totally wiped.*"

"*Me, too.*" Johari wet his lips, or tried to, anyhow. "*What did he send?*"

"Hang on a minute ... he sent Armstrong's diagnostics. Norgay made it down there, but can't repair Armstrong by himself. Those frackin' sea monsters. More and more of them, and the conventional armaments don't work underwater. He can't even get close."

Like the damned dragons. Did Savior even want to talk with Johari, or had it just been waiting around until Norgay returned and they could spring the trap? *"I have to get him back."*

"You can't go after them — what are you, nuts? I can send Eriksson."

"What, so they can kill him, too? We can't afford to lose bots! We're already down by three, until Earhart can get here — Fleet needs those bots." For a moment, he just lay there, breathing hard and hoping the oxygen system hadn't gone over the edge. *"And he's my friend."* His family, but he didn't say that.

"You're lucky. Eriksson and me — we're not like that." Another beat passed, then Shawntelle said, *"Johari ...* "drawing out his name. *"I'm afraid for you."*

"Thanks," he whispered. When he had mastered himself, he crawled over to the scattered heap that Savior had made of his belongings. The medipak sat sideways, precariously close to the edge, but he hauled it back down and dragged it a few feet further. Gasping for breath, he fumbled out the mask and jabbed the control. Nothing. He slapped it, jiggled it, finally noticed the kink in the tubing, and uncurled it to a glorious breath of fresh air. His chest ached as he sucked in.

"Still there?"

He sucked in another breath. *"Yeah."*

"You okay?"

He took another hit. *"I'm okay."* A few food bars and packets of medication littered the surface. One of the blankets waved over the sea from a pinnacle of stone, marking his surrender. No. Bandages wound across and dangled over the edges. The generator had vanished, but the evaporator stood not far off, dented, but apparently functional, and it still contained a blessed liter and half of water. Johari wet his lips and drank deeply. The medibot's fried remains stared back at him, a mute reminder of what Norgay would become, what he already might be. Ruined. No better than stone. Johari's rock. *"You said Savior can enter the Realm. Its implant —"*

She started objecting before he'd even finished the thought. *"Probably make the thing go bonkers."*

"It needs to listen to me. You can't send Eriksson or Zheng He — the dragons would fry them, too — and the rest of you, even Tolui, don't have any experience with these creatures. Besides, they trust me. You can't lay an ambush like that unless you trust your bait." He smiled faintly. *"If nothing else, it proves their intelligence."*

"You can't seriously be defending them."

The oxygen mask dangled from his hand as he stared over the alien sea. *"We attacked first. Then we attacked harder. Any half-way civilized culture would do exactly what they've done."*

"Johari ... Fleet needs this planet. Humanity needs it."

"Thought you didn't even want to live planetside."

"It doesn't matter what I want, or what you want. We're here because our people are depending on us. That's why Fleet rolled back the regs about intelligence. Tranquility lines up eighty-seven percent. What are the chances we ever find another planet like this?"

"I know. But it doesn't belong to us." He hung his head into the mask and took another deep breath. *"The Founders knew the Fleet, and even the scout program, were a last shot for mankind. We played god on our own planet until we ruined it, then we killed each other fighting over the wreck. That's why they wrote the oath the way they did. If we're the conscience for the bots, Shawntelle, we're also the conscience for the Fleet, for the whole fracking race. We're not gods anymore, we're penitents."*

"We're desperate."

"Children do what they want. Animals do what they need. Humanity used to do what was right. Or we tried to, anyway."

She made no reply, and he drew in a fresh lungful of oxygen. *"Can you get Savior connected to the Realm or not?"*

"I've been running the subroutine already, making the portal. Right now, it has an unregistered implant, like a baby. Once I create the registration, it should be possible."

"I thought only Fleet could do that."

"I have an admin ID. Don't you?"

"Nope." Weird. Fleet doled out that kind of access only to high-level personnel and those with special privileges. *"How do you rate?"*

"Who knows? Fleet logic. You want to come in?"

Johari settled himself, imagining sitting down with his cello between his knees and trying to remember how tranquility felt before he rashly named a whole planet for it. He triggered the VR handshake. Shawntelle's crazy geode world blossomed around him. *"Not the Realm?"*

She shimmered into being nearby. "Fleet's hot to get hold of you. If they catch your signature online, they'll beat down the door."

"In that case, thanks. For this, for everything."

Her gaze flickered over him, then returned to his face and she let out a long breath.

What would this place even look like to Savior's eyes, with their different blend of rods and cones? Disorienting, to say the least, but VR gave Johari the mother of all projectors, a whole different way to communicate. "I'm gonna need to display image files, can we do that?"

Shawntelle's eyes narrowed. "This is my kingdom, where I rule, and make the rules."

"Let me be your court jester, then. I don't need full access, just group files."

"What the hell is a jester?" She sighed. "Never mind. What else?"

"Can it be … maybe a simple analog of Tranquility?"

"I've got a few test environments. Hang on." She glanced up and to the side. The world around them shifted into puffy clouds, a roiling volcano interior, a wash of ocean blue —

"That one, the ocean. They seem to use blue when they're content."

"And we want our monsters happy. Got it." She glanced up and to the side — accessing again. "The implant is registered. You want me to grab it and suck it in? No guarantees on this. We may not even get its attention."

"Can we ping it first? Make Savior get woozy or something? Last I saw, it was swimming, and I don't want it to —" He broke off as her expression hardened.

"Stockholm Syndrome: remember that from the military training unit? That's where a hostage falls in love with his enemies."

Their eyes met. "Thinking of them as the enemy isn't helping anyone."

"Right. 'cause thinking of them as magical, wise, fantasy friends is super helpful."

The truth stung. "The anthropological term for that is 'Noble Savage'."

"Ha! You think they're noble, I think they're savage." She prodded him in the chest.

"We can't go around wrecking other people's worlds the way we wrecked our own." He spread his hands in a pleading gesture.

"I'm not leaving you alone with this thing, Jo. You takin' too many risks." She stepped back. "Best I can do is send something that disorients it, then give it a minute to get to safety. Gotta have that kind of instinct, right?" Nodding to herself, she faded, turning into sparkles in the air. "This set-up's gonna make you look like some kind of wizard. Is that your plan?"

"My whole plan is to get Norgay back."

"And maybe save somebody else's world." Her voice echoed in the blue around him. "Maybe you're the noble one."

26

JOHARI LAY BACK into the soothing ocean of Shawntelle's creation. Motes drifted around him, and he glimpsed shadows in the distance, simulated fishes far off. Rays of sunlight filtered down, as if he floated just below the surface. The effect of water dampened all sound.

He called up the dragon puppet and it took form around him, larger and more detailed in the full-immersion VR realm. He tried accessing their cloud-storage, the image directories, and scrolled through the file for Norgay. An image of the bot about as tall as his arm flashed into view a short way off. He blinked through a succession of pictures, from Norgay in flight mode as they slid through the edges of a nebula, to standing on the rocky surface of a barren world, to hovering in the murk of the swampy planet they had last considered. Earhart hovered behind him, holding up two fingers. Maya's idea? Norgay seemed oblivious as he reached for a sample siphon. Johari barely made out himself inside, a tiny figure.

He remembered that day vividly: the five bots divided the planetary sphere to investigate, sampling the air, water, and what passed for earth. They worked across the atmosphere together, then deeper and deeper, a slow downward spiral, methodically pursuing their tasks — exactly what they hadn't done here on Tranquility. Every sample, every test, every scan reinforced what they didn't want to hear. They moved closer together as they worked, coming within sight of each other, drawn together against the emptiness of the planet and the futility of their task.

"This planet is shit!" Shawntelle called across the comm space between them. "Bet it even stinks like shit, with all those farting gas pools and decaying crap."

Tolui giggled. "Given the biological density of the surface, and its exothermic nature, you're not wrong."

"There might still be something, right? Some kind of... Solid ground?" Maya's very young voice piped up. "Maybe we could build floating cities, like giant boats?"

"The engineering for that would be intensive, Maya, but it's not a bad idea," Emm put in. "If we keep searching there could be the potential for... something." Emm trailed off, their tone aiming for hope and not quite hitting the mark.

"And we have yet to locate any viable supplementary protein," Tolui pointed out. "This place could support an outpost, maybe, but not a colony, no way. If we can't find something more sustaining than just floating around in space, we might as well stay there." Armstrong performed a slow rotation, taking in the vast green expanse of nothing.

"Fine by me — let's blow!" Shawntelle waved as Eriksson's jets gave a burst. His human form grew sleek, shifting to flight mode as he shot up through the atmosphere.

Johari asked Norgay to pause, his engines shivering the surface of the muck. "Face it, guys, none of the tests are bringing back more than 43 percent. We're wasting our time."

"I am forced to agree, Johari," Norgay's voice murmured all around and within, resonating in his chest like a stroke across the cello.

Maya sighed. "It's super green, though. Was your planet like this, Johari?"

Johari couldn't remember how he had answered her, or even if he had. Viewing the bots like this, in miniature, they appeared to have traded places with the children they carried, bots playfully exploring a strange new world, with little sign of their human partners. But Johari knew the truth. They were not explorers, they were warriors, every one of them, as if Fleet had planned for an invasion all along.

Johari chose an image of Norgay in atmospheric mode, viewed against the sky, an image Savior should recognize.

A keening emission of sonic chaos. A dark form streaked past him, trailing bubbles. Huge in the water, the creature flew past again, going the same direction, distance and transit all a trick of the small VR world they occupied. He glimpsed flashes of color near the creature's head and his implant buzzed with electrical pulses. Confusion and despair flooded his sensors. At least, that's how he wanted to interpret Savior's wild signals. Shawntelle's speedy programming snared it, and only she could let it go. Stockholm Syndrome or the Noble Savage. In here, the salamander became his prisoner. Did that mean it had the potential to care about him, if only he held on long enough?

In a rush of bubbles and electric tingles, the salamander spun about. The force of its movements pushed him away. He tumbled in the water beneath, above, around Savior's madness. In this tiny realm the colossal salamander dominated, huge and graceful in a way it had not been on land. Imaginary or not, water belonged to Savior. Its limbs spread away from its body, slowing the rush, and it curved back on itself. The electric pulses grew more focused. Its jaw gaped open, easily wide enough to swallow him whole. Amphibious eyes focused on Johari, rounded slits reflecting the miniature image of Norgay still hovering nearby.

Johari arrested his own movement with a reflexive reorientation to VR. No matter how often he stepped around and over that VR dog, in the end, it didn't exist, and neither did any of the rest of this place. It was a shared delusion, and now he had dragged Savior inside.

Savior's frills drifted in a nimbus, silent for a very long moment. Finally, it closed its mouth, and spoke in a cascade of colors and pulses. "Johari ... take Savior ... water not."

Johari pointed toward the image of Norgay. "Norgay," he said, exactly as if he were teaching the word.

The salamander lashed itself into a vertical spiral, thrusting upward with its muscular form. It appeared below him and pushed past, then it turned hard and made straight for him.

Johari blinked his avatar away and appeared behind, the image of Norgay tethered to him. He pointed again. "Norgay."

Savior surrounded him with a storm of tiny electrical pulses. Johari refused to respond. Finally, the salamander aimed its chin at the image and made a pattern of white and yellow streaks. Its artificial voice said, "Norgay."

"Savior take Norgay. Savior give Norgay to Johari." Johari held out his hand.

Savior dove in a circle and pulsed at him, lifting its chin in one direction then another, as if seeking something to bounce them off of. Amphibious eyes aimed at him, pools of gray-green flecked with gold.

Spreading his arms, Johari said, "The Realm. Johari's world." The VR puppet flared and buzzed. "Savior give Norgay. Johari give Savior."

Savior flicked itself in a tight circle, then circled the other way, not frantic energy, but meditative. It came to rest in the water in front of him, and its frill signaled at the same time that its assigned voice said, "No."

Johari crossed his legs and sat, hovering in front of Savior's eyes. "You hurt Norgay. I need him back."

Savior's frills rose up shifting from pink to gold like a nuclear sunrise. "Norgay break dragons. {an inflection of light on the verb} Dragons break Norgay."

Johari's breath stopped, and Shawntelle whispered, "*Oh, shit.*"

"Johari give Savior," the salamander went on, with a few flashes that couldn't be interpreted. "Norgay break." {that same inflection returned: past tense? broken?}

Inside his skull, Johari said, "*Tolui said you could sync our implants, mine and Savior's.*"

"*And you said it was nuts because it is. My program's set up to map Savior's brain function as best I can — that was Tolui's idea, natch — but we're parsecs away from getting an accurate sync. Even with people, it's kinda iffy.*"

"*Language learning takes months or years, even if you share the same anatomy. If we can't communicate, this is gonna take forever. They're breaking Norgay, and we're losing Armstrong as well. Then what happens? Fleet burns in here and flames the world.*"

"*You say that like it's a problem.*"

"*Come on!*" He slashed his hands through the air, and Savior twitched back from him.

"Johari give Savior." It flashed the pattern he'd seen it use before, the one that might be an apology.

For a long moment, they hovered in the imaginary ocean, each surrounded by a familiar environment, and at the same time, utterly outside of their element. Johari whispered, "*Okay, if the world will end in fire and not in ice, then I might as well go down with it. Sync me. Let me at least try everything I can before I give up Norgay for dead.*"

Motes of nothing real drifted between them as Savior curled in the water, waiting.

"*Eriksson is preparing for a mission to Armstrong, to see what he can do. Zheng He is still on guard here. Earhart is incoming in about seventeen hours.*"

"*Unless I'm getting bad at math, that's hours after Armstrong is dead, and at least a few minutes after Fleet's window of choice. Are you gonna do what I asked?*"

"*This could fracture your mind, you idiot. Jeez. You gonna pull rank or something? News flash, you're halfway an outlaw: you don't have any rank.*"

He sagged. "*Please, Shawntelle. It's not like I had any real power anyway.*"

"*Ever think maybe I don't want to be responsible for what happens to you?*"

"*Me going insane? Maybe it's too late.*" His implant buzzed and tickled. "*You're already working on it, aren't you.*"

"*Yes, moron, I'm doing this for you. I'll be monitoring whatever's left of you. Right? This is gonna be — like dropping that thing in VR, but worse, you get me?*"

"*Thank you.*"

"*Don't thank me until you survive. Oh, and by the way, pretty sure direct interface with an alien life form puts you waaaaay over the line for military discipline.*"

Savior gave a graceful shiver that re-settled its frills somehow projecting a sense of menace, reminding him of a cobra about to strike. Its frill flashed and sparks of electricity passed between them. "Johari give Savior."

"*It's not a war, Shawntelle — at least, it's not meant to be.*" Then he thought of Norgay's secret weapons. Maybe it was a war. Maybe it always had been. Had his mother known Norgay was packing? His father had clearly been suspicious. Or jealous, of her relationship with the bot who had raised her. How would she feel knowing that her own child had taken the place that once belonged to her? "*I'm ready.*"

"*No, you're not. But I'm pulling the trigger. We can map visual, that's what we're used to, and that's where we'll start, but they've got six freakin' eyes. Good luck in there. Out there. Whatever.*" She paused, then, more softly, "*Bye.*"

Weight suffused his limbs and Johari dropped out of the world.

27

S TREAKS OF LIGHT — blinding, incoherent — shattered images overlaid — a charcoal shadow shaped like Norgay, colossal indeed, ringed with lights like swirling fireflies — blood spooling into water — the spines of a leviathan {seabreaker} as it chomped a friend in half, a salamander — a curving sweep of pearlescent sky — the dagger shapes of orbital vessels — Maya as a tiny girl climbing Earhart from toe to head — powerful hands decked with claws stripping a dragon's light — thrashing in pain and terror in a dragon's grip — standing over the sea, lines of power radiating, learning to speak to the sky — scrolling lines of data that describe a thousand incomprehensible things — coiled in transformation beneath a translucent shield of wings.

Johari fled the bombardment. Light poured in a thriving mass beside him, around him, a network of strands and pulses. It spoke to him and he reached for it, desperate to escape the madness —

The world cracked.

It broke open like an egg sucked by a groundbeater. Pulses of light unraveled and fractured — danger! Faster! Seabreakers — messages that made no sense.

Heat words shot across the water-that-was-not, and the water retreated, sinking into nothingness as if into sand or shadowed caves. Shades-of-darkness dove for the retreating water, then it spun about. The wrongness receded.

Three Skins drifted above, a queer four-limbed thing without tail or gills, speechless. Black tendrils waved from its head in a meaningless scrawl. Its failure to die in the water had been one of the signs that this world was not the world. A world without world. Three Skins, too, shattered. Were they dying? The space between them, where the not-water had been, dissolved. In the gaps, chaos. Shades-of-darkness forced itself to see. Hunting eyes, knowing eyes, ancient eyes. Ancient eyes ... only nothing could be seen, but a nothing more empty than anyplace in the world. No movement flickered, not the slightest floating {insect}.

Danger pulsed within. Something had gone wrong with this false world, like the wrongness that brought Shades-of-darkness from the threshold to this not-place. Three Skins caused the wrongness. The image shifted: Three Skins in focus for an assault. Hunting eyes pinned the creature.

Three Skins brought Shades-of-darkness here, tore it from the world the way a flier snatches lubbers from the sea. That danger could come from such a small and feeble thing. The fliers spoke true when they referred to it as food, yet it could speak, it had a voice unlike any other, and it had made itself a new voice for the sake of sharing.

Between them, Three Skins and Shades-of-darkness built a story as strong and bright as anything of the Revered. {Fracture} Three Skins brought danger and not-danger, bound together in one fragile, unfamiliar shape. More than merely not-danger. Danger and gift, danger and greatness.

Shades-of-darkness opened its knowing eyes. Three Skins hung in the nothing, and opposite, an image of the nothing itself, as if Three Skins belonged there. In the vision of knowing eyes, Three Skins' neck glinted and flashed as if it spoke of its own accord, more so than before, a frantic pattern, the source of the panic and urgency. Shades-of-darkness spoke to that, sending heat words. Three Skins' soft body jerked and thrashed, Shades-of-darkness felt the pierce of a sharp heat word and —

Johari screamed. For a moment he had too many eyes. He saw the immensity of the emptiness and fought against it. He saw himself dangling there, hair floating around him, head tipped forward, then the streak of pain at the back of his neck and now —

Fliers and food. A broken egg, patches of sky that suddenly spoke in fire —

Fliers {dragons} dipped and dove over the ocean. Streaks-of-gray Firstborn swept downward, screaming rage, spewing heat words of loss, of the broken sky and broken land. Knowing eyes saw the truth — too many eyes. Images overlapped, flickering in and out, layering up into a fragmented world, a broken stained-glass window remade into a nightmare.

Cathedrals leapt into being, swelling with towers, statues, stone, a hundred images of — {not-food, skin-shedders}. What could such a thing be named? Living, speaking, like the ancient, learning to speak and to share in speaking. Not alone — the rock called Norgay — a dozen other rocks, moving through the not-sun {darkness, night}, giant shells each holding several-several more like Three Skins. Not rocks, not shells, eggs that could birth entire tribes of shedders — {space ships, Fleet}

Johari fought the onslaught of images. Every tiny thing he thought of, every reference point in all of his study sprang into being. Alongside his own racing thoughts, Savior's mind raced, too, their images dueling in virtual space, and in their linked implants. He fought for some way to break the flood and deliver what he needed Savior to know, and find what he needed to find. Savior, the creature who called itself Shades-of-darkness. Norgay. Johari gasped for breath, for sanity, and brought his focus to his friend, his partner, his home and his world, pushing the image toward Savior.

Norgay's appearance at the edge of the chimney, weapons ready, viewed through a single set of eyes in grays and patterns, a spectrum of light Johari had no access to. In this view, Norgay's power nodes flickered, relaying messages and commands. No wonder the dragons got the jump on the bots — they could see the energy the bots produced, even the tiniest spark of their lives. Wouldn't Tolui be fascinated? Wouldn't Fleet be terrified?

Savior lured Norgay close, staying with Johari, then assaulted the bot, closing the net with a pattern of light and pulses Johari felt as if they flowed from his own skin.

"*Johari?*" Shawntelle ventured. "*Are you still — are you there?*"

Savior answered with a thunderclap of electricity, a swarm of pulses in which Johari's pattern — Three Skins — linked with Norgay, pulsing with danger, then linked with Shades-of-darkness in a brilliant rainbow, a rush of speech.

"*Savior can hear you now.*"

"*Damn — should've known.*"

Speaking without speech. Voices from within. As the Revered would claim. Shades-of-darkness waited, listening.

The pulses of Savior's thoughts moved through Johari, and he eased himself away. Too much, too intimate, seeing and knowing things he should not know. What secrets had he already betrayed? Communication went both ways.

"*But you're okay?*"

Johari opened his eyes and lifted his head. The soothing ocean evaporated during their shattering, and now he and Savior simply hung in space, the void Savior feared because there was nothing to sense. No matter how often or in what direction it sent its heat words, it would receive no reply. The void that felt, to Johari, so much like home.

"Give back Norgay," he said. "Please."

"A rock is your broodplace," Savior replied. Its frills still rose and shimmered with light, but its voice ran through Johari's mind, commingling with his own thoughts. {broodplace, family, home}

"A robot, yes." {robot: rock person, a being who was a tool}

"Cannot be given. Norgay not-mine."

"How did you lose him?"

Savior saw gold, the flash of Johari's fury, and the subtle shades of his fear. Savior coiled in the void, its frills drifting gently, neither of them injured, here, as they were in the world beyond. "Norgay broke fliers. Fliers receive the honor of his death and leave their wings behind. Shades-of-darkness ... makes Johari {Three Skins} his tool." {regret, decisions, confusion, pain, wonder}

With every message came the buzz of alien emotion. Something like awe, the mingling of fear and wonder. Savior in awe — of him? "Shades-of-darkness, please tell me how to get him back."

"Johari alone, not-alone. Spaceships. {eggs full of shedders: people} Voices within."

"I have friends here you haven't even seen, but I know you've felt them. More could be coming — many more. I don't want them to kill you."

"People seek the honor of my death?"

"It's not for honor —"

"*Hey, Jo —*"

Shawntelle's voice within, just when Johari needed to focus on Savior. "Give me a minute, okay?"

"*Johari, I can't —*"

In a rush of color and texture, lighting effects and subroutines, Fleet Comm flowed across the void to envelope him, a wave that tingled through his implant. He suddenly floated in the virtual ready room of the admiral's flagship. Fleet Commander Roxanne Shen stood before him, across the table.

Breaking the illusory sleek plastic and conforming metal of the ship's outer hull, Savior dwarfed the commander and all that she had, dwarfed in turn by the ship that stretched beyond it. As if they had tried to squeeze a legend into the tight quarters of an interstellar vessel, Savior's head and shoulders thrust inside, and out the arched porthole, its tail flicked with {aggression, hiding fear}. The salamander reared back its head and flared its frills, mouth agape like a carnival ride come to life.

28

"*S*HAWNTELLE, *GET IT OUT OF HERE!*" Johari dropped to the floor, pushing back his hair, struggling to conjure up a uniform, or at least a shirt.

"Johari — what is that?" Commander Shen glared at Savior. "Is this what you've been doing while you ignore your duty? Making up monsters and walling off the Realm? Enough." She slashed a hand through the air. "How long did you think you could keep us out? Who do you think authorizes VR storage?"

"Sorry, Sir, truly, I had no wish —"

"You have no standing to speak before me, am I clear? 'Yes, sir.'"

He squared his shoulders. "Yes, Sir."

She flicked her gaze again at the intruder. "Lieutenant Martinez, please remove this anomaly. I will have order."

Martinez sent an avatar through the door, a hatchet-faced man who dodged Johari's gaze. "Sir, this is not merely an anomaly. This —" he indicated Savior —" is associated with the unauthorized implant."

"What the Hell have you been doing?" Shen jabbed a finger at Johari's chest, and his avatar recorded the impact.

He opened his mouth to reply, then closed it gently. Savior blinked out of existence, and Shen gave a tight smile. "Good work, Martinez."

Martinez pursed his lips, and glanced at Johari. His brow furrowed, and for a moment, Johari felt like he knew the lieutenant's thoughts as well. Better to tell her the truth, that Martinez had no idea what made the monster vanish, or wait for a more opportune time? A time when she wasn't already primed to rip someone's head off?

Shen composed herself more carefully. "Refusal of Fleet communications. Deliberate unauthorized interaction with alien life forms while under military protocols. Denial of contact protocols. Inappropriate deployment of colossus technology. Illegal division of virtual space for clandestine purposes. Unauthorized activation of an emergency implant. Did someone have a baby? If there is a problem with the fertility suppression regimen, Johari, I expect to be informed." She cocked her head during this aside, then straightened. "How do you plead?"

Some of those were Shawntelle's crimes, directly, some were spread among the team as he brought them into his crusade to get the bots back while preserving the lives of the dragons. Johari's throat felt dry. Any one of them was enough for a charge of treason. Would she kill them all and reclaim the bots for another round?

"You may answer," she prompted.

Johari met her eyes, but he envisioned the frills of golden fire rising all around him. "Commander, I take full responsibility for my decisions and for the orders I gave my team."

"Johari Colossus Norgay, you are hereby remanded to custody."

His implant struck cold through his body as Fleet's controllers triggered their own embedded routines. "Sir, wait — Two colossi are in danger, if I don't —" His avatar froze. On the chimney back in the world, his body went rigid as he entered lockdown. Who would they dispatch to arrest him, to collect his paralyzed body and place him in a sled to await trial? Or would he receive summary judgment, locked forever: hearing and seeing, and never speaking again?

Tears stung in his eyes. They joked about being made into protein bars, but the team lacked the facilities for that conversion. Place him in a sled and turn off the power, letting him suffocate. Suffuse the chamber with poison and kill him outright. Who would they send? Which one of his friends would get the task of collecting his paralyzed self like a bit of space debris ripe for recycling? Which one of them would trigger the subroutine for his execution?

A chime sounded through the chamber, then a new door opened, a wood-paneled doorway into a modest suburban house that didn't exist. Emm stepped through. They wore a uniform and stood at attention. "At your command, Sir," they said, but their eyes flicked, just for a moment, to Johari's still avatar.

Shen pivoted away from him, to face his friend. "What is the compatibility rating of the planet Tranquility?"

"Eighty-seven percent, Sir." A factual answer, delivered in an even tone. At their back, Emm's fingers intertwined.

"What evidence do we have of civilization?"

"None, Sir." Emm swallowed, and added, "There is clear evidence of intelligence in a local species our reports will refer to as dragons. Sir."

"Dragons. That seems a little whimsical."

"Yes, Sir, however there are clear similarities." Emm broke off before saying more.

"Please send a tight beam of the reports immediately, Emm Colossus Zheng He."

"Yes, Sir."

"Is it true that one or more of the colossus units is suffering catastrophic failure?"

Another glance darted at Johari, the slightest wince. "Sir. Colossus Armstrong was damaged in an altercation with the local life forms. During the effort to retrieve and repair him, Colossus Norgay suffered an attack. His current whereabouts are unknown, Sir, but he reported that a single colossus unit could not alone perform the retrieval of the Armstrong unit."

"Thank you for that very concise briefing, Emm. I think I'm going to enjoy working with you." Shen's avatar softened around the eyes, a touch of humanity.

Johari watched as if through another set of eyes {knowing eyes? Ancient eyes?} Commander Shen bore the responsibility of finding a home for the human race. The choice might have been his, but the urgency was hers. If a few children, or a few aliens, must be sacrificed for the good of humanity, Shen would take that bargain. When Johari partnered with Norgay, he had agreed to a duty that might require him to die for the Fleet. He had never imagined that meant being killed by it.

"Yes, Sir," Emm whispered.

"Your first priority must be to retrieve and repair the colossus units by any means possible. When this process is underway, please dispatch a sled to take custody of the traitor, Johari ne Fleet. Colossus Norgay reported isolating him pending our investigation: I trust you have access to his location information?"

"Yes, Sir."

"I will send a direct order to the colossus units. If the native life forms endanger your mission, they must be eliminated. I will not tolerate additional losses."

On a viewscreen to the commander's left, statistics from Tranquility scrolled and flickered, and Martinez stepped into her line of sight, holding up a finger. She gave a regal nod, and he said, "Sir, we are close to the margin for deceleration. What are your orders?"

"In light of all the information at our disposal, order a slowdown, plan our trajectory for Tranquility. If the wildlife continues to be hostile, we can provide the necessary means to subdue, and establish facilities for the conversion of the resulting resources." She saluted, and he replied, his eyes gone round and lips twitching into a smile as he hurried from the room.

Conversion of resources: protein harvesting. Savior, Fury, Fracture and all the rest, "converted" into food for the ravenous Fleet.

"Please give my regards to your team, Emm Colossus Zheng He. We'll be seeing you as soon as possible." Shen turned and strode from the room. The door slid shut behind her, closing down Fleet Comms and leaving Emm alone in the corridor with Johari's frozen avatar. Emm sprang out of their military posture and appeared before him. They stroked back his hair, then folded him in a quick embrace. "Johari — I am so sorry. Fleet needs this. You've got to see that. We need this place."

His implant conveyed the warmth and pressure of their embrace, but he could make no response. They released him and hurried away to do Fleet's bidding. The virtual dog trotted up to him, tail wagging, and pressed its head beneath his unresponsive hand. Imprisoned in his own mind, Johari screamed into the silence.

The scream burst from his lips into reality. Atop the broken seal of the chimney, Johari shivered awake, his body tremoring from head to toe as if he'd just woken from hypersleep. How long had he been in VR? Thirst burned his throat and mouth, hunger knotted his stomach, and pain stung the back of his neck. He reached up and found blood, the base of his skull a seeping wound. He jerked back his hand, blood droplets flicking across him. Wait — he was moving! The implant that seized control of his voluntary muscle function must have failed.

"Hey."

Johari scrambled to sit up, someone else's hand caught his shoulder to steady him and he cried out.

"Hey, you're awake." Shawntelle examined him, her brow creased. In sharp — perhaps deliberate — contrast with Emm's immaculate uniform, Shawntelle wore fingerless gloves and a fitted tunic with swirling patterns that made him think of the semi-precious stones she nurtured in her private world. Her left hand gripped his shoulder. Her right hand gripped a small metal spike dripping blood.

He pulled away from her, kicking. "Get away from me!"

His kick, supported by the cast, sent her sprawling and the tool tumbled out of her hand. "Frackin' space wreck, Johari, I'm trying to help!" She caught herself on an elbow.

He crouched a few feet away from her, heart thundering and breath squeezed in his chest. "Help? I should've guessed you'd be the one sent to do it."

"Shit, Johari, I'm not here for them. You gotta focus," she snapped. Righting herself, she inched closer, keeping his attention on her face, dark skin lit by an alien sun. "There's two ways to sever an implant's uplink. One of them's remote, but I couldn't do that — they've got control of the whole grid. I had to do it physically. In person."

His fingers rose again to the back of his skull. "By stabbing me in the neck."

She tipped her head in a sort of shrug, coils of hair bobbing against her shoulders. "Had to be a precise strike to the control center. Good news about you being paralyzed, I could count on you not moving during the procedure. I was still monitoring when you got called on the carpet — you took the fall for my crap as well as your own."

"No point in all of us being traitors."

"I've been a bitch half the time you've known me, Johari. Anybody else would've chucked me over to save himself."

In VR, she had been fierce but strong, almost kind sometimes, almost...She had touched him, helped him, cared for him. Would betraying Shawntelle have gotten him a reduced sentence? It made no difference. That wasn't who he was, and it never would be. "I'm in charge of civs — I'm supposed to be the civilized one."

She snorted and shook her head. "What's that make the rest of us, barbarians? Forget it. You need to scram and so do I. I've got the mini-sub — on the way to check out Armstrong. They'll know you're off-grid. With any luck, the blood might convince them you're dead."

He cradled the fresh injury, the severed connection with all he had ever known. "Thanks."

"Thank me when you live." Her gaze tracked over his face, then she slipped her hand over his, knotting their fingers together in his blood. "Promise me you're gonna live."

Johari found himself smiling. "Do my best. What about Norgay?"

"Maya's scanning, but we got nothing. Something is shielding his emissions, if he's still got any. Fact is, we don't even know where to look."

"You'll never find him without the dragons."

"Without you. Emm's counting on that." When he recoiled at the name, she continued, "We got orders, remember? Step one, secure the bots. Step two, deal with the traitor. No way we can secure the bots without the traitor." She squeezed his hand.

"And Emm —"

"Has no idea what I'm up to. They're working on a bureaucratic solution, cramming legal files for a precedent to get you free, even if it's temporary. You and I both know it would be too late. Seriously, gotta go." Their foreheads rested together, just for a moment, then she did break away, retreating from him in careful steps, not taking her eyes off of him.

"Don't die." She spun away and ran a few steps toward the edge where an auto-belay device locked a rope to the top of the chimney. Black dreads haloed her head as she dropped away from him.

Johari brought himself back to the present. Get out of there — but how? Easy for her to say, she had the mini-sub. He didn't even have a link back to the others — when he probed the part of his mind where once he could call them at will, he found it empty. If he found Norgay, would he even be able to talk to him? If. When.

Johari clambered to his feet and found a big packet of supplies from the medipak. He emptied everything out of the pouch and stuffed in a few food bars, the portable oxygen, the core processor from the broken medibot in case he needed a signal boost, and the evaporator — after eagerly drinking down the water it already contained. The large metal reflector would be a pain to carry, but he couldn't see a good way around it.

He devoured a few bars. Fruit bars. The protein bars he left as they'd been scattered. With an emergency tourniquet, he fashioned a strap for the makeshift pack. He had no recourse to the Fleet or any of their technology. What did he have? His wits, his knowledge — knowing eyes — and a jumbled heap of images from a salamander's mind. Johari stilled himself. One scene, he had witnessed from two different views: Norgay's video, and Savior's memory. When Norgay came in search of him atop the chimney, Savior summoned help. Speaking to the sky. Between the two, Johari knew the way, the only way, he could get off this tower of stone and maybe find his partner.

Summoning all he had learned, conjuring a stream of electricity that tingled along his arms and across his throat, Johari called a dragon.

29

T HROUGH SAVIOR'S KNOWING EYES, the chimney cap radiated with lines of power. Johari assumed they congregated here for the warmth or safety from the sea. In fact, even broken as it was, the cap served as an amplifier, adding energy to his call.

It buzzed through his feet and knees, making him jittery. Its shattered state revealed the cords that held together the shells. No civilization? Bullshit, and every other kind of shit. Animals might build nests and howl of loneliness or danger — they didn't build an amphitheater to converse with their elders.

Among the pulses he played, Johari used the signals for Fury's dragon name {Sweeps-with-the-tide Lastbreak} Would it come to him? Johari's muscles twitched and shivered with the effort of calling. The wind picked up and he shivered, the blood drying at the back of his neck. In the distance, a rising hum. That was no dragon's sound, not the rush of wings or the cry of anger. Someone was coming — one of his own, if he could call them that any more. From the direction of the camp, a small shape grew, glinting silver.

Not one of the bots, a personal flier, from the span of the wings. It angled slightly, revealing what trailed behind: an evac sled.

Johari spun about, searching around him. He had nothing but the wreckage of his bivouac and a few spits of rock. Nowhere to hide, and no way to get down, not without breaking a few more limbs.

Calling up his internal menus, Johari altered the message, adding his name {Three Skins} and the signals for danger, urgency. Signals likely to send the wary and wounded dragons even further away. His heart sank. A few feet off, he spotted the probe Shawntelle used to free him. And just out of reach, the surgical kit, torn open, where she had gotten it. He dropped down awkwardly and dragged the kit toward him, spilling sutures and needles in plastic packets. Retractors and other tools he didn't recognize, and there, in its own sealed package, a surgical scalpel. With his teeth, he ripped open the package and slipped the knife against his thigh inside the cast, flat and hidden.

With a grinding end to its hum, the flier landed, shuddering the tenuous cap. Whoever it was would expect him to be paralyzed. If they hadn't seen him moving —

"Johari ne Fleet, hands on your head." A microphone modulated Tolui's voice, rough and deep, almost a man's. Johari's stomach clenched and his eyes burned. Tolui, his first friend among the team, his long-standing ally. The one who'd gotten them into all this. Tolui ordered, "Turn around slowly."

Slowly, Johari placed his hands atop his head, the scalpel pressing against him. Tolui stood taller than Johari and outweighed him by a dozen kilos. He envisioned jumping on his friend, getting the blade up to something vital, a threat, only a threat. If he could just get to the flier and get out of there — the last thing he wanted was to hurt anyone. Rising to his feet, he turned as if in a dream.

Tolui wore a full suit, helmet and all, making it hard to reach any vulnerable part of him. His extended hand gripped a pistol, an effective portable firearm ideal for dispatching local vermin. Framed by the helmet, Tolui's normally deep-bronze skin sallowed from his time in the sled, the whites of his eyes off-color, dulling their contrast. His Adam's apple bobbed as he swallowed hard. He needed a rest. Johari's condition was no better.

"I'm glad to see you're recovering."

Tolui's jaw knotted. His elbow dipped a little, then rose, the gun straightening. "This isn't what anybody wants, Johari. If you just, if you come quietly. Nothing's decided yet."

Johari met his eye, holding his gaze. "Pretty sure that's bullshit."

"I know a hell of a lot more about bulls and shit than you do." Tolui's voice cracked. "My screw up dragged you into this. I gotta make it right with Fleet. My term's up, Johari. I'm graduating. If I get out of this clean, I can take my pick of jobs Fleetside. I could be the chief biologist for all of Tranquility — me. A disposable fracking orphan. I can ditch the fertility suppressants and pass on my own genetic material. I could have a family, for once. You had that, Johari, you know what it means. Please, let me have it."

Johari mastered his voice. "Nobody wants that for you more than I do." It hurt to speak, to even look at Tolui. Their whole lives lived in metal boxes, they finally stood on a planet where all mankind could make a home, families, children, the brave new world they had been searching for for two hundred years. Johari stared down the barrel of the gun, standing between humanity and their future. All he had to do was die.

The black eye of the gun rose just a little and gestured toward the sled. "You'll get stasis for a little while, few months, long enough for Fleet to get here. Then you plead your case. We'll support you, Johari. You talking to dragons, man! That counts for something. They'll see it, they'll know you're too valuable to —" he clamped his lips and the unfinished sentence hung between them.

His palms sweated against his scalp. Johari walked carefully forward, letting his limp carry him. The slim metal of the scalpel pressed into him with each step, as if urging him to action. The sled opened to a command he could no longer feel or issue. "My implant is damaged, Tolui. It might not be able to interface for stasis."

"Emm and Shawntelle will figure something out," Tolui answered, relief flooding his voice. "We'll take care of you until Fleet gets here, just like you took care of me."

"And when Fleet gets here, they take care of me." He stood abreast of Tolui, the barrel of the gun turning to follow him, maybe a half-meter away.

"Come on, man. There's ways. They don't waste resources. That's the whole point about the protein bars, isn't it? They're not gonna — just because you went a little nuts about the dragons." Tolui's voice begged for understanding.

"And if they're developing civilization?"

"Fleet is coming! Nobody can stop that any more. It doesn't matter."

"If they're people, then killing them is murder. And killing them all is genocide."

"Johari. If there's no civilization, they're just animals. Humanity gets its colony. I get my family. If there's no enemy, then you're no traitor and they've got no reason to — execute you."

Johari absorbed his words, his desperation. If Tolui were right about all of this, any of this, they both won. Johari knew what he had seen and heard and felt. Tolui could wish and hope and argue all he wanted, and it wouldn't change the fact that he was wrong.

Johari turned his head. If he reached out now, he could set his hand on Tolui's and maybe still the slight shaking of the gun. "You know more about bulls and shit than I do, Tolui. You really believe Fleet lets me live after all of this?"

Drawing himself to his full height, standing square, Tolui worked his jaw, but said nothing. His eyes glittered as if the sheen of tears had hardened them. His Armstrong-style hair grew in a little shaggy, showing less kinship with his bot every day.

"Zheng He and Eriksson between them might get Armstrong back. There is no way they find Norgay until it's too late. The dragons are going to break him, Tolui, that's their plan, and I am the only one who can stop it."

"They're animals, Johari — they don't make plans! Besides, I have all your records, including the puppet. If you think you're the only one who can track the monsters, that's just your fracking arrogance talking." Bits of spittle struck the inside of the helmet. Tolui's fear and tension taking a solid form.

Johari stared at him.

Tolui's breathing escalated as he went on, "Yes, alright, Fleet regulations state that no alien species should have access to our tech, especially to the colossus units. Stronger measures may be —"

"Stronger measures? Like blowing the aliens off the face of their own planet, and Norgay along with them? Maybe Maya and Emm can put him back together, too. From scrap metal."

"Get in the sled, Johari. We're all doing what we have to do." He thrust out the gun so that it jabbed Johari's chest.

Johari's heart pounded. What they had to do. To save Norgay, and maybe the whole of dragonkind, to help them understand what was coming. All he had to do was attack a friend. Then the sickening thought struck him. Without his implant's interface capability, he couldn't even fly the damn thing. Johari's skin buzzed and his bare feet tingled with a growing awareness. He suppressed a smile. "You're recording this, aren't you?"

"It's evidence. Everything you say and do. The fact you care so much about Norgay and Armstrong, how hard you're working to get them back? That's gotta be in your favor. Now get in the sled." His voice hitched a little when he spoke his bot's name.

Nodding slightly, Johari winced and looked down at his cast. "Give me a minute to adjust this thing, would you?"

A hesitation, then, "Yeah, sure." Tolui took a half-step back, the gun held slightly lower.

Johari bent down to the cast, to where the scalpel lay. With a push and a click, he tugged the cast free of his leg and swung it upward against Tolui's outstretched arms. Tolui stumbled back, his arms pushed upwards. The smartcast writhed and worked, already conforming as it wrapped around Tolui's hands, encasing the gun and all, straight down to his elbows.

"What the Hell!" Tolui fell, struggling against his own arms, and nearly rolled off the edge.

Johari grabbed him and hauled him back to where he couldn't fall off the chimney and die. "Sorry." He gripped his friend, keeping him safe.

The scalpel winked in the sunlight nearby and Tolui glanced at it, then at him, shrinking away. Johari retreated, hands held high and empty. "You're gonna be fine. You'll get your job and your family, everything you've ever wanted, except me in that sled."

A shadow swept the chimney, and Johari reached upward, sending a call of welcome as Fury stalled in the air above him, claws flexing. Moment of truth: was he about to get shredded? The dragon dropped down beside him, watching with its knowing eyes. It leaned downward, extending its wing in a wide arc behind him. Johari caught hold of the dragon's shoulder and pulled himself up. Reflected in Tolui's helmet and in his awe-struck gaze, Johari and the dragon soared away.

30

JOHARI LAY ALONG THE DRAGON'S NECK. Without the cast, his leg ached, and his other injuries chimed in like a poorly-trained chorus, a dissonant distraction. Should've grabbed some extra meds, too. He crept his hands down, clinging to the ridges along the dragon's throat and seeking the electro-sensors.

Fury {Sweeps-with-the-tide Lastbreak} hummed and sparked beneath him. "— broodmates danger Three Skins."

Broodmates, those who shared a nest. "Yes. They are angry and scared."

"Angry over scared," Fury replied. It spiraled over the chimney, allowing glimpses of Tolui's little craft and the sled gleaming like someone's lost toys.

Angry over {layered, the use of frills and pulses at the same time}: angry because they were scared.

"Lastbreak also. Angry over scared." Then the glowing cascade of an apology that washed from Fury's frills down along its throat to sizzle beneath his hands.

Johari rested his cheek against the dragon's back. "My word for Lastbreak means angry."

Sparks touched his fingers, fizzing and popping, without translation. As they tickled, he laughed, and he needed no translation. Johari let the moment stretch, laughing with a dragon, an alien monster that had nearly killed him. A monster that somehow became his friend.

When the tingling died away, he said, "Can you take me to Norgay? Shades-of-darkness says the fliers have him, that they will have honor from breaking him."

"Lastbreak speaks the Revered." Other words hummed beneath his fingers, but he did not understand them all, and the program had access only to the concepts already discussed or revealed by his glimpses into Savior's mind. The Revered, the dragon he called Fracture, who heard? saw? visions and set them out in bones.

"Does that mean no?"

"Those of the Revered step outside. Beyond fliers, beyond ancients." A few more words Johari didn't understand. "Lastbreak take Johari. Johari speaks {place?}"

Apparently, the dragons with Fracture had a separate role in their society, a role that placed them apart from either dragons or salamanders. "I have to tell you where to take me, but I can't ask you to take me to Norgay."

A brief radiance of assent.

In all the wide world of Tranquility, how was he supposed to know where to go? He wanted to ask why they wouldn't tell him, and why Fury had come for him in the first place if it wouldn't help him.

Johari sank against the dragon's back, reviewing the flashes of ideas, memories, inspirations he'd gotten from Savior. He thought of the bone gallery where he'd met Fracture, where the parts of the dead could be reassembled into something new and meaningful. But if they intended to break Norgay, surely his "bones" would not be included in a place like that.

Both salamanders and dragons had been in the entourage that carried him away, that suggested a beachhead, someplace both halves of the species might be comfortable, yet Maya's scans revealed no sign of Norgay. Something blocked the signals; that eliminated the beaches. Dragons lived principally in the air, while salamanders lived underwater. They came together around the chimneys, where salamanders could swim below and dragons soar in from above. What else? What other interfaces existed to join water and sky? Waterfalls, mountain pools: too high, too hard on the salamanders. He could think of lots of places where the water came into the sky, but every one of them was a challenge, and there wasn't anywhere the sky came into the water, so —

Johari's head shot up. There wasn't: not on Earth or in any story he'd ever read, but on Tranquility? Holes in the water, Shawntelle described, sending vids of a patch of regular openings in the surface of a cove not far from the structures he'd mistaken for huts. Holes in the water close enough for the dragons to carry the stricken bot. "Holes in the water," he transmitted through his hands, desperately searching for any equivalent word for "holes". "Void," he had captured from Savior's experience in VR, but that carried a suggestion of fear and urgency. Would it mean enough to Fury? He sent it anyway, along with "darkness" and "not-water."

"Darkness in water," Fury echoed, then it tucked its wings and dove. Johari hung on with all his strength, the muscles of his arms trembling from the effort as wind blasted his face. For a moment, he hovered weightless over the dragon's back, tempted to let go and soar, arms outstretched, accepting the wind as his challenge and his companion.

Fury swept in low to the surface of the ocean, then unfurled its wings in a rush. Its neck dipped downward, lower eyes beneath the water and jaw opened. From the water, it snatched a thick-bodied fish and bolted it down as they soared on. Water splashed over Johari's face and hands. Ocean spray scattered against him as they stayed low. Shadows flitted over them, sometimes matching their speed and direction. Another dragon dipped in front of them, letting its chin slide along the surface. Fury dipped its face as well, and a buzz of conversation passed between them. Three Skins, Shades-of-darkness, a hundred other words he didn't know, along with a sense of warning from the other dragon before it rose up again into the sky.

"Am I endangering you? Johari dangers Fury {Lastbreak}?"

"Fury hunts danger," it replied, using the word for "anger" rather than its own name. Johari didn't know whether to be flattered or concerned.

Low islands rose up, curiously smooth and strangely whorled. What would Shawntelle, or even Tolui, make of them? Not volcanic, certainly, in spite of their dense texture, with cracks along the waterline where a whitish mineral showed through. Small plants or animals grew in the margins, living in the merger between land and sea and eating whatever nutrients battered against these curious shores.

Broadening his focus, Johari struggled to make sense of these strange landforms. At one turn, they resembled humps, then revealed deep ripples or flattened areas. They showed in clusters, some with cave-like openings. When Fury turned around one of these islands, an opening glinted with that same white mineral. Quartz? Diamond? Then, below them, a dark breach in the surface of the sea, almost perfectly round as if they had bored a hole in the ocean. A slight rim showed around it. Ahead, another hole, this apparently at an angle, with a ridge of stone emerging from the water.

In the shallow seas between the openings and the islands, salamanders moved, great dark forms sliding over the raised surfaces. A bay barely deep enough for a salamander to swim held hundreds of arthrosnails, and a half-dozen salamanders apparently tending them, moving with flicks of their tails, transporting the snails, lifting and turning them. Snail farmers. Animal husbandry, an early marker of civilization.

Beneath the shade of a huge, rounded island, an opening more broad than tall cut the surface of the water. A pair of dragons clung to the ridge above it. At the sight of Fury, they spread their wings, arcing with streamers of light. They drummed their feet against the ridge so hard that the water shivered around the opening, disrupting the pattern of waves. Whatever message they meant to convey, Fury gave no reply. Instead, it trimmed its wings in close and dove into the hole beneath the sea.

Salamanders and a few dragons gathered at the entrance, many of them still in motion, summoned by the guardians at the gate. Fury swept up its wings and settled lightly on its hind legs, neck arched to fit inside the passageway before them.

From the chaos of arrival, a welcoming committee of sorts emerged, moving a half-salamander's length in front of the others, communicating with brief flashes and sometimes leaning toward each other to direct their heat-speech. The space itself curved overhead, smooth and glossy, until it curved again to the floor, crossed with grooves and gouges. Pearly-white swirled with creamy pink, the tunnel dazzled Johari's eyes with the sparkle of light-words as the salamanders spoke.

The effect bewildered him: a dozen salamanders, with that many dragons looming above them, their frills flashing and sparking. How could they understand anything that was being said? Fury's neck expanded and relaxed with breathing, but so far, it made no reply. Johari sat up carefully, working to maintain his balance on the slope of the dragon's body. From here, he took in the creatures arrayed before them, blocking the way in a semicircle, then he caught his breath.

What he had taken for cacophony, two dozen aliens talking at once, resolved into — what — a rainbow? The light moved in a wave like an old-fashioned stadium crowd fanning their excitement. The chant, for such it must be, began at the center where the arc of aliens bulged toward him, and rippled in both directions. A distinct pattern of light from pale green to vivid orange passed from the center to the ends and began again as soon as it had reached them. A chant, or a round as in music where one voice took up the song when the first singer reached a certain point, overlapping the melody and creating harmony in the interstices.

Johari focused on the chant leader, the salamander he had dubbed 'Gandhi' for its intervention in the apparent conflict between Fury and Savior. Ignoring the rest, he watched the pattern from beginning to end. A fusillade of green sparks flowed like raindrops among the upper layer of frills. These dripped into changing shades, shifting yellow, then orange in sharp flicks throughout the frills. Thankfully, they never reached the deadly gold of an electrical assault. He recognized few of the words except "break" and "honor" and something related to tools or making.

Johari once more let himself drink in the full chorus. By the time Gandhi reached the orange, the dragons to either side of it spoke in green droplets, a radiant gathering, and an unmistakable warning.

Leaning into his hands, Johari said, "Fury, let me down."

"Danger ahead." The message warmed his palms.

"Yeah, I figured."

Fury bent carefully and Johari clambered off, slithering along its foreleg and catching himself just before he landed on his injured leg. Breath held a long moment, Johari relaxed a little and let go of Fury. It rose again above him, leaving him to stand, shaky, on the grooved floor of the passage.

The texture of the floor, cross-hatched in his view from above, now revealed its pattern, the surface roughened by the scrambling of claws. Long, sharp claws scored into the material of the tunnel, creating chips through the layers. The groves channeled rivulets of water as a few more salamanders heaved themselves inside from the ocean, shrinking the space inside with an ever-increasing density of aliens. Six-eyed, their heads haloed by fireworks, they now hemmed him in from both sides.

His chest ached, his lungs feeling tight as his heart hammered within. He wiped his damp palms against his ragged pants and took a step toward Gandhi. "Where is Norgay?"

The salamander stood on all fours, tall enough that he might have walked under it without his hair brushing its chest. Its head stretched forward. Its ancient eyes reflected his tiny figure framed by the flickering of salamander stars.

He stepped forward again, his feet slipping a little, and he spread his toes to grip the scarred floor. "I'm sorry for intruding on your home, but I need him back."

With a rubbing sound like leather on leather, Fury leaned its head down beside him, watching with one knowing eye. It tipped its chin up, then stared at him again. Chin up, stare. Johari reached out to touch it, letting his fingers find the receptors hidden in the ridges of its jaw.

"Johari speaks heat words. Fury speaks light Stone-{small movement}."

Shift? Stone-shifter? Johari pointed toward Gandhi, and Fury rippled blue agreement. "You're offering to translate for me? To tell them what I say?"

Another brief blue flash of assent.

Right. Johari said again, "I apologize for coming here. I need to find Norgay and bring him back."

Instead of the wire-frame and graphics puppet Tolui made for him, Fury's enormous head and glowing frill echoed his words, the essence of them, in any case. Fury's frill unfolded over Johari's head, the fleshy tentacles waving slightly with the transmissions of light that passed along them.

This close, he saw the channels of light and the tiny flickers deep within. The frills were really a single organ, folded back on itself like a thick ribbon. A few of the tendrils brushed against him as Fury spoke, trails of warmth, delicate and almost tickly. Their warmth hovered at his back, like a gentle hand that had been supporting him, and now waited for him to move on alone.

Gandhi flashed his answer, including a few words Johari now recognized: his name and Fury's, Norgay, Savior, with a strong overtone of anger. Again, and again, the wave of pink denial. No, no, no.

Fury's own anger rose in answer, and it spoke in waves of color: Fliers, honor, break, no, Savior — the focus of the anger, from what Johari could tell — Johari's broodplace {home, Norgay}.

Sitting back on its haunches, Gandhi flashed, "Go."

The salamanders to either side took up this chant, a single word in an urgent spike of red. Go, go, go, beating at him from all sides now, the white walls of the passage made red with their message.

"What's going on?"

"Gandhi speaks Johari go," Fury told him, its frills rippling to the same effect, then, through Johari's hand, while his frill said nothing at all, Fury continued, *"Gandhi speaks {void} knowledge Norgay. Gandhi speaks Fury speak Johari {void} knowledge."* Heat words without light.

"Gandhi told you he doesn't know where Norgay is — no, wait, he told you to tell me that he doesn't know."

Fury's enormous eye stared at Johari, a gold and black emptiness ready to swallow him down. *"Gandhi speaks —"* a burst of anger, and more, that almost scalded his hand. Johari didn't know what it meant, but it felt like cursing. *"Savior speaks fliers take Norgay. Savior speaks —"* that same intense burst. {shit} Johari thought. Savior claimed the dragons took Norgay, but it lied, and now Gandhi wanted Fury to lie as well. Johari's jaw knotted and a sense of betrayal burned. Of course they could lie — why shouldn't they be able to? They were intelligent: that had been Johari's entire point in trying to communicate with them, to establish their intelligence. And, incidentally, their worthiness as a species. Why shouldn't they be doing everything they did for their own selfish reasons, and not remotely the motivations Johari's team postulated for them?

"Johari goes," Fury said, but almost tentatively. "Johari not go, Johari food."

The flashing red demand for his departure throbbed all around, giving him a headache. Johari squinted at the ground, water seeping beneath his toes, trickling down and making the floor slick. Go, go, go. Get out of this place and forget about Norgay. Admit defeat, go home and take the punishment that waited for him, letting his teammates off the hook for his escape. Fleet was coming to make of Tranquility their new home, and to them would fall the vengeance for Norgay's death.

Only one problem: Norgay was home. He always had been.

He looked up at Fury's massive eye. *Tell them Johari goes.*

"Johari hunts no more {a question}"

"Tell them that. But it is {shit}. Johari hunts danger."

Fury tingled with laughter and surprise. Then it raised its head and delivered Johari's message.

The flashing red ceased, and Gandhi replied with assent, rising again, the others shifting around. A few at the edges backed away, then turned, curving themselves in half to reverse course down the passageway. Johari released his toes, and pulled the flat plate of the solar evaporator from his makeshift pack. Behind him, the salamanders at the entrance too were moving, some of them sliding back into the water with a series of splashes. They sent a fresh sheet of water down the passage. Johari ran three painful steps and let himself fall forward, chest to the metal plate as it slid along the rushing water. It swept him between the salamander's legs down the passage toward his death, or Norgay's resurrection.

31

T HICK TAILS LASHED OVER HIM, clawed legs stomped and leapt as he slid by on a curving path slightly down, sharply turning. The passage spiraled — and Johari suddenly made the connection. Shells full of shedders — that had been Savior's context for the idea of Fleet's spaceships. The pearlescent surface, the layers within the material, the shape of the opening and now of the passageway itself. He slid along the inside of an enormous shell, a remnant so massive that the idea of its occupant terrified him. His metal plate ground to a halt, squealing and tumbling him sideways as the water dispersed so thinly it could no longer provide enough lubrication. Johari stumbled to his feet, missing the smartcast already, missing even the bone he had leaned upon at Fracture's cove. Fracture, the Revered, the one Fury served.

His momentum carried him against the wall of the passage, his hands outstretched to catch himself on — nothing, as it turned out. The inner wall curved here into columns and arches, carved out of the shell material to link the next turn of the passage. He flung his arms around the nearest column, then pivoted to the side, tucking himself into a notch at the base of the column.

The architecture — what other word could there be? — was formed on a giant scale, the scale of dragons and salamanders. Something pulsed beneath his hand, and Johari jerked back. Thick, rubbery filaments wrapped the columns and ran along the walls, partially embedded in grooves like some kind of scrollwork decoration. The material resembled the cords that held together the plates of the chimney cap.

A continuous length of something wound tight and as thick around as his thigh marked the outer wall as well, and beneath this, broad, slick grooves as if huge claws scraped a pathway there every day for decades. The filaments nearest him buzzed and crackled, then went still. Johari held his breath. It hadn't stung. Reaching out carefully, but not emerging from his nook, Johari set his finger on the filament. Nothing happened. So it hadn't been directly responding to him, nor did it seem alive, though the texture of it suggested organic matter. He wished he could take a sample for Tolui. Next time he saw Tolui, Johari would be shot on sight.

In the passageway, salamander claws scratched on shell, pacing methodically downward. Johari grabbed the metal plate he'd abandoned and stuck it back in his pack. Then he froze, listening. A soft, rhythmic clatter came from beyond the pierced wall, and grew louder as he listened. He pressed into the crevice, drawing his feet up tight, in spite of the protest from his leg. Another series of pulses shivered through the filament. Heat words. He placed his palm against it, but could not make out what they said, save for the sense of urgency. The salamanders communicated through these filaments.

The clatter reached him clearly now, accompanied by a subtle grinding. He tipped his head, peering into the gloomy beyond. It grew brighter by the moment as well, with the unmistakable glow of a salamander's frill. By this eerie light, he made out the shape of a curious contraption. It followed the outer wall, along the thick cable. A salamander rode on top, moving slowly, its head bent toward the inside, all eyes open. It lay on a sling mounted on a framework with broad runners underneath, fitted neatly into the tracks Johari had noticed earlier. Its hind legs walked steadily, propelling it upward at an even pace while its forelegs remained free. Whatever components of the implant Shawntelle's surgery had damaged, Johari prayed that it had left his recording cameras intact.

One of the main arguments against other creatures developing intelligence revolved around the upright posture of man. Had humans developed because their posture gave them the ability to manipulate their world? Or had they grown more upright as they worked with their hands: hunting, tool-making, painting on caves or playing bone flutes.

Certainly, back on Earth, chimps and other Great Apes used twigs as tools to gather ants or honey. Crows used their beaks to manipulate all kinds of things, and octopus, with their eight clever arms, could unscrew jar lids, even from the inside. Still, in order to make lasting changes to their world, hands made all the difference. Hands made it possible to weave, to hammer, to saw, to shoot. To write a book. To play the cello.

With their long bodies and thick tails, salamanders could not stay upright for long. At his rudimentary campsite, Savior took the medibot to the side of the chimney cap, using the drop-off to free its hands to examine the bot more carefully. They appeared to be as four-legged as their namesake, but these salamanders had used their hands to create a sled to make using them even more effective.

As it drew alongside, the vehicle revealed itself as a rather crude thing of hides slung over bone and shell. The hides cradled the salamander from its armpits to its hips. Beneath this sling a few compartments held objects, salamander tools or specimens, mysterious, except for one: a glinting shard of metal, the inner curve of one of Norgay's giant fingers.

Johari tensed to leap out and confront the creature and take back the piece, but the last thing he needed was to attract the creature's attention. Johari go, or Johari food — those were the choices. Norgay was here, somewhere in the spiraling hive of salamanders. Johari pressed himself into his notch and held his breath as the sled passed and continued its journey upward. The occupant's frill lit up not far beyond, its flare of light reflecting strangely off the walls in muted tones of green, orange, blue, pink.

Cutting through to the next turn, Johari hurried as best he could. He found another series of openings pierced through, then a darker opening beyond. When the filaments embedded in the walls buzzed, they also produced a soft sort of light, enough for his enhanced vision to make the passage bright as dawn.

Johari limped toward the opening, glancing up at the cable as he stepped beneath. In a cubby carved out of shell stood an empty sled. A set of grooved tracks led out and merged with the main line a little further down, like a lay-by on a railroad track. He leaned against the thing, catching his breath, and listening. Movement rumbled up the passage, growing closer, and here stood his salvation.

They already knew he was there, somewhere, inside their home. Stealth would be nice, and his size clearly helped, but stealth was hard to manage given his injury. Speed would have to do. He forcibly set aside the image of Norgay's severed finger. If he had already been broken, so be it. They could break Johari, too. If not, then Johari needed to reach him, and fast.

A small stone wedged the sled in place. Johari studied how to get it moving and back on the track before he kicked the stone away. The sled moved slowly on the flat surface, and gained a little momentum when it reached the slight pitch of the spiral. A pair of round clamps dropped into place over the cable held the sled to the side. Once he engaged them, Johari climbed underneath the sling, crouching with his injured leg extended along the front of the sled. The pockets attached to the sling hung down far enough to cast him into shadows — he hoped. The sled ground softly along in its channels. Another salamander, on foot this time, hurried past on the inside wall. It glanced over at the empty sled, but took no action. Excellent. A little while later, another pair of salamanders passed, their frills flickering as they conversed in silence. One of them paused and tipped its face toward the filament in the wall, placing a cheek-side electroreceptor against it and causing the line to buzz. Johari slid by, circling inward, sometimes crossing other openings into dark spaces or chambers occupied by salamanders eating, grooming, resting. The enclave was too complex to be contained within a single shell, no matter how vast. Next time he passed a chamber entrance, Johari studied it as long as he dared. A combination of smooth stone and shell formed these sub chambers, a process only sustainable until the great shape wrapped back around on itself.

A flickering cascade of light poured in on the other side, and Johari peered out. The walls within completely vanished, opening into a vast space where the heart of the shell had been carved away, from where he entered up to a central pillar still linking the top and bottom. Communication filaments dangled down from above to around the height of a salamander's head. The slightly bowled chamber contained a dozen salamanders, many propelling themselves on sleds like the one he rode, not guided by any cable, but moving freely among stone and shell constructions serving as tables, bins and benches. The salamanders' frills flashed and shimmered as they worked, hands clutching various tools of stone, bone, wood and shell. At the nexus of all this activity lay Norgay.

His limbs splayed like a sacrificial victim, a cluster of salamanders worked over him, crawling across his chest and legs, prying at his right hand with their sharp claws. Already they had flayed his palm and fingers, revealing pistons, cables and actuators as well as the tools and weapons hidden inside, ready to deploy at a moment's notice. That hand cradled Johari to carry him from the water, warming him through and holding him close. Salamanders examined the bot closely with different sets of eyes. They probed him with their claws, and moved their chins over him, sending and receiving pulses that mapped Norgay's prostrate form.

Johari felt ill and furious all at once. Dragons would break him, Savior claimed, for their honor. Because he had killed and injured several dragons, because the humans had damaged an egg — a narrative Johari could understand. This was no breaking, it was a dissection. Then came the idea that made Johari's skin go cold. This was not vengeance, it was science.

Johari's sled rocked to a halt, bumping gently against another parked sled already attached to the cable. For a moment, he did not move. This was exactly why military protocols forbid the sharing of technology, what he had been trying to prevent when he went after his helmet, a technological peashooter compared with Norgay. What had they already learned? What more could they discover about the humans and their technology as they disassembled his friend, piece by piece. And how long would it take them to employ that knowledge against Johari and his team, against the Fleet on its arrival?

Even as he wondered all of this, part of him simply wondered at this moment. His team discovered an alien intelligence, one with language and architecture, with a curious spirit of discovery not much different from humanity itself. Fleet intended to destroy it and claim its planet for their own. Humanity needed a home. Their interference had already affected the dragons, first by breaking an egg and injuring its mother, then everything that came after. The salamanders had stolen technology, and they knew it. At any other moment, their examination would be admirable, a bit of cultural espionage intended to help them understand their enemy, except that Johari's people were their enemy, and their technological prize was his family.

He tried to ping Norgay, the way he'd always done, but felt no reaction: because of Johari's damaged implant, or because Norgay himself was damaged? Down below, one of the salamanders stirred, lifting its head from an examination of Norgay's neck joint. Another one reached for a filament and sent a series of pulses. Others turned toward it, expectant, and it gave a little "talk" in flashes and sparks. Still under the sled, Johari wriggled free of his makeshift pack. He had the evaporator, oxygen and some medical tools, the remains of the damaged medibot, and a number of fruit bars. Devouring one of these, then taking a hit of oxygen, Johari considered what to do next.

He had synced to the medibot before its destruction, maybe... Johari found the battery and the camera assembly, a timer-transmitter for sending distress calls. Before, he rewired his helmet and suit to emulate dragon heat speech, he had the parts here to do something similar. A distress call indeed, the burst of furious gold that indicated urgent attack.

He set the timer, then crept from the cover of his sled and dodged behind the next one. He left most of his gear behind. Either he'd wake Norgay, and they would escape together, or they would both die trying. Creeping forward again, Johari reached the closest filament. He linked the dangling leads from the battery to the organic filament, digging in the ends so they wouldn't come loose. Setting the trigger, he crept onward.

The salamanders' primary light came from their own activities, leaving the rest of the chamber mostly in gloom, plenty of shadows for a small and slender food creature to slip among. He worked his way toward Norgay's left foot, his toe rest against the outer wall. The robot was longer than the salamanders, and infinitely more rigid: it couldn't have been easy getting him in here, nor was it likely to be easy to get back out, unless...

Johari glanced toward the ceiling. He had not descended very far in vertical feet. Accessing his internal processor, he found an estimate of current position, at one hundred fifteen feet below sea level. Meaning the top of this chamber likely broke the surface of the water in the form of one of those curious islands.

If that were true, the islands together with the holes in the sea, comprised an entire bed of giant shells emptied of their inhabitants. He pictured sharp-clawed, curve-toothed, duplicitous salamanders devouring giant snails to steal their shells and claim them for their own. Like Cro Magnon men using their spears and fire to hunt cave bears not only for the meat, but to claim the best caves for themselves. Apex predators.

Who would win when the Fleet arrived? Maybe the real question was, why did he still care? For Fury, and Fracture, and even for Savior who shared with him as he had shared with it. He came representing his own people. If Savior's lies constituted a betrayal, then what about Johari's presence, breaking the world he named Tranquility?

The filaments all around buzzed with sudden vigor. Every salamander twitched to a halt. A few touched the filaments, only to be shocked by what they found there. Their frills flashed danger and Johari's name.

Those on the downed robot stopped what they were doing. The one who had spoken earlier flashed its orders, the red of "go," and many of them began to gallop or scoot their sleds toward the upward path. Johari slipped further downward, and finally reached Norgay's enormous foot.

Deep scrapes marked the metal from dragons' grip and salamanders' claws. A few marks punctured the skin, and a little stain of hydraulic fluid marked their edges. He placed his hands on the multi-metal and tried to ping again, this time using the enhanced electroreceptor system. Nothing. The metal vibrated slightly with a rhythm like footsteps. Johari dropped down, stepping to the outside where he'd seen fewer salamanders working. Staying close, trailing his fingers along Norgay's leg, he worked his way toward the access port at the bot's hip.

Something moved nearby and Johari pressed himself against Norgay, cringing a little at the cool metal. Norgay felt dead.

A tingle in the air and Johari's hair stood on end. The pressure from above increased, as if he were being pressed downward by an invisible weight. He held his breath. Salamanders depended on sight and the pulses from their electroreceptors, like the ones poised over him now, a system developed for "seeing" in the darkness of a sedimentary sea. Smell and hearing were lesser senses, or so Tolui claimed — Fleet's fortune that he was right. The sensation receded, and the slight shiver of footfalls moved away slowly. Was the salamander searching for him, or just continuing its examination?

Johari shifted into motion, leaning into his hands, letting his injured leg drag behind him as he inched toward the port, a slight indent above the hip joint where Johari's touch could trigger an opening wide enough to climb inside and close the door behind him.

His sweaty palms slid along Norgay's surface. He ducked beneath a shell construction at the bot's side, then spotted a rod lying across his path and took an exaggerated step over it, leaning in to support his weight, as ever, with Norgay's help. His palms slipped and his head rapped against the metal with a dull thump and a sudden pain. He bit back a curse as the footfalls ceased, then turned back.

Again, his hair tingled, every tiny hair along his neck and arms, as if they were called to rise up and betray him. At the same time, the gloom above pressed down against him, and his enhanced electrosensors sparked with recognition. Shit. He was only a few feet shy of his goal. Dropping his posture of stealth, Johari leapt for it, staggering and clawing his way along the bot. His outstretched hand snagged the handle, ready to turn.

Claws swept around his side, dragging him upward, gasping, like a fish in a net. The claw dropped him against Norgay's torso and pinned him there, the outside digits easily spanning his ribcage, the inner ones at his throat and each shoulder. One claw extended against his ear as if to spike out his brain. Savior's ancient eyes glared and its frill rose into ominous gold.

32

A NGER, SOMEONE ELSE'S ANGER, flooded Johari's implant, still synchronized to Savior's.

"Release me — release us both — and you might survive this," Johari said, translation and desperation inextricably linked.

Savior's head gave a sinuous gesture as if it tried to shake something away. "{small food item, morsel} do not speak here."

"I have and I will."

"{urgent thing, moment: emergency} Three-skin words."

"I sounded the alarm, yes." The grip tightened, and Johari gasped as his chest compressed within the cage of claws.

{knowledge, admiration: clever}

{gratitude} At least he would die at Norgay's side, and his teammates need never taste his protein.

The claw kneaded his chest, releasing, compressing again, but not as hard. Johari's image had been fleeting, but Savior had felt it: longing, despair, kinship, meat.

"Let me go. Please. Fleet is coming, and they will kill you all. The bots have orders to kill you all."

"{Johari's tools, bots} not here. This bot is already dead. The alarm will cease. This bot, we will {knowledge eat: study, learn}"

"And Johari?"

Savior loomed over him, breathing, its frills flexing slightly and retracting. Its ancient eyes closed. If other eyes opened, Johari could not see them for the dark bulk of the monster overhead. It reached up, stretching its neck, and brought a filament closer. "Alarm lies, shedder trap. There is no attack, no danger," it relayed into the filament.

"Shades-of-darkness." Johari lay his hand against Savior's, a tiny, fragile thing upon the strength of ages.

The ancient eyes opened again, and the creature's throat worked. "Will you eat me?"

The filament ceased pulsing, then broadcast some reply, accompanied by the renewed light of salamander voices returning and the approaching scritching of their claws.

Savior's body shifted, sliding Johari a little further to the outside. Keeping his presence a secret? "Shades-of-darkness. This is not your word."

His throat went dry, though his eyes stung. "Savior," he whispered. {lifts above, takes from danger, brings to honor}

Savior lifted Johari a little off of Norgay's body, his limbs dangling, injuries throbbing all over again. "This word a lie."

"I know," Johari told it. "It's shit."

Savior twitched at the sense Johari conveyed and the heat word that accompanied it. A rumble passed through its body, and Johari felt cold. Would his blood slick Norgay's sensors? Would the bot know that he had died, or was it already too late? Better, perhaps that Norgay never woke to find Johari's corpse. He had gone half-rogue to bring Johari back from the cove; what would he do if his boy were dead in truth?

"Your name is Shades-of-Darkness. Three-skin made you something else, something not of the world." {sorrow, regret, apology}

"Shades-of-Darkness {takes, knows, wants} Three-skin world."

"By killing my friend."

"{object, thing, not-food: this} tool. Many tools." Savior tipped its chin toward the things around them, the tables and sleds and shaped pieces of shell. "Tool and {important object: treasure?}"

"Norgay's not just a tool, he's my friend — he has thoughts and feelings. He is my family {broodplace, flier, egg}. That's why he came for me. That's why he got so angry, thinking the fliers hurt me." Johari wasn't sure if anything he was saying even made sense to Savior, in spite of the implant's attempts at translation. Did the salamanders even have family? He knew hardly anything about their lives. Another reason they shouldn't simply be destroyed. "You want to study him, to know how he works. He doesn't have to die for that. We can share knowledge in other ways."

Savior tipped its head, casting a knowing eye over Norgay's body. "This is not the first dead. This is only one. More dead are fliers and ancients."

Johari's heart fell. "I would rather that they lived. If you kill us, even more will die. More fliers, more ancients, more eggs."

"Fliers make more eggs. All they care for is flying, eating, playing, {creation of eggs, gripping each other: sex} Fliers have {the opposite of knowledge}"

Sounded a lot like teenagers, really. No wonder he and Fury got on so well once it decided not to kill him. Savior's dismissive tone stung, but if only fliers could lay eggs, then ancients — salamanders — would die without them. "They're not stupid. What about the Revered, all of the things that she makes?"

Savior's frill stilled with tiny specks of colors radiating through them, as if it were considering what he had said.

Overhead, the filaments flared again to life, transmitting urgent fear and danger. Savior thrust Johari back to the metal a little too hard, knocking the breath from his lungs and knocking free his hand to slap the surface of Norgay's chest. "Three-skin stop the alarm."

Johari struggled for breath, his mouth gaping and lungs burning. He tried to shake his head, then rerouted past his mouth, letting his skin do the talking. *"Not my alarm. This one's not mine."*

Ancient eyes focused on him, and the returning salamanders halted. The air flickered with conversation, Johari's arm hairs tingled. Savior looked away, and its frills rose. "The danger is real — what comes?" it asked of those entering.

What reply it received, Johari couldn't tell. The huge head swiveled back to focus on him. "Norgay. How many? How many Norgays do you have?"

Only one. Only Norgay adored British television and delighted in Johari's laughter. Only Norgay remembered his parents, and only he had chosen Johari for his own. The team had been given three priorities: first, get the bots back and running, at any cost; second, apprehend the dangerous criminal Johari ne Fleet; third wipe out all the hostiles. In this one battle, they might succeed at every goal, at the cost of an entire city of aliens and Johari himself. "Five. And they will fight for us, for him. You have to let him go. If they can, they will kill you all. They probably hunted me, to find you."

Savior's frills percolated with tiny spots of color, a hundred rainbows sparking to life, glowing, falling away. "Norgay dead."

The filament lit up again and Savior touched it, the message passing through it into Johari's battered body. "Come, come, come Shades-of-Darkness speak {several} Norgay. Norgay Johari-speak {Johari's mouth?}." Flooded with urgency, tinged with fear. It sounded like one of the other bots was employing the VR puppet Tolui made to try to talk to the dragons. How many — Eriksson and Zheng He?

"You have to go and do what you can. Leave me here, let me try to wake him."

"Three-skin come. {Several} Norgay won't kill Johari." Savior shifted its bulk in a sinuous movement and started for the door. Johari slapped its hand, wrapped his fingers around a claw and tried to tug it free.

"No, they will. They need Norgay. The others don't care about me."

It had reached the ground on the other side of Norgay where a few other salamanders gathered, buzzing and flashing with danger. It raised Johari in its grasp, bringing down its head. Its hot breath, reeking of rotten things and the ocean ruffled Johari's hair. "Three-skin lies."

"This is the truth. The other robots will not hesitate to kill me."

Gandhi wriggled forward, staring at Johari in Savior's grasp. "Good ... Three-skin to the Norgays."

"No, not now," said Savior's frill, and its heat speech probed Johari's skin. Of course they could lie, they could speak two different languages at once when they wanted to. "*Why? Why is this true?*"

Johari kept his touch firm, staring up at Savior's ancient eyes. "*Because I came to you. Because I met the Revered and flew with the dragons. Because I asked them to help me speak with you instead of letting you die."*

The salamander settled back for a few long breaths, the alarm flashing and buzzing all around them. Distant blasts sounded from the direction of the entrance. *"Savior,"* it said on a whisper that tickled Johari's skin.

"I'm sorry. I chose —"

It interrupted with a sharp frill of denial. "Johari word. Johari to Shades-of-Darkness. To me, Johari is savior."

33

T HE ENTIRE CHAMBER SHIVERED with an impact from beyond. "Shades-of-Darkness," said the others, calling out to it.

"Go," it told them. "Shades-of-Darkness comes."

Two of them turned about and ran. The others pushed their sleds into motion, their light vanishing up the passageway.

It lowered Johari to the smooth floor of the shell, and released its grip. That single claw lingered near Johari's cheek. "The shell breaks at the water, the water comes in. Johari dead."

"If they break the opening, I'll drown."

A flash of blue assent.

"I'll be careful," he answered. "You, too." Then he clasped the claw in his hand, and sent gratitude.

The salamander pulled away and ran up the corridor, plunging Johari into darkness aside from the muted flashes of terror from the filaments that carried their words. He slumped against Norgay's leg, running out of time with every labored breath. The pack clunked, almost forgotten. He fumbled out the oxygen mask and breathed in deeply. Two breaths, three, then it hissed to the stillness of an empty cylinder. Dropping his lifeline, Johari clambered up Norgay's side and got to work.

When the dragons attacked Norgay, they shot him with thousands of volts of electricity, overwhelming his system and forcing a shut down. Had he shut down voluntarily, entering a safety mode, or had the assault been too sudden, sweeping through his defenses and damaging his processors? One way to find out.

Johari climbed the familiar terrain of Norgay's leg and hip, up to the smooth shell of his chest, Johari's home — not so smooth now, but scraped by stones and claws. Dozens of deep, deliberate marks scored along every seam and joint as the salamanders tried to find their way inside and pry him into pieces. Had they seen what Tolui and Zheng He did to the dead dragon and salamander? Apparently scientists in every race thought the same way, that the best way to learn from something was to slay it and take it apart.

Johari had no time for anger, though fear ebbed and flowed with every crack of ammunition and shudder of the giant shell around them. He thought of drowned Armstrong — all but dead, now — becoming a plaything for sea monsters. He imagined Norgay, spread-eagled in the wreckage of the salamanders' home, like an idol in a shattered temple, while alien algae greened over his faceplate and eels slithered in and out of his ruined arm. And Johari would be an alien skeleton settling on the floor of an alien sea.

He refused to let it happen. He found the outline of the upper hatch and prodded the trigger point. Nothing. It required power to open, and Norgay had completely powered down. Johari forced himself onward. Easiest to start the process from within — safest, too, given the chance of drowning if he stayed out here, but there were other ways. He dragged himself onward, his chest constricted and limbs aching.

For a moment, he lay alongside Norgay's nose, catching his breath. Norgay contained oxygen, pain killers, a bed — everything Johari so desperately needed would be found within if the bot could be made to wake up. He crept a little further, his fingers sweaty. Losing his grip, he slid on his stomach, then slithered down over Norgay's cheek to land in a heap beside the bot's giant ear. Panting and aching, Johari patted Norgay's ear. Just where he wanted to be. Maybe not how he wanted to get there.

An enormous boom echoed down the corridor, shaking the floor beneath him. Johari took hold of Norgay's ear and pulled himself to sitting, then felt for the access panel on Norgay's temple, just below a curl of flexmetal hair. His eyes burned. He felt like he was preparing a corpse for burial, the body cold and unresponsive, every lock of hair in place. "Don't be dead," he whispered.

His fingers slid into place in a series of notches keyed to his fingerprints. He pressed gently, and the hatch popped open, a small emergency light flicking on. Johari let out a breath. All he had to do now was ...

He squeezed his eyes shut and wiped them with the back of his hand. All he had to do was trigger his implant, and activate the re-ignition codes. Assuming that Norgay's core processors remained undamaged, that would begin the start-up sequence. His hand crept to the back of his head, to the slight wound where Shawntelle freed him from Fleet control — by ruining his transmitter.

His head bumped gently against Norgay's as he fought to control his breathing. This wasn't the only way, it couldn't be. What happened when a bot lost its child? When they were damaged in battle or by an asteroid strike or something? Yes, their partner was the first line of access, but that couldn't be the only one.

By the feeble green emergency light, Johari searched the small array of panels, ports and read-outs, all still and silent. One port, capped with a red seal made gray in the dull glow, bore the inscription, "Cable uplink". A way to directly link the bot's brain with an external computer in the event that wireless became unavailable. Like if a kid's transmitter had been stabbed.

Johari popped the seal and stared at the tiny hole. He scanned the area around him — the abandoned sleds, tables and tools of the salamanders' project, and above it all, the dangling filaments they used for distance communications. It could carry a signal. Maybe, just maybe, Johari's bastardized communication system could convince Norgay's processor to accept it.

Pushing to his feet, Johari climbed onto one of the tables and found a long slab of shell with a sharpened edge. Grabbing the filament in one hand, he tried to wield the shell against it like a knife, but he couldn't manage the weight with one hand. He bit gently on the filament. {Danger! Battle! Injury!} sizzled between his teeth as he sawed through the filament with both hands on the salamander's blade.

The filament came loose and he tumbled backward, the shell blade shattering as it fell from his hands. Snatching the filament, he let himself roll, fetching up against Norgay's side with a splash. Johari gasped at the touch of the water. Only as deep as a fingertip, the water soaked into his pants and crept steadily higher.

Johari fed the thin, uncut end of the filament into the port, praying he wouldn't need any significant power source. He had only himself, after all. He pressed the filament between his palms, and allowed a bit of his enhanced power grid to flow down the line. He flicked to his internal menus, tiny figures dancing before his left eye. A series of winks and eye twitches brought up the hardware menu, a thing he hadn't used since training. [Unknown connection. Connect?] Unknown connection: an organic one. Johari agreed to the connection, waiting a long moment for the menu to go green.

[NAME THIS CONNECTION?]

Dragonspit — who cared? He reached across the filament to Norgay's emergency center. [INITIATE HANDSHAKE]

[SIGNAL NOT RECOGNIZED]

"Oh, come on!" Water lapped at his ankles. Adjusting his grip, he tried again.

[INITIATE HANDSHAKE]

For a moment, he feared Fleet had already blocked his codes, but no, Norgay's abduction had happened before Fleet declared him outlaw. He shifted the connection with the filament, settling it deep into Norgay's resting form.

[JOHARI COLOSSUS NORGAY IDENTIFIED]

[INITIATE RE-IGNITION PROTOCOL, COLOSSUS NORGAY]

Something hummed gently through his palms, then:

[SYSTEM OFFLINE]

"Yeah, that's the point! Oh, for —" He took a deep breath, and let it out slow, imagining the soft strains of cello music. System offline. He needed Emm or Shawntelle, or both of them, but he wouldn't know which one to strangle first. Re-ignition wasn't working. What came next? Emergency protocol, the minimal re-boot that allowed the bot to function as a sort of oversized drone. He could figure out how to recover Norgay's personality and updates later. Somehow.

[INITIATE EMERGENCY OVERRIDE PROTOCOL, COLOSSUS NORGAY —]

No, that designation wouldn't work. The Norgay he knew was an artificial intelligence occupying the utility framework, the way that a person occupied any kind of body. The ghost in the machine. Still, 'Norgay' was an overlay the bot had been wearing for a couple hundred years, as far as Johari knew. What was he before that, when he was just a thing, and not a person? Johari scanned his menus again.

[FLEET COLOSSUS DESIGNATION UA 27 UNIT 512]

Another long hum. Johari bent his head over his clasped hands, water lapping against the bot's ear, its chill touch stroking over his bare waist above his beltline. Praying in the drowning temple. Praying for a miracle.

[PRIMARY INITIATION ENGAGED]

A series of metallic whirrs spread quickly through the downed robot, then sensors flicked up, down, back and closed methodically from the forehead down.

The floor shuddered and a wave splashed up to Johari's shoulders, making him jump. He pulled out his filament and slapped the panel closed. Just in time — another wave doused him, lifting his feet from the floor and smacking against Norgay's side. Johari kicked upward, getting his face free of the water and gasped a breath. How long would the reboot take? He grabbed the top of Norgay's ear and hauled himself from the water, scrambling out of its clammy reach to sprawl across the bot's forehead like a human cold compress.

The process went on beneath him, the robot's body emitting flashes of light and sound, pings of sensors, clicks of internal adjustments. His intact left hand whirred and lifted as if the bot wanted to shake, but the fingers rotated through a series of tools and weapons as they came on line.

A wave rushed over Johari from feet to head, lifting him slightly, and he scrabbled for purchase. "Wake up, wake up! Come on!"

Next wave, he reoriented himself, and let it carry him back to the robot's chest, still dry for the moment. He flailed and snatched a safety handle on Norgay's shoulder, clinging to it as the wave receded.

"Norgay! Open up!" He grappled again with the upper hatch — a panel that should slide free as if he were to perform open-heart surgery on the bot.

Water rushed over him, for a moment lifting him from the surface so that he hung there, suspended. Below him, linked to him by the desperate grip of his hand, Norgay glowed faintly in the water as the system diagnostics worked through their inexorable list, heedless of his need. Holding his breath, Johari rapped his other fist against the bot's chest.

Vast blue eyes lit, radiant in the murky water of the shattered room. The water receded abruptly, dropping him once more to the robot's chest. "UA 27 Unit 512 awaiting re-assignment."

"Let me in!"

The hatch slid open and Johari floundered inside just as another wave rushed over them. A bit of water poured through before the hatch slid shut. Shuddering and gasping for air, Johari fumbled his way to the hammock and collapsed into it. "UA 27 Unit 512. Your designation is Norgay. Get us out of here."

Norgay sat up out of the water, sending waves rushing to either side and raised both hands. He fired off a volley of rockets, then triggered his jets.

Pressed back into his hammock by the acceleration, Johari hung on tight as Norgay exploded through the ceiling in a shattering of pearly white.

"Woo-hoo!" Johari grinned as they soared upward. Not like a dragon's flight, certainly, but still, the power harnessed all around him exhilarated him. He closed his eyes, breathing in the familiar atmosphere, the soft sounds of Norgay's operation, the feel of the cloth beneath him, cradling him. A little mocha, a little Bach — and a lot of aspirin. He'd be all better — as soon as the battle was over.

They launched into a spatter of liquid and a hail of bullets that broke off immediately.

Johari dragged himself to a seated position, clinging to one of the straps. "Norgay, window."

"Please clarify." A flat, metallic voice, a flat request for more information.

Any sense of comfort, of home, vanished in that moment. Norgay wasn't here. He might still be buried somewhere within, his personality, tastes and memories preserved in a back-up. His friend was gone, leaving Johari with just a tool.

"The main window. Make it translucent."

"Copy."

The big window cleared in an instant, aside from the streaks of blood. Dragon blood.

A dragon slapped the sea below in a froth of blood and a churning of monsters underneath. The shattered island jutted from the water in places, surrounding a pearlescent bowl of broken shell. The hole in the water led now to a ruin. Huge shards of shell, the outside rough, the inside smooth, rocked in the waves. Chips taken from the other islands and the other holes hinted at a complex of giant shells joined together like a coral colony.

Salamanders sheltered in the remnants of their home, seeking the shallows where the leviathans could not follow — only to flee for deeper water when the bots turned their attention downward. The bots. Three towering figures, positioned backs together, hovered over the scene. Zheng He's chlorophyll coating showed streaks of gore across the green. Eriksson's lower leg showed a deep trough lightly banded with extruded tools to strengthen where the mini-sub should have been. Shawntelle must be still out somewhere. Johari hoped she was safe, wherever she was. Earhart arrived just in time for the battle, no doubt receiving the Fleet's orders about destroying the salamanders. Orders Norgay had not received.

"Unit 512, access personal back-up and activate. I need AI back on line immediately." He needed his partner, Norgay. It felt like issuing orders for CPR, pounding on the chest of a dead man and hoping he'd come back to life.

"Working," came the bland reply. The system scroll at the left-hand side of the screen showed continued diagnostics, including a diagram of Norgay's body, his right hand a flashing image of distress. Rockets had only fired from the left, Johari realized. Major sensors remained off-line, the ones closest to the surface and most likely to be damaged by a lightning storm like the one the dragons unleashed. "Firefight in progress. Accessing Fleetcoms —"

"Delay that! When we're out of danger, then Fleetcoms."

"Copy. Firefight in progress. Engage?"

"Negative — do not engage. Internal gravity off — don't copy every order, just do it, okay?" Johari drifted upward, grabbing the bars and handles to reach the command center. "Increase oxygen level by twenty percent. And if you've got an airborne analgesic, I'd love some

— and get me a new smartcast." At each order, an acknowledgment flashed across the screen, overlaying the view of Eriksson drawing down on a large piece of shell where a group of salamanders hid.

The air vents hissed around him and his breathing eased, along with the pressure of gravity dragging at his leg. The smartcast popped out of a medical panel, rotating toward him, and he caught it with his free hand, applying it to his leg. "Comms to me, broadcast frequency."

"Johari, are you in there? Is Norgay online?" Maya's face appeared on the right of his screen.

"I'm here, he's not — not yet. We're under emergency protocols."

"Oh." She swallowed, face troubled. "But you're an outlaw."

"We've got to stop this, Maya."

Emm's face popped into view alongside Maya's. "Johari ne Fleet. Your assistance in recovering Colossus Norgay will be noted in my report." The words sounded formal, but they flashed him a smile, eyes alight.

As the smartcast finalized its fit, he held up his wrist as if he could show them his watch. "We've got less than an hour to retrieve Armstrong before he's in full shutdown. Break off the attack."

Eriksson pivoted, arms raised and bristling with weapons. Tolui's face joined the others, his mouth set in a line and eyes narrowed. "We don't listen to outlaws, and we sure don't negotiate with them."

"This is wrong!" Johari shouted. "You, of all, people, have to know that! You wanna be chief biologist of a planet we've already ruined?"

"I wanna live," he shot back.

"Me, too, man. And so do they." Johari pointed to the sheltering salamanders. For the moment, the dragons had withdrawn, circling upward while Earhart tracked them with her outstretched array of micro-missiles. One bot they could surround and fry, as they had Norgay, but three together apparently was too much.

"Johari ne Fleet. We have orders to apprehend you and hold you for justice," Emm said, almost softly. "Our bots have direct orders to remove the alien threat."

"The team has three priorities, Emm, I heard her say it: Number one is, get the bots back at all costs." While he spoke, Johari tapped and slid a few more commands across his screen. Tight beam: offline. Unit 512 wouldn't be getting any orders from Fleet. Life support system: automatic, and lockdown. Even if Fleet, or one of his teammates, managed to get control of the bot, they couldn't just suffocate him. Setting in coordinates. "If you stay here, killing the locals, you lose. You fail at goal number one because Armstrong's battery fails, and he's not even capable of emergency function. It goes from being a rescue mission to a salvage operation. You've already got me, Emm. You know right where I am."

"Waiting to frackin' attack us again the minute we're distracted," Tolui said.

"He's got a point, don't you think? Johari does?" Maya asked, leaning in toward her screen.

"What would you have done, Tolui? You're being asked to commit genocide. If history has taught us nothing, it has shown us this: we have a moral obligation to disobey immoral orders." He swallowed hard and continued, "We're not animals working on instinct; we're not machines, just running programs. We choose. That, more than anything else, is what makes us human. I'm trying real hard to make the right choice."

Tolui dropped his gaze.

"Meantime, priority one. Catch me if you can." Johari tapped off the broadcast and said, "Unit 512, all speed to these coordinates."

A smooth voice inquired, "Are we returning to the scene of the crime, Master Johari?"

Johari's eyes flew wide, and he felt weightless in truth, already soaring. Norgay thrust out his damaged hand, tucking the other fist near his side and, in the attitude of Superman, sped to the rescue.

34

"THEY BETTER FOLLOW US," Johari said. "You already figured out that you can't do it alone." He pulled himself into the command chair even as Norgay extruded it, anticipating his need. He buckled in for safety, but let his injured leg simply rest upon the air.

"Indeed. I believe that they will, although many of my sensor and communication units remain offline. I have accessed the file of your speech. Brief, but to the point. A hint of Martin Luther King, Jr. perhaps?"

Johari exhaled, as if he could at last empty all of his fears. He leaned his head against the flexmetal, and it conformed with a gentle warmth. "Oh, man, it's good to have you back."

Norgay swept over the surface of the sea, heedless of anyone knowing he was there. He performed a roll between a pair of outlying islands. Even from here, Johari made out their shapes. Another shell cluster, but this one had no visible entries, like a beaver lodge. "I do believe I'm beginning to enjoy flying. Or perhaps it is that my period of stasis has caused me to reanalyze my priorities."

"Or I'm under house arrest and you're just flying around to convince me you're still on my side."

A pause, then Norgay's voice, softly. "I have tried never to lie to you, Johari. I have tried to be the mentor you deserved. It has been said that a man cannot serve two masters."

Johari tried a laugh. "And the important one is supposed to be God, isn't that right?"

"I have determined, in spite of my programming, that the important one is you."

Johari's throat felt tight in spite of the oxygen boost and the lack of gravity. "You know I'm a traitor."

"I assumed that is why you shut down tight beam communications, so that I could not receive orders during my … incapacity."

"Not long ago, you told me that you serve Fleet, humanity, and me — and that Fleet and humanity are one."

"You and I together have studied the history of mankind, Johari. This is a history that Fleet is forgetting. Without you, they are losing their humanity, and it is my hope that you can remind them that humans used to dream of more than conquest. They — you — know that we are machines of war. When we were reclaimed, it was with optimism, or with vision. I have no wish to return to what I was." A hint of warmth and humor entered Norgay's tone as he continued, "Even if I must cast my lot with outlaws, Master Johari. Or shall I call you, Johari the Kid?"

"I was thinking more like Butch Cassidy and the Sundance Kid — y'know, the Hole-in-the-Water gang?"

"We are a rather small gang."

"We're elite! Besides, I think we might have some recruits." He tapped the upper part of the screen and tried to zoom, but the function was offline. There, at the top of the screen in the rust clouds, moved the shadow and slice of wings.

"We have arrived. Last time, I simply submerged and attempted to rotate Armstrong away from the chimney to reinstall his pack, however, it is not possible for me to both defend against the incursion of sea monsters, and also effect the mechanical repair." Before them rose the broken chimney, surrounded by the choppy wash of the water. If he stared hard enough, Johari could make out the gliding shapes of sea monsters. More than one.

"Task list," Johari began. "Rotate Armstrong, or simply raise him. Reinstall the nuke pack and perform a power-up."

"In my present condition, I regret to say, I will not be capable of these tasks without additional colossus support."

Johari scanned the diagram of Norgay's damaged systems, the right hand still flashing red. "Then we'll have to hope the others get onboard with Fleet priority one. You guys are talking, right?" The constant flicker of bot comms edged into one of the readouts.

"Indeed. We are waging a conversation of demand and refusal. They are demanding that I give you up. Particularly Eriksson and Tolui. Earhart remains neutral as she has only just arrived and has yet to fully comprehend our ... situation."

"And Zheng He?"

"Awaits further action, at ease with Emm's command."

"Right then, let's give them something. What do we need to do first?"

"It will be significantly easier to raise first and reinstall in a more conducive environment. The inside of the chimney could be ideal for this purpose. I placed Armstrong's nuclear pack within rather than to be burdened during my prior flight."

Inside the chimney — he stared down into the writhing mass of sea monsters below the churning water. "Norgay — where's Shawntelle? She came out here with the mini-sub, right? Can you get her on comms?"

A status dial appeared in the comms corner, a yellow ring, endlessly refilling itself, then a crackly voice: "— repeat, Shawntelle Colossus — inside a fracking — anyone —" the visual showed a square of static: jagged streaks of white that sometimes resolved into the contours of her face only to dissolve again as if he'd seen the image only in a cloud.

"She's down there somewhere —"

"Attempting to enhance."

"We need a monster-wrangler, Norgay. Let me out." Johari fumbled with his strap.

"If you are revealed, there is a significant probability that Eriksson will attempt to recapture you."

He took a deep breath, savoring the enriched atmosphere.

"My implant's damaged, you know that, you've got to find her, and get Armstrong out of there. Zheng He will know what you're up to. If they commit, Earhart goes along."

"And Eriksson attacks, thereby saving the day."

"Kinda hoping that, between Shawntelle and Armstrong being at risk, Tolui will at least argue the point. We're running out of time, let me do what I can." He drifted up to the hatch and lay his hand against the warm panel.

"You intend to speak with aliens."

"They know those leviathans, we don't. They know the ocean, we don't. We need their help." He rapped lightly against the hatch. "Open up."

"And they would help us because we have yet to complete our genocide?"

"They're smart enough to know that killing us doesn't win them the war. The more we learn about each other, the better the chance for us all." Johari projected much more confidence than he felt. "Besides, they've got free will, same as we do. One of them helped me find you. One of them let me go. That's Fury up there, waiting to see what happens next."

"How can you be certain it is not waiting to kill you?"

"Because even when they come in alien bodies, I know my friends."

On the screen nearby, Shawntelle's face suddenly drew into focus. "— on a loop. I'm inside a monster. It swallowed the sub. I'm giving it some fierce indigestion, trying to saw my way out, but I don't know how long —"

"Shawntelle, it's me! It's us! We're coming to get you."

"Johari?" She glanced up, her eyes very round, and flashed a grin that trembled. Or was it just the failing quality of her comms? "Don't — risks —" the image broke apart again and her voice faded into static.

"I believe the creature containing Miss Shawntelle has gone out of range."

Shit. "Let me out! And get ready to sink."

The hatch gave a pop and a hiss, but did not move aside. "Johari. As Miss Shawntelle says, do not take unnecessary risks."

"Right. You, too." The hatch slid aside, and Johari climbed out onto Norgay's shoulder. His leg in the cast supported his weight, but sent streaks of painful protest. Johari raised his hands and allowed the tingle of electricity to flow over him. "Did you get the programming for the puppet? Can you project it as long as I'm in contact with you?"

"I feel uncertain about the medical safety of your implant enhancements." Norgay swiveled his head up and the wireframe dragon appeared around them. Parts of the image flickered where Norgay's systems remained semi-functional.

"I'll talk to my doctor — unless she gets digested first." To the dragons beyond, Johari began with a humble apology. He added the names of Fury, and of the Revered, invoking her acceptance. The dragon puppet's frills radiated their light. A handful of dragons sank through the clouds, circling warily and flashing to one another in little bursts with far too much gold. Stung by the fighting, wary, they remained at a distance. Norgay hovered above the ocean, hands down and spread, though his skeletal right hand merely hung, unresponsive.

In the air not far away, the other three bots waited. Eriksson held both hands, guns displayed. Earhart stayed a little further back, and Zheng He took a posture of deliberation between them, balanced, palms held lightly together. Zheng He's chest screen went transparent, and Johari made out the figure of Emm, seated in their control chair. They raised a hand in a slight wave. Johari raised his hand in reply.

To the dragons above, he said, "Please help us. If we can raise our {kin, broodmate: friend} these others will not fight." He didn't know the conditional tense in dragon-speak — didn't even know if there was one — and felt sure the translation included only a few nouns and verbs, but he hoped they would be enough.

One of the dragons circled lower, letting streaks of light sweep along its wings as it offered a brief, full display, then came lower still. Fury.

"Greetings, my friend," Johari told it.

"Greetings ..." The dragon's frill replied, "friend Johari."

The tension that gripped his shoulders and tightened the muscles all the way down to his toes, released just a little, and he grinned. "Will you help?"

"What do you ask?"

"The seabreakers must be driven away."

Fury abruptly changed course, shooting straight up to rejoin its kindred. It circled among them, flying fast. Eriksson tracked it with two banks of weapons, while the others remained on Johari.

Norgay said quietly, "The negotiation appears to have broken down, sir. Have we considered an alternate plan? Aside from merely dying at the hands of the Viking atop the grave of the astronaut?"

Johari stared up into the sky, holding his breath as Fury wove among the dragons. It tucked its wings and dropped downward, an arrow toward the sea. It hit with a splash, sweeping its wings along the surface. With a muscular lunge, an enormous sea monster broke the surface and rushed in that direction. Fury's speed carried it along the water, tail lashing.

"What are you doing?" Johari shouted.

The sea monster lunged, mouth gaping, and its dozens of brethren followed, a churning wave of gnashing teeth.

35

"I T'S DRAWING THEM OFF, I must go. Get in."
Fury's mad flight, half in the water, swept the monsters away.
His friend's wings, already damaged from previous encounters
with the bots, worked hard to keep it just out of reach. "Right."
Johari bent his knees, preparing for re-entry.

A net shot over him, snagging his arm. Johari toppled, arms
flailing. Norgay's right arm reacted, rushing up to catch him — but
his hand dangled, useless, as Johari slid along Norgay's shoulder.

"Johari ne Fleet, stand down. Colossus Norgay, you will give
up the fugitive," Eriksson's voice pounded across the distance
between them as Johari rocketed downward. Stand down? Was
that meant to be funny? Johari tried to turn himself, to gain some
purchase on Norgay's smooth surface.

"I think not." Norgay cut engines on one side, and dropped
sideways, arresting Johari's fall by shifting from a wall into a floor.
Johari slithered into the awkward clutch of Norgay's ruined hand.
Norgay's airlock irised open and Johari scrambled through,
tangled in a net of slick plastic fibers. He kicked and pulled the

thing off, then bounced through the upper hatch, gliding on his back.

Over them, the sky filled with lightning, golden streaks that sparked from a storm of dragons. Fury's companions soared over the ocean, raking the waves with their claws and the electrified tips of their wings.

"Woo hoo!" Johari pumped his fists at the air.

"Indeed," said Norgay. "However, we have work to do." He tipped steeply downward and dove. Water rushed past the window, choppy waves, then murky sea.

"Give me comms, open channel." Four boxes appeared, one of them empty, two of them displaying a Fleet 'busy' emblem, and the last one filled with Emm's face.

"It is advised that you surrender and turn over your Fleet technology promptly," Emm said, a slight smile playing over their lips.

"Come and get it," Johari said. "We could use the assist."

"Well, you asked for it." Their hand moved off-screen and they leaned back with sudden acceleration.

The light dropped off quickly as Norgay dove, the green-blue water turning a leaden shade drifting with tiny particles and flat, flexible things that resembled seaweed, or bits of dragon's wings. Norgay slowed, turning in the water, and Johari re-oriented himself. He strapped into the seat. "Where's our external lighting?"

"Alas, it is principally dysfunctional."

"You dove down here without lights?"

"Not entirely." A vivid blue illumination streamed down over the canopy. Norgay amplified the brightness in his eyes, casting a glow over the scene.

Tumbled rocks, broken off from the chimney above, reminded Johari of ancient ruins or sunken amphorae from some giant's civilization. There, among the rocks, his back to the tower, stood Armstrong. Rags of seaweed draped his form, obscuring his stern metallic face. Small creatures flitted in and out around his legs and slipped beneath his arms. Strange worms clung to the fingers of one hand, waving in the current, pulsing with light as they trapped smaller things with spread fronds, then devoured them.

"Tow cables," Emm suggested. "One of us to each side."

"We'll have to thread the needle — get down to his legs and —"

Maya's face popped into view in Earhart's comm square. "The dragons' power is depleting, and the monsters are starting to lose interest — you'll have incoming pretty soon."

"Nix the cables — too long to set-up. If only we could — Wait!" Johari tapped on Norgay's diagnostics. "You still have your emergency shelter?"

"Yes, I think I see. Stand by for capture and guidance, Zheng He."

"A lasso of some kind," the other bot replied.

"We'll get him up, you get him there safely." Johari slid the diagnostic chart to a larger view, a full schematic of Norgay's right side. "The nuke pack is inside the stone chimney."

"Confirmed. You get him moving, we'll get him home," said Emm as they worked over their displays.

"They're coming, Johari! The monsters! They've turned back!" Maya's hands pressed Earhart's window as she stared through at him.

"Eriksson — Tolui — we need you," Emm shouted. "Forget your grudge and get down here."

Norgay moved closer to Armstrong, hunching himself into the space between fractured pillars of stone. "Ready."

"Ready," Zheng He answered.

Norgay leaned in. The cargo panel on his side opened, and he used the manipulators of his left hand to pluck free the bundled emergency shelter, then placed it between Armstrong's locked knees. "Johari."

With a swipe and a tap, Johari triggered the self-inflating structure. For a moment, nothing happened, then the casing billowed open. Compressed air pumped into the shelter and it bounded from the casing in pillows of silvery material. Armstrong shifted against his unsteady mooring, and Norgay moved a few rocks, then pulled back abruptly as the shelter's inflation accelerated, yanking Armstrong toward the surface with it. Norgay bounded up the slope, giving Armstrong's feet a shove in the right direction, away from the chimney.

He slammed forward, hard against the stone. His entire frame shuddered and the blue light dimmed by half. Norgay swiveled his torso, bringing up his arms as the leviathan curled in for another strike. It flung itself against him, mouth gaping and tentacles slapping for a grip on the metal.

"Shoot it!" Johari urged. "Light it up!" The monster lacked a few tentacles already, and he wondered if it was the same one he'd tangled with on their first visit, or if Shawntelle had done some damage before it sucked her in.

Norgay fired his left arm guns, scoring a series of stripes across the monster's face. It jerked back with a ripple, then curled away, maybe searching for the safety of Armstrong's shadow, but the bot was gone. Writhing the length of its body, spinning a dozen powerful flippers, the monster dove toward them again. Norgay dodged left and fired. The monster fled into the darkness.

"— electrical —"

Johari's head snapped up as Shawntelle's link went suddenly live only to fail again. "That's it, Norgay, that's the one! Don't let it get away."

The diagnostic chart at the side of his screen blinked with red in a half-dozen more places, including Norgay's shattered eye. Norgay pivoted and pushed off from the stones, launching himself after the monster. Bubbles streamed past and ribbons of gore. Putting on a burst of speed, Norgay reached ahead into the gloom that rushed toward them, dizzying. A huge paddle-shaped tail slapped at Norgay's hand, and he grabbed for it, fingers tearing into the fin.

With a wrench of its body, the monster swung about, half-wrapping Norgay in its muscular form. Its mouth surged open, enveloping the bot's right hand.

A huge metal foot reared up, slamming the monster's belly. The tentacles grabbed, yanking Norgay's arm further down its gullet, the mouth swooping open, then closed, up to the elbow now. Teeth ground against metal. A siren whistled as red flared around the joint.

"Shawntelle, can you hear me? Are you there?"

"— hari —"

Or was that "hurry?"

"Shoot it or crash into it. Something. Show me where you are."

Norgay pulled hard, hauling on the monster's tail as it clamped higher onto his arm. "Master Johari, I fear this situation is untenable."

"Yep — gotcha." Johari snapped free and pushed for the airlock where his spare suit waited. "You've got a toolkit on the left, yes?"

"This hardly seems the time for general maintenance." Norgay kicked again, and the creature thrashed against him, fins lashing and scraping free bits of his broken visual sensor array.

"I'll get it."

"You will do nothing of the kind."

"Shawntelle, raise your hand!" Johari urged as he pulled into his suit and locked on the helmet. Without his implant, he couldn't hear Norgay inside the suit, could only wait a long moment between slapping the airlock control, and Norgay allowing it to cycle open.

Johari dropped into the water, the suit's lights activating promptly. He swam between the combatants, thinking of that Greek statue where the anguished father wrestled a giant snake, desperate to keep it from devouring his children. He kept one hand to Norgay's surface, sliding his fingers along until he came to the access panel. It popped open at his approach and he grabbed the toolkit, an unfolding belt with each item in its place, meant for use in space. It slung about his hips and he turned to face the monster. Its vast side heaved as it strained to devour Norgay's arm. Then its belly bulged with an awkward shape, as if it were pregnant with missiles.

Johari dove. He pulled a prybar from the kit and dug into the monster's side above the bulge, anchoring himself. In the other hand, he grabbed the drill, cycling it through a series of auto-attachments for the biggest damn hole he could make. How thick was the thing's hide? Who knew, but he and Shawntelle were about to find out.

He jabbed the drill and carved a vicious groove as the creature struggled to escape this new pain. A huge fin smacked against him, nearly knocking him free, but for the magnetic cling of the tools to his suit gloves. Using the drill on a diagonal, Johari carved into the monster again, pushing hard. Dark liquid streamed out, obscuring his vision. Another strike, digging in, and the drill chimed against metal.

The monster convulsed, then flung itself sideways, smashing Johari into Norgay's chest. The breath whooshed from his body. Something cracked and water trickled across Johari's cheek. How could it hit him so fracking hard? His head rang.

The beast thrashed, smearing him up and down as Norgay tried to pull it back.

In Johari's addled view, Norgay surrounded him, metal and glass on both sides. Johari gasped for breath and swallowed sea water, coughing hard. In front of him, the minisub protruded from the creature's ripped belly. Shawntelle bent over the controls and pulled back. The sub's manipulator arm, broken and dangling, jammed forward and back, tearing the flesh, widening the gap. The sub thrust forward again, and the creature writhed in agony. Norgay tugged on its tail. The creature arched away wildly, finally releasing the pressure on Johari's chest so that he plummeted downward.

The minisub popped out, motors whining with the effort. It wobbled over him, then, in a tower of bubbles, rushed down to meet him.

Johari kicked frantically and caught hold of one of the skids. The damaged manipulator reached in a series of jerky movements, and pressed around him, holding him close as the sub pushed for the surface. They raced upward along Norgay's back, his right arm entrapped in the monster's gullet, left hand grappling with its head. His saw gashed into it, revealing scrapes of bone as they sank together into the darkness.

36

THE MINISUB BROKE THE SURFACE, bobbing, Johari's arm wrapped around the skid, the sub's arm wrapped around him in a crazy embrace. Choking and coughing, he yanked off his flooded helmet and gulped at the air. His body still dangled into the water, but he no longer feared the monsters.

At last mastering his breath, Johari looked up to find the transparent nose of the sub just over him, and Shawntelle's hands pressed against the inside, framing his face as she stared at him. When their eyes met, she laughed, teeth flashing, then sank forward, her head resting against the window. He reached up and patted the outside, as if he could pat her shoulder and reassure her that he'd be alright. He would be. Someday.

Spitting out sea water and wiping his mouth, Johari pulled himself up onto the skid, or tried to, until Shawntelle scrambled back into the driver's seat and gave him a power assist. The water all around him tossed with the wreckage of the fight, shreds of tentacles and bits of dragon's wings. Already scavengers above and below pocked the surface of the waves to snatch up tasty morsels. Norgay was down there, somewhere. "Come on," Johari whispered. "Come back."

The sub motored drunkenly through the chop, its lower props barely cutting the water as it angled toward the broken chimney. A large chunk of stone, slightly arched, lay to one side atop an ancient heap of rubble. A bot waited there, then rose and stepped forward, striding a few paces along the stone into the water. It reached out to gather the sub into its vast silver hand. Eriksson. He lifted the sub with both hands, bringing it to eye level, head slightly bent to examine it. No doubt, he and Shawntelle communicated over their own frequency. Without his transmitter, Johari remained deaf to such communications. At the moment, he was simply too wrung out to care. He let go of the skid, and let himself slide into Eriksson's palm.

The bot's impassive broad receptors aimed down at Johari for a long moment. Finally, Eriksson said, "Consider yourself apprehended."

Johari managed a laugh that scoured his throat and ached in his chest. "That means," Johari gasped a breath, "you can go for Norgay. Find him. See if he's. Okay."

A series of bangs echoed from the mini-sub, Shawntelle gesturing vigorously from the inside. Shorn of most of its external structures, the little submarine lay bent and scraped in Eriksson's hands.

The bot strode back to the pier of stone and knelt to deposit Johari, and, more gently, the sub. Eriksson's giant fingers prodded at the submarine's hatch, then pinned down the vessel as a series of manipulators and tools emerged from his wrist. Something like an oversized can-opener pried up the lid. Shawntelle clambered out, a little wobbly, and Johari empathized with her dizziness. She leaned on Eriksson's hand. "Hey, big guy. Didja miss me?" This ended on a breathy snort of low expectations.

"Tolui lacks the willpower for strong action," Eriksson told her, his head tilted down toward her.

Shawntelle held her hair back with one hand to stare up at him. "Wait a minute, was that a 'yes?'"

For a moment, Eriksson made no reply, then he said, "I did not select you to be ordinary."

She blinked a few times, her eyes turning glossy.

Johari pushed himself to sitting. "Turns out you're not as unlikeable as you seem. Or maybe, as you want to seem."

She snorted again, but a smile twitched the corner of her mouth. Shawntelle strode toward him. "Didn't I tell you not to take crazy risks?"

He tapped the back of his head. "Sorry, my transmitter's out. Can't hear a thing."

She sank to her knees next to him and pulled him into her arms. Johari hugged her fiercely in return. "I couldn't have done it without you. Any of this."

"You mean wrecked the bots, defied Fleetcom — and almost got yourself killed a half-dozen times? Next time, leave me out of it."

Johari's chest ached from the embrace, but he didn't want to let go. "I need to find Norgay," he whispered.

"I know." They held a moment longer, then released each other and she offered a hand to pull him to his feet, both of them unsteady.

"Johari." Tolui's voice, almost tentative, as he approached.

Johari took a step back from him, his hand rising automatically to fend off whatever might happen next.

Tolui tucked his hands into his armpits. "Eriksson relayed what happened to Norgay. Tools. Scientists. Architecture. A biotechnical transmission system." He swallowed, worked his jaw, then said, "You were right. The dragons, the salamanders — whatever we should be calling this race — it is a culture. One we tried to kill before we could even understand it." He glanced toward the sea, still strewn with fragments of dragons and monsters. "I'm sorry."

"I know."

With a slight nod, Tolui said, "You're the one who looked after me when I started this whole mess. Maybe you should've just chucked me out there with the monsters."

"We're a team, remember?" Johari let go of Shawntelle's hand and walked the few steps to Tolui's side. "An orchestra, we're best when we play together."

Tolui's face tipped up, dark-gold eyes watching him with a worried expression. "Fleet's coming, Jo-jo. What do we do now?"

"Whatever we have to. Humanity needs to survive, but not at the cost of another world. We'll find another way." He put out his hand.

Tolui took a deep breath, and accepted the clasp. "Man, I don't know where you get your faith, but I hope you're right."

He'd been raised that way, by someone who thought himself to be irredeemable. Johari deflected the thought and asked, "How's Armstrong?"

"Earhart and Zheng He are affecting repairs, with Maya's guidance. He'll make a full recovery. Thanks for that, too." His brow furrowed and he scanned the sea again. "Where's Norgay?"

Johari's chin dropped, and Tolui gripped his shoulder as Shawntelle came in beside him.

"There's been salamander activity. Eriksson doesn't want to leave us while the enemy might be on the prowl," she said.

"They aren't the enemy," Johari said wearily. He scrubbed a hand across his face. "I don't even know what they are." But even as he said it, he knew that he did. Curious, noble, emotional, strong, devious, clever, fierce, communal. In a word, people.

"Johari ne Fleet. Scan west," Eriksson ordered, swiveling in that direction, but revealing only a modest complement of weapons. Maybe he was learning restraint.

To the west, coming in low, a single dragon soared. Johari limped toward the vacant end of the stone where it sank beneath the sea. Fury drew up, and let his wings soften to land perfectly.

Hands outstretched, his aching chest full of joy for this, if nothing else, Johari offered his gratitude.

Was it truly a victory, if they had won the life of a single bot, at the cost of another? Fury rested its chin lightly on Johari's hands, cycling through its three sets of eyes as it regarded him — a gesture Johari had only seen before in the salamanders. How soon before his friend made that transition? The question made him realize how very much he still had to learn. The dragon wore something at the base of its neck, a torus? He'd never seen the dragons with any kind of personal decoration before.

"The ocean hides. The ancients reveal. Treasure from the deep." Fury regarded him steadily, but Johari frowned, trying to puzzle out the meaning. Maybe his system wasn't functioning, or the translation was imperfect. He had no idea what the dragon meant to tell him.

It lifted its head and settled back, wings folded to reveal the scene beyond. A riffle in the water grew as it moved toward them, not fast enough for a monster, too broad for a salamander. Johari enhanced his vision, focusing on the disturbance. Pushing a bow wave before them, a dozen salamanders came, towing something behind them, half-submerged.

"Norgay!" Johari shouted, as if the bot could hear him. He ran to the edge of the stone in that direction, then a claw gently wrapped his shoulders. Fury leaned in, dipping its neck. It drew back its hand and tilted downward, an invitation. A ropy coil of some strange material hung by its shoulder. Weird. Johari took hold and pulled himself up. At its throat, resting against its narrow shoulders, the dragon wore a yoke made of bones linked by gobs of ... Johari reached out to touch the material, white and leathery, yet rigid. Egg shell. He hooked his feet underneath the bones.

Fury lifted off with a few flaps of its wings, then swept over the ocean and back in a smooth curve that brought them alongside the raft of salamanders as they towed their prize toward the broken chimney.

On one side of Norgay's face, the many reflective disks and sensors that formed his eye serenely reflected the sky. Stone crushed the other side, shattering sensors and scraping the metal, gouging him so deeply that water seeped from wounds. Hints of cables, cams and actuators glinted within. His right arm ended at the elbow in a jagged ridge of torn mechanisms.

"Norgay," Johari whispered.

The remaining eye flickered. A pattern of broken light and crackling electricity washed over it. Finally, it lit up blue, and most, if not all, of the sensors trained on him. The dragon keeping pace, Johari clinging to its makeshift harness as he stared down over the edge.

"I feel that we must review the naming conventions of planets, Master Johari," Norgay rumbled, his voice sounding a little watery, an affectation that drew a laugh from Johari's lips, and stinging to his eyes. "Upon due consideration, I feel obligated to challenge the designation, 'Tranquility," Norgay continued. "Unless, of course, you wish the name to be taken in jest. In which case, I approve." He raised his left hand into the sky, pointer finger elevated.

Resting his head along the dragon's neck, Johari reached back. He lay his palm against Norgay's damp, silvery skin, the image of his own face mirrored there. The robot's metal features reflected the shadowy shape of the dragon above, while salamander speech sparkled along his body. Together, they bathed in lights beneath an alien sky.

ABOUT THE AUTHOR

Elaine Isaak writes adventure novels inspired by research subjects like medieval surgery, ancient clockworks, and Byzantine mechanical wonders. Published works include *Drakemaster* (Guardbridge 2022), The "Dark Apostle" series (DAW), as by E. C. Ambrose, and the "Bone Guard" archaeological thrillers. One recent adventure is the interactive superhero novel, *Skystrike: Wings of Justice*, for Choice of Games.

While researching her books, she learned how to hunt with a falcon, clear a building of possible assailants, and pull traction on a broken limb. A former adventure guide, Elaine lives and writes in the Granite State. To learn more about her works and world visit her website: *RocinanteBooks.com*.

YOU MIGHT ALSO ENJOY

SKY CHASE

BOOK ONE OF "THE FLIGHT OF SHIPS"
by Lauren Massuda

Travel to a vast world of airborne ships and floating islands.

THE SMUGGLERS

FROM THE "TRUCK STOP AT THE CENTER OF THE GALAXY"
by Vanessa MacLaren-Wray

Attachment is everything.

Available from Water Dragon Publishing in
hardcover, trade paperback, and digital editions
waterdragonpublishing.com